THE SIBERIAN CANDIDATE

THE SIBERIAN CANDIDATE

JOHN HOULE

BookPress®

publishing

Published in Des Moines, Iowa, by:

Bookpress Publishing
P.O. Box 71532
Des Moines, IA 50325
www.BookpressPublishing.com

Publisher's Cataloging-in-Publication Data

Names: Houle, John Christopher, author.
Title: The Siberian Candidate / John Christopher Houle.
Description: Des Moines, IA: Bookpress Publishing, 2023.
Identifiers: LCCN: 2023915472 | ISBN: 978-1-947305-79-3 (hardcover) | 978-1-947305-85-4 (paperback)
Subjects: LCSH Providence (R.I.)--Fiction. | Elections--Corrupt practices--Fiction. | Politics--Fiction. |
Politicians--Fiction. | Political campaigns--Fiction. | Crime--Fiction. | BISAC FICTION / Political |
FICTION / Thrillers / General | FICTION / Crime
Classification: LCC PS3608.O85543 S53 2023 | DDC 813.6--dc23

First Edition
Printed in the United States of America
10 9 8 7 6 5 4 3 2 1

To my wife and family,
you're everything to me.

1

"It's not business, this is personal," Henry Mercucio said calmly into the phone as he leaned back in his chair.

"This is my family's business. My grandfather started it, my father took it over, now I run it. I have kids, a family, why do you need this?" the shell-shocked, thirty-something owner of Magellan Management questioned.

Henry's top lieutenant Danny Conroy let himself into Henry's office with a package under his arm. He was feeling more comfortable walking right into Henry's office, and he knew Henry would want to see what the Magellans had overnighted him in response to the latest offer.

"Hold on, you sent me something. Open it, Danny."

"Golf balls," Danny told Henry.

"Golf balls," Henry's tone said it all.

"I know you golf. So, go out and play, but leave my company alone," the young Magellan fired back.

"You're right, I love golf. You know what I love more? Irony, and maybe just a little bit of revenge added on top. This is what I'm going to do. I'm going to stand on your family's Jamestown estate, connect it to the municipal course, and play through your backyard. Then I'll drain a twenty-foot putt on the new 18th green where your family used to watch sunsets."

Danny held back his laughter as he watched Henry kill the call. He saw how Henry, who meticulously maintained his toned 6-foot physique and slick, full head of hair, was boiling under his calm exterior. "Boss, how do you want to respond? You offered more than enough."

"I want you to go down there and tell them I own the majority shares. I'll dump their stock, and they'll have nothing. Sell me the property, or I'll fuck them. Danny, unless someone takes a swing at you, no violence. It's not what we do. We're lawyers, not criminals. I know your old boss probably told you we're all the same. Remember what Michael said at the beginning of *Godfather II*, we're both part of the same hypocrisy, but never think it applies to my family."

"Yes, I know. I don't get why you're doing this. I mean, why this one? I don't mean to question you. This just seems so much smaller than your recent stuff."

"Never question your Don, but this one time, I'll let you know about my business. I always said when I was big enough, I would fuck over the people who ruined my father. How many times do you have the chance to do that? Old school, my friend! You fuck with my family, I take you out. And remember it's not my stuff we're talking about anymore, it's our stuff now."

Henry's father had been manhandled by the Magellans for years. Henry recalled his mother in tears telling his father how he had to get away from them. Henry was not some great crusader looking to avenge old "C," which was how he referred to his father, and he knew some of his father's misfortunes were self-inflicted. He wanted to send a message to the Mergers & Acquisitions community that he was not some second-tier lawyer and Providence political consultant looking to play in their world. And even more importantly, he was showing anyone who questioned whether Reggie Sinclair's son-in-law could stand on his own, without the backing of the mighty titan, that he was his own man. The Southern industrialist father of Henry's beloved wife Lyndsay was a legendary reverse carpetbagger. There was a new player on the stage, and he was setting the rules.

Henry lived by his own code: only players, never innocents. And he only fought at his current weight. Amateurs attempting to take a swing at him were simply dismissed, or a warning shot was fired across their bow. If they retreated, they were given reprieve. If they challenged the new natural order, they were swiftly dispatched with overwhelming force.

Such was the case with the Magellans. Henry had offered young Magellan thirty percent above market value for his Jamestown, Rhode Island, estate in advance of his plan to link it to the public golf course to build a golf revival for the public. It was to include an amateur training facility and feature a combination links style and Donald Ross layout, all with sweeping views of Narragansett Bay and the Atlantic Ocean. The acquisition of the property by Carl Mercucio's son was enough for his small act of vengeance. When Magellan dismissed him like that family had done to his father, it was time to make a course correction.

Danny Conroy was selected to deliver the final message, an important, personal mission that elevated his own status. Not since his days as an operative for Terry Silberman, the mastermind of Mayor Jack Donovan's Providence criminal enterprise, had Conroy felt his self-importance. He enjoyed being at the center of the political and business world again. After the fallout of the Donovan administration and the new era ushered in by new Mayor John Campagna's administration, it was not difficult to see that Henry Mercucio was the new political Godfather pulling the strings that his mentor Ray McNally had mastered. McNally, the former congressman from Rhode Island, was off on another of his partnership perks in the British Virgin Islands with another young assistant. Henry's other father figure, Mayor John Campagna, was already talked about as the next Rhode Island governor, a position long sought but often denied to Providence mayors.

***

It had not been by pure chance that Danny Conroy had met Henry and his new bride in the Cayman Islands two years ago. To get the goods on Henry, Conroy had followed Henry's assistant for weeks after the mayoral special election to replace the disgraced Donovan. He befriended her during a casual bump-in at a bar and slowly began working her for information. He had asked her where she wanted to go on her next vacation, and she'd quickly named the Cayman Islands, because if it was good enough for her boss, Henry, who only stayed at Ritz Carltons, it must be the best.

As Conroy drove his five-year-old BMW M5 convertible up the long driveway of the Magellan estate, he recalled how much his life had changed since the fateful meeting on the beach with the Mercucios and his girlfriend, Jana. He'd remembered their kindness upon seeing him the next day, when like Bogart's Rick, he looked like that sorry sap at the train station realizing his Elsa was never coming back. After having spilled his guts to his friends from Providence, he had been amazed how they took him in while on their own honeymoon. They had him join them for dinner and drinks by the pool. Henry's long stories about Providence politics and his new business development plans had helped distract him from his own feelings of betrayal and sorrow. Danny had confided in Henry and Lyndsay that the love of his life was never coming back. He had left out the part about Jana taking off with all of his money, and not just the cash in his wallet, but the millions he had siphoned from the Silberman-Donovan extortion racket.

With little time to wallow in his mistakes, Conroy had a new mission. Henry had given him a job and a new sense of purpose. He tightened his tie and disembarked from his beamer. There was a peculiar smell on the grounds, an aroma of wildflowers and weed. Rhode Island had legalized marijuana, and everyone was eager to get in on the new gold rush. He walked fifty feet to the door and noticed it was slightly ajar. He could hear yelling and screaming, then boasting and taunting, though not the malicious kind. It was the type that Danny knew all too well with his own boys. "Of course," Danny thought to himself as he walked through the open door, "Fucking video games."

"Good afternoon," Danny said as he knocked on the door. No one was ever shot for saying 'Good afternoon,' he thought, knowing at the same time to never underestimate your enemy.

"Who the fuck are you?" challenged some Vineyard Vines clad douchebag.

"Daniel Conroy from Warner & Isikoff, on behalf of attorney Henry Mercucio."

"Yeah, he's here for Prince Hal," the young Magellan said to his cherub-faced friend, who confronted Conroy with more attitude than muscle.

Danny had no idea what he was referring to and made a mental note to look up Prince Hal. He monitored the room like he had learned in his previous life, assessing the situation for guns and dogs, anything preventing him from executing his task.

"Mr. Mercucio asked me to hand deliver his final offer."

"So give it to me, delivery boy." Magellan started reading and then tossed the papers at Danny. He called over his sidekick to assist with the attempted intimidation.

"Mr. Mercucio expects your answer by close of business, today."

"He can have it now. How's this? Nothing. Not even the garage his drunk daddy built for my father. You run back now and tell him that, delivery boy."

"I will. Mr. Mercucio likes to hear bad news in person."

"Tough guy, what are you going to do now," cherub-faced interjected himself into the stand-down, "You going to kick his puppy or something?"

"You know what they say about how we either fight or flee when faced with challenges. Just so you know, I intend to fight," Danny told him. His words were not needed for intimidation. His presence handled that for him.

Danny retreated after his last jab at him. He turned around slowly, trying to remain calm as Henry had taught him, although what he wanted to do was put these kids through the glass window overlooking the bay.

"Rage."

"What?" Cherub-face was stumped.

"War," Danny informed them, looking into Magellan's eyes. "Mr. Mercucio has made you a very fair offer. I will not allow him to be disrespected. He is not like you and me. I know what you think, you're above me, and maybe you are. I didn't grow up like you, I get it. But Mr. Mercucio, he's above us all. Smartest guy I've ever met, and I worked for Silberman, yeah, that guy. Mr. Mercucio beat them at their own game," Danny said, letting his line linger so the boys could understand what he was saying. By dropping the Silberman name, he was dog whistling, another tactic Henry had taught him.

"Man, cut this Mr. Mercucio shit, his name's Henry…"

"It's called respect, asshole."

"So, are you telling me I should respect the kid whose daddy was my father's errand boy? You think I'm selling out my family? This estate has been with the Magellans for 50 years. You tell your master he can pound sand."

"I won't," Danny replied. He paused, letting the silence linger for a moment. "Boys, the way I see this, you have two choices. I can walk out of here with this signed document and drive the 45 minutes back to the office. Or I leave with my dick in my hand, and what follows is the end of you. And I'm not talking your frat boy shit with a few bruises that your pretty little sorority chicks nurse you back from. I'm talking end-of-days kind of shit. Because Mr. Mercucio is about to go biblical on your ass."

Danny let the words sink into their pot-infused heads. "I actually think he's hoping you don't sign, so he can erase your father like he never existed. Honestly, I'm kind of hoping you don't sign, because I have to tell you, I can't wait to see your smug faces after he sends me down here with your eviction notice."

"Whatever, tough guy," cherub-face retreated.

"Have you ever seen an eviction notice, buttercup? I have," Danny said, turning around for the final time.

"Wait," Magellan responded.

"What are you doing," cherub-faced said. "This guy's nothing. We can take him."

"Give me the fucking papers and tell Henry I still think he's a little piece of shit."

"Mr. Mercucio will be pleased. Thank you."

***

Danny had wanted to lay out Magellan when he made the closing remark about his boss. If Henry had taught him anything, it was to control his emotions. As he made the drive over the Jamestown bridge back to Providence with his sunroof down, soaking in the July sun and ocean breeze, he had to smile. He was driving Henry's old BMW convertible and was blasting Metallica's "Nothing Else Matters" at a decibel level that was shaking the car. He knew this job was a test by Henry to see if he could use his mind, not his hands, to beat a competitor. He would go to war for his prince, never questioning Henry if he asked him to beat the shit out of the two frat boys, something he would have enjoyed. Just like Henry, Danny had larger ambitions.

As he took the elevator to the top floor of Providence's Superman building, the art deco 1920s building the Sinclair group had recently revitalized, Danny wore a grin on his face from ear to ear. For a guy who had been kicked in the gut, he was slowly rehabilitating himself. He walked through the glass doors of Warner & Isikoff straight to Henry's assistant. Haley looked at him differently, and maybe one day he would ask Henry if it was acceptable to ask her out. They had become friends ever since he had bumped into her in the coffee shop on the first floor. She had no idea Danny was in the same league as her boss, a kid from similar streets who also had risen up.

"He's expecting you, Danny," she said, giving him a smile, and then adding, "You look different."

"Thank you, Haley," Danny said, throwing her a wink.

"How'd you make out?" Henry asked, getting right down to business as Danny walked in. Henry had told everyone on his team to come right into his office whenever he was needed. The caveat was that anyone who entered should do so with all their issues, not just a single one, to ensure efficiency at Henry's problem-solving school.

The sunlight was behind Henry, making him appear even larger than he was. Danny knew Henry was not the same as the old boss. Only Terry Silberman from his confines at Danbury Penitentiary was a worthy adversary to this warlike Harry. And even though they may have played the same game, Silberman was the Cleveland Browns to Henry's New England Patriots. Everyone had their time in the sun, and it was just how they used it, Henry told his disciples.

"Did he bring up my father?"

"He did," Danny said. Henry's eyes were glossed over with the first hint of tears. Henry was a hard man, and his family was an emotional trigger. A vulnerability, Danny noted, filing away the information.

"What did he say?"

"Something about a garage he built, I didn't really understand," Danny lied out of respect. He turned over the signed purchase and sales agreement to Henry, and explained, "The money will be wired and the excavators are on tap for Monday morning."

Henry walked over to the renderings of the new development at the center of his office. "Look at this, Danny. This is where the eighteenth green is going, and on the ninth hole on a clear day you'll be able to see all the way to Providence."

"I think I need some new weapons," Danny said a bit sheepishly, referring to new golf clubs. He was also relishing the thought of his enhanced wealth.

"Not just you, Danny, anyone who's ever wanted to play a world class course. This one is for us. Average guys like you and me who were shut out, it's for us."

"Love it, boss. However, you're not exactly average."

"What do I have to do to get you to stop calling me boss? Jesus, Danny, we're the same age."

"Age has nothing to do with it," he said, turning to walk out the door.

"Danny, why don't you ask out that nice girl, Haley? I see how she looks at you."

"I don't know what you mean."

Henry held up his hands. "Okay, sorry if I overstepped. Not my business."

"I have your permission?" Danny asked.

"My permission?"

"I mean you're OK with that? I was thinking about asking her to get a drink or dinner, and I wasn't sure you'd be OK with it."

"Don't think, just do," Henry instructed, walking him the rest of the way to the door with a hand on his shoulder. "Today, we make the rules."

"If you say so, boss… I mean, Henry. Anything else?"

"Yeah. Burn down that fucking barn those assholes had my dad build for their fucking cars."

Danny nodded, already envisioning the flames that would be seen from Narragansett Bay.

2

Charlie Braverman was not your typical lieutenant governor. He made this ceremonial position into one of influence. Traditionally thought of as a steppingstone for higher office, which it was, Braverman was transforming the LG's office into Rhode Island's new economic muscle. This little Revolutionary state was the spark of two major revolutions. After igniting the first hostile act against The Crown with the burning of the Gaspee in 1772, the new American state held out longer than any other to sign the U.S. Constitution. Samuel Slater's first water-powered cotton mill triggered the Industrial Revolution, and now the state was making another leap forward in the renewable energy sector.

Rhode Island's governor, who had inherited the position himself when the state's former dynamic first female governor took a cabinet position, was all too happy to sideline his ambitious subordinate by letting him take over the state's troubled economic development office. The head of economic development had also followed the former governor out of state, resulting in a brain drain of top talent throughout the governor's office. At 70 years old, the current governor was looking to hold on to power for another year and then turn over the reins. While the governor was no fan of Braverman, he did appreciate the optics of having the do-nothing lieutenant governor's office take over a key executive area. He touted how he had saved the state over $1 million by eliminating top salaries on economic development and having them absorbed by the lieutenant governor.

Braverman knew he could make the office into anything he wanted. A Brown University educated liberal from the East Side of Providence, Braverman's father had died when he was young and his mother had moved them from Brooklyn to Rhode Island for a fresh start. Braverman became a great student, earning his way into the state's Ivy League school. He was a political science major at Brown, and became one of the university's most ardent activists, no small feat at Brown. He had torn down signs, had defaced a statue of Christopher Columbus, and had marched for Free Tibet.

Now as the leading Progressive voice in the state house, he was starting to relish his new role as the state's cheerleader-in-chief for economic recovery. He knew his new bona fides as econ-chief would increase his stock with the state's wealthy elite and hard-working class if he could deliver a few wins. He was hoping to hit one out of the park in Prague. First, he needed a savvy Dutch investor to see Rhode Island's burgeoning offshore wind market as the place to deposit his millions. Braverman was not easily intimidated; when you started with nothing that was usually the case. He had outfoxed many of New England's rich and elite and was ready to play on a bigger stage.

His nostalgia pangs for Prague from backpacking through Europe after college had led Braverman to a cavernous restaurant in Old Town. He arrived early with his state aide who had made the trip with him. He really liked Christine, and he knew he would need to settle down if he was going to run for governor. It was one thing for the state to elect a 38-year-old chief executive, but his indulgence of different women each week would be an optics issue. On these trips abroad, he always brought his seasoned chief of staff, Ernie Rossi, to help him avoid youthful indiscretions.

Braverman and Christine had a drink at the bar as they waited for their esteemed guest. He arrived with all the pomp that was expected for someone at his level. Karel Jansen, CEO of Dutch Wind, appeared like a man on a mission. He was impeccably dressed, something Braverman was understanding projected a man's status. Braverman retreated from the bar toward the table with Christine, and he watched as his guest pulled out the chair for her. There was still chivalry in Old Town.

"Thank you for meeting me here, Mr. Jansen."

"Always a pleasure to come to Prague, Governor Braverman," he retorted, with the proper greeting for a lieutenant governor.

"Please call me Charlie, that's what my friends do."

"I'm glad to hear we're friends, Charlie, and this lovely lady, she is your…"

"Friend, I mean, assistant, this is Christine Smith, my special assistant, and my chief of staff will also be joining us. In fact, here he is."

Ernie made his way to the table. His suit was two sizes too big, and his belly protruded over his belt, though his sloppy appearance hid a brilliant mind.

"Gentlemen, Christine, this seems like a fitting place to discuss Rhode Island's future," Ernie said, getting right down to business.

"Yes, the future is bright in Rhode Island. Now that your legislature has opened up your Block Island Sound to an expanded wind farm, we are ready to commit to your state. You have the only working offshore wind farm in the country, and we want to get in on the ground level, as you say," the Dutch executive said, putting his cards on the table. Much of the leg work had already been done, and tonight's dinner was meant to christen the deal.

"I just want to make sure the new turbines go up farther behind the existing five. Block Island is one of our top tourist destinations, and I want to ensure we maintain its integrity."

"Governor, we Dutch know a thing or two about windmills, and I assure you, our design will blend in with the landscape."

"Then I suggest we order a bottle of champagne, don't you think Charlie? I mean, Governor," Ms. Smith offered.

"Absolutely, this is a big deal for Rhode Island," Braverman acknowledged.

***

A couple of bottles of champagne later, Charlie and Christine made their way to the bar. The Dutchman and Ernie were long gone, and it was just the two of them. Christine went to freshen up in the lady's room for the second round of celebrations she anticipated. She was hoping that this trip and win for Charlie would seal the deal for him to announce for governor, and as the political pro she was, she also knew he needed a wife on his arm. She hoped to clinch her own deal in Prague.

On the urgings of Christine, Charlie ordered absinthe. He was thinking the same thing as she, and he needed a little confidence juice to ask her the questions. Should he run for governor, and would she want to be beside him? They had talked before about announcing to staff that they were an item, and he also knew he would have to end his other trysts, which would be hard. It was time to grow up and settle down. He still had an eye for talent, and the sultry brunette at the bar kept looking at him, even more when Christine left. They both looked up at the same time and caught each other's glance. She demurred, and then Charlie broke the ice and ordered her an absinthe to be sent over. She took the offer and came over to Charlie, just as Christine exited the bathroom. Christine at first was taken aback, but the alcohol and excitement took over and she opted to play along. Why not one more night of debauchery, she thought, and then on to reality.

Charlie and Christine entered a new phase of their relationship, and the sacrifice she made ultimately delivered her what she wanted. After the pretty Russian girl left Charlie's room, she confronted him and told him this was it for her. Not a prude, and equally as experienced as her partner, she was just not prepared for the night's outcome. She enjoyed pushing her boundaries to a place she had not visited since college with an equally curious coed. These late-night drinking escapades and their subsequent fallout were weighing on her sensibilities. As soon as their sultry guest left their bed, she gave him the ultimatum. If they didn't announce after Prague, she was gone. Knowing he better go big after this night, Charlie one-upped her and offered her his grandmother's ring. He had brought it with him on the trip, anticipating this moment was coming, just not quite after the night they had shared.

"Let's not announce we're going out, but we're engaged," he said with a grin. She then slapped him, and said, "not like this, you asshole. You're going to do it properly when we get back. And I'm never doing this again." Charlie knew she was right. He had figured he would need to do something special for her.

He retreated in the morning to his hotel's foyer, letting Christine sleep off the night. He was drinking some strong Czech coffee in the hotel coffee bar, when an older man approached him. He had a manila folder in hand and asked if he could join him. He seemed harmless, spoke flawless English, and honestly Charlie didn't know if he was part of the Dutch team investing in his state's future.

"Mr. Charlie, it is great to finally meet you. I remember you only as a small boy in Brooklyn and to see how far you have come."

"You know me from Brooklyn?"

"Yes, I know your mother, a lovely woman, who would be devastated to know her son was with a Russian prostitute."

"What?"

"Yes, I know they like their liberals in Rhode Island. Not sure the taxpayers would be so understanding to see what their lieutenant governor is doing with a state worker on their dime."

"I don't understand, who are you?"

"My name is Alexi Antipov. GRU."

"Fuck me, Russian Intelligence."

"Yes, I knew your father, we served together in Afghanistan."

"My father died in a car accident when I was two."

"Yes, that's what your mother told you. Your father died in Afghanistan. He was Spetsnaz, like me."

"I don't understand," Charlie admitted. "My father was a Ukrainian immigrant. He got killed crossing the street in Brooklyn. He wasn't Russian, definitely wasn't special forces."

"There's a lot you don't know about where you come from. I want to tell you about your father, what he believed, what his dreams were, what he sacrificed, and what he did for you."

"You're talking about a man I never knew."

"You will learn about his sacrifice, what he did to protect his son, and why I am here to protect you today."

"You have an interesting way of showing it," Charlie threw back at him.

"You can't be so reckless. Right now, let's just say these pictures are an early wedding gift," he said as he handed them over.

"Wait, how do you know I'm getting married?"

"It's my business to know things, Mr. Charlie. You and your

lovely bride don't have to worry. That is the only copy. I know a thing or two about discretion. I just wanted to meet you," Antipov told him.

"Well, you certainly have a great way of introducing yourself."

"I got your attention, didn't I?"

"You certainly did, so what do you want?"

"Just your friendship, Charlie."

"You're Russian Military Intelligence. What could you possibly want with the lieutenant governor of Rhode Island?"

"You're a man on the move, one with many talents. We're looking for friends who have a connection to Mother Russia."

"I'm Ukrainian. We know something about Russian help."

"We come from the same place. Let's just say I want you to know you have friends looking out for you."

"Showing me these pictures is a funny way to start a friendship."

"Better in your hands than all over social media, wouldn't you say? I intercepted these photos before they could be used against you," Antipov lied, which was appropriate for the type of relationship he had initiated.

3

Yuri Turgenev was far from his home in Yekaterinburg, Russia. He had been christened in the Russian Orthodox Church built upon the site where the Romanov family had been executed in 1918. Every time he visited St. Petersburg's Hermitage Museum to see Rembrandt and Matisse he could not help but think of the Czar and his family. The bloody history of Russia touched many average people in different ways. He relished living in their seat of power in Russia's most European city, and like so many of his comrades he longed for the day of further integration with the continent. Just across the border in the Baltics, his compatriots were experiencing greater freedom. Not him, not his fellow countrymen. No, they lived under a dictatorship, and though there was plenty of window dressing of democracy, Yuri understood that for Russia to turn away from her autocratic history it would take revolution again from within.

Like so many other Millennials, Yuri had never experienced Russia's brief democratic experiment and yearned for freedom. It was all around him, from Vilnius to Riga, Tallinn to Kiev, so why not St. Petersburg, he and his friends questioned over their vodka. Though the Russian government tried to snuff out the voice of freedom from across the border, the desire to be free could not be caged forever. And Yuri planned to do something about it.

"You need to stay with the baby; I'm going out tonight," his wife, Alana, told him.

"Is that tonight?" Yuri asked her, without even looking up from his laptop.

"Yes, I told you yesterday. I don't get why I have to keep telling you. You just assume you can take any night off because your cause is so important. I have to ask you for a night to go out with my friends and dance."

Alana Turgenev was no Russian babushka. She had a Ph.D. in molecular biology, and both her parents were acclaimed scientists and professors at St. Petersburg State University. She was following in their footsteps and was accustomed to the lifestyle afforded to her family as a member of the intellectual elite. She had met Yuri her freshman year, and though many of her friends thought he was just another ruffian from the Urals, she fell in love with his passion matched only by his impressive intellect.

"Are you even listening to me? What are you working on anyways?" she asked, both interested and annoyed with him at the same time.

Even though Yuri knew similar conversations between husbands and wives with young children were happening in many different places at this very same moment, he had to hold back unless he wanted to risk her Russian wrath. He measured his words, simply replying, "Yes, honey. I'm working on our child's future, that's what I'm doing."

"You and your great future, Yuri. How about you pay attention here instead of your unrealistic dreams? You know nothing changes here."

"It doesn't have to be that way. We can change."

"What are you going to do, start a revolution?"

"Maybe, someday. Right now, if people like me and you and our friends don't speak out, our son will live in a world we don't know anymore. Russia is dying. Brave men and women need to save it."

"And you're the one, Yuri? There's no one else? You know if anyone heard what you're saying they would take you away from us. Are you going to risk leaving your son without a father? And me a widow?"

"No, I want to help give you a Russia that is free, that has opportunities for our son, for our family."

"Oh, my husband, you're so naive. What can one man do?" she asked him, rubbing her hand across his cheek. She was both mocking him and loving him at the same time, experiencing the dichotomy of pessimism and hope ingrained in so many Russians like her.

"I can do this," he told her, pointing to his blog post from the website they had launched for their local chapter of the Anti-Corruption Party. In every major city local chapters were popping up to expose the corruption rampant throughout the local and national Russian government.

"To what end, my love?"

"The Russian bear needs a little poking from time to time. He'll go back to his slumber, and when he wakes up we'll throw so much at him that he won't know where to run. We're going to set up a trap and catch him with his paws in the honey."

"What do you have, and on whom?" she asked, her intrigue replacing her annoyance.

Yuri turned his laptop toward her so she could read it, and before she was even finished he told her, "And this is just the beginning."

"I'm not surprised, nor will anyone else be. These bastards have been stealing from us for years. You really think anyone is going to care?" she echoed what so many other Russians felt about their so-called public servants.

"It's bigger than you think. It involves every sector…engineering, construction, IT, banking."

"And the government knew about it?"

"Not only knew about it, they were part of it. Shell companies no one can trace with money diverted from the Russian treasury. It's fraud at an unprecedented scale, state contracts rigged, tax evasion at the highest levels. The money was supposed to go for our roads and ports. Money to modernize our healthcare system instead goes into the pockets of the oligarchs. We have seniors living in poverty, kids who can't get vaccines, because our country has been looted."

"And you can prove this, Yuri? You know they'll come after you."

"These bastards made up debt from these shell companies. They paid off Russian judges. They had companies laundering money and then paying back debts to a court-controlled account. The Bank of St. Petersburg held the debt and was then flooded with cash from these companies. Then $10 billion is withdrawn and spent around the world. On what? Yachts, dachas, you can only imagine."

"And again, you can prove this?" she asked, her Russian cynicism at work again.

"Yes, we have signed documents from Russian judges, and we can show the bank transfers. Ten billion dollars of our money, gone."

"When you break this, they're going to come after us. We've gotta get out of here."

"We're not leaving; we're staying," he insisted.

"Be practical, my love. Even Lenin knew when to get out, but then he came back."

"You've got that conference in Prague you're lecturing at. We could just go early," he rationalized.

"A month early?" she questioned, starting to see that it could work.

"They won't question why a couple of professors are going to Prague, and I release the story from there, where it's not as easy for them to get to me, or my family."

4

"Hello, Beako."

"You got me, Henry. What are you going to do, whack me?" Beako threw up his arms. He sipped his mojito from the dunes bar at the Ritz Carlton in Key Biscayne, Florida.

"Wasn't exactly hard," Henry admitted. "You and the rest of the Northeast elite hide out here in the winter."

"Don't really need to hide, Henry. I have your new daddy's money that set me up here pretty good. I have a villa on Key Biscayne. I've got a new girl, play golf, and drink by the beach, while you're playing powerbroker back in the cold."

"I didn't come here to hear about your new life, Beako. I came to ask you something," Henry admitted.

"So shoot, what is it? I have a couple more mojitos 'til my girl's done with her pilates, then I have to take her to dinner."

"Campagna's niece, did you sell her the drugs?" Henry came right out with it. The question had lingered in his mind ever since he had faced off with Beako in the last campaign. Campagna's niece had mysteriously taken some fentanyl-laced Oxycontin and had died the night of the mayoral primary. Beako had pictures that tied Henry to the scene and had tried to blackmail him.

"C'mon Henry, even you know that I'm not that fucking ruthless. I'm no different than you are. And I know you would have done the same thing to me if you had what I had on you. I wanted to win, and I used what you gave me against you. Really, you think I would knock off a girl in a mayoral race? You've been hanging out too much with those conspiracy whack jobs."

"I know you had connections with the Lombardo family…"

"Really, Henry, the Lombardos went straight decades ago. They're not mobbed up anymore, certainly not into drugs. You heard what you wanted to hear about me. You think I've got mob ties…man, you're just like everyone else. Just 'cause I'm from Providence doesn't mean I'm mobbed up. C'mon Henry, you know better than that. You let your own feelings for me misguide you."

"You released a picture of me before you left. You agreed to lay low. I could've had Sinclair pull your money. One phone call."

"Yeah, I did that, posted your photo on Instagram. It was hard to tell it was even you. That's not why you're here, is it, Henry?"

"The devil you know, Beako."

"Yeah, Henry, there's no room for the holy ghost between us. So let's have it. What d'ya want?"

"Let's just say, Beako, I may need a man of your talents down the road, and I want to know where I can find you," Henry admitted.

"A man of my talents, huh, so you're up to more skullduggery, are you now, Henry?"

"Ya know Beako, you're right, we're not that different. We both came up from the same mean streets."

"They weren't that mean, Henry. We're both kids from the 'burbs; others had it much worse than us. We're the ones who had the balls to do something with what we had. That's how you and I are alike. No one gave it to us. We went out and took it. You know that. So tell me what do you have in mind," Beako questioned.

"In due time. I just wanted to see if you and I could work together again, and I can see you're still the Beako I knew."

"I'm just sitting in Florida, a little before my time, waiting for the call to put me in the game."

"Ya know what Sun Tzu said, Beako, keep your friends close."

"And your enemies closer, yeah, I know that one."

"Oh, the devil you know…"

"Is better than the devil you don't know, know that one too," Beako reminded him. "I'm curious, Henry, what are you really up to?" Beako pressed.

"Like I'm going to tell you, Beako. You think I was born yesterday. C'mon?"

"You flew down here, for what, to show me you could get to me, is that it?"

"Yeah, something like that," Henry admitted, as he also sipped a mojito, since while in Rome, why not blend in and fully understand the landscape ahead of him.

"So you really think we can put our history behind us, you and me, Henry?"

"Yeah, Beako, I think so. I've got bigger fish to fry. And there aren't that many of us left."

"Yeah, the last of a generation, a by-product of McNally, his legacy. We're like his two sons fighting for daddy's attention and love," Beako admitted, referring to Congressman Ray McNally, whom they had both worked for and who had schooled them on the finer art of politics.

"How is the Congressman, anyways, still running things at home?"

"Always. I see him every couple of weeks since I moved out of Warner & Isikoff," Henry explained, referring to the firm he still held partnership in, thanks in many parts to McNally. "I spend most of my time at my office in the Superman building. McNally, of course, secured us the funding from the state."

"He does know how to grease the right palms. He taught us well, Henry."

"Yeah, Beako. It's our turn now, and your chance to make things right."

"Is that what this is, Henry, you're my savior, you're going to help get me back on the righteous path?"

"I guess that's up to you now, Beako," Henry told him, standing up from the bar, and downing his last sip. "I'm just the messenger."

5

Henry promised his wife, Lyndsay, his side trip to Miami would not delay him from their trip to Raleigh, where they were attending the wedding of Lyndsay's oldest sister, Bridgit. Lyndsay was the matron-of-honor, and the wedding was set at her father's country club, a giant spectacle that dwarfed Henry and Lynsday's own wedding. Mary Sinclair, Lyndsay's mother and matriarch of the powerful Southern family, finally was afforded the opportunity to showcase her family's far-reaching political and financial status with a wedding for the ages. Senators, governors, and fortune-500 business leaders all attended, as the Sinclairs married their second daughter to the heir of another elite Southern family.

The groom, Brad Dumont, had graduated from Duke University and then Harvard Business School and was in line to take the helm of the banking empire his father had cultivated from the ashes of the financial meltdown. The merger of the Dumonts and Sinclairs brought high-tech manufacturing and banking together and was the seedling for a Southern conglomerate that could impact the futures of both families for generations. His daughter's happiness was always on Reggie Sinclair's mind, but this business titan also wanted to assure his family's legacy for the next hundred years.

"Henry, glad you could make it. I was worried your side show in Miami would delay you," Sinclair said to his son-in-law. "Come grab a scotch with me." he offered, but it was really a demand.

"Yes, I saw Mr. Beako set up quite nicely in Key Biscayne," Henry said with a hint of sarcasm that did not go unnoticed.

"I've given you plenty of latitude, you know. I knew you were going to see him. I've watched that project with that golf course you want to build. I went with you on your Superman building, and I have to admit that was a good one. Bought us tons of good will rescuing that signature building in Providence. Nice little profit thanks to the $80 million in subsidies you got us over the next 30 years. My boy, I need you to start playing on a larger stage."

"That golf course is nothing small. It's going to be one of the top destinations in the Northeast for golf when I'm finished. I'm going to have a ferry that shuttles guests from both the Newport and Providence hotels. It'll be a gold mine when I'm through."

"Yes, it will, and it was also your final act of retribution. I know your real game was to take out that family that you think messed up your father. Actually, I'm pretty impressed. Now, I need you to turn that passion toward helping your new family."

"Whatever you need, you know I'll do anything for Lyndsay."

"I want your child to sit on top of the empire we build, not them," he pointed to the Dumont patriarch. Sinclair knew that the Sinclair-Dumont merger was not solely built on love, and that old man Dumont had his sights on the Sinclair fortune for his family.

"We're really going to do this at your daughter's wedding," Henry said as he saw Lyndsay eyeing them as she made her way over to remind the two most important men in her life of their pledge to her.

"Dad, remember no business, this is Bridgit's wedding. Can you turn it off for the night and just enjoy?" Lyndsay said to her father what only a daughter could get away with both publicly and privately.

"Of course, honey, no business. Right, Henry," Sinclair said looking directly at Henry.

"Today is about family," Henry announced.

As the matron of honor, Lyndsay had many official responsibilities steering clear of inter-family dramas and making sure her aunts, uncles, and cousins felt their self-perceived worth based on their seating arrangements. This gave Reggie Sinclair his chance to talk to his son-in-law about his true intentions as Lyndsay's attention was taken away for more important matters at the moment.

"I'm glad Bridgit is marrying that kid; she's happy. That's always a father's primary concern, his children's happiness. I want you to keep an eye on him. I want him to work with you."

"With me or for me?"

"Does it really matter, Henry?"

"It does. You know how these rich kids are. No offense."

"None taken."

"They come in thinking they own the place. Treat people like shit. It's been hard enough for me to convince people I'm in charge, and now I've got some new kid coming in to challenge my authority. No, thank you." Henry was becoming comfortable enough with Sinclair to express how he truly felt.

"Do this for me, Henry. You'll be able to use those political instincts of yours to smell out if he's up to something, what their true intentions are. You can keep an eye on him. Let's see how he makes it up in the Northeast, away from his insulated world. It will be good for him, and you. Plus, Lyndsay and Bridgit can be together again."

"Are you asking, or telling me?"

"I'm asking, Henry. He works for you, but you have to ask him.

Sell him like you sell so many. Tell him your dream, what you think the company will become. It's where you shine."

"I shine when I'm putting things together," Henry shot back.

"Yes, I know, with new mergers and new deals come more complexities. We need to know who our allies are, who we can trust."

"And you don't trust them?" Henry asked, looking over in the direction of the Dumont tables.

"Dumont and I," Sinclair started, referring to the patriarch who he had battled, "let's just say we've had our run-ins over the years. Doesn't mean his son is the father. I mean look at Lyndsay, she's way better than me, more like her mother. All my girls, especially Bridgit, so kind, honestly, don't know why she..." He cut himself off as he saw his eldest daughter and his own wife glare over at him. He understood their look, knew it all too well, and translated it like he had learned on many a family vacation, "Dad, you're working, you promised." He heard them again. It was difficult for Sinclair types to just turn it off, even at his daughter's wedding. He sincerely hoped they never saw, nor did he ever want them to see, what he had to do to keep everything he had built afloat. The difference today for Sinclair was that he had his strongest ally yet by his side. He had chosen wisely.

6

"I'm getting married, Ma."

"What? Who is she? When did you meet her?" The interrogation had begun, and Mrs. Braverman was not happy, though not for her son's engagement. She also knew he needed to grow up. "You haven't even introduced me to her. Is she pregnant?" she asked her son, as they sat together in the great room in a senior cooperative on Providence's East Side.

"No, ma, she's not pregnant, it's just time for me, and with all you have going on here it's hard to get on your social calendar."

"Yes, turn it back on me. You're the one who thought it was a good idea for me to come here."

"C'mon, mom, I gave her the ring you gave me, grandma's ring."

"That ring, that's the only thing we had worth anything when we came here. My grandmother hid it when she was in a concentration camp in Ukraine. It's our family's legacy," she reminded her son.

"That's what I want to talk to you about, our legacy," Charlie admitted. "Ma, you told me dad died in a car accident."

Mrs. Braverman looked away, knowing she couldn't make eye contact with her son. She came back to her precocious son's favorite topic, himself. "Tell me about your trip. I always loved Prague."

"Ma, I met someone in Prague who knew my father."

"Prague is a beautiful place. I went there with your father when we were first married."

"Ma, I met this guy who told me he knew my father." Charlie was not going to tell his mother what they had on him, and he could tell she also was holding something back.

"KGB," she muttered.

"Actually, GRU. Ma, who is he?"

"You met the Colonel, that's what I knew him as."

"Ma, he said my father was in the Special Forces. He said he died in Afghanistan. What really happened to my father?"

"I'm not feeling well. Please take me to my room."

Charlie walked his mother back through the winding hallway of her cooperative to her expansive apartment. It had three bedrooms that she boasted to her friends were to be filled by her grandchildren staying over someday. Charlie had questioned how his mother could afford such a large living space, having assumed she would have settled for one of their more affordable one-bedrooms. Whenever money came up, his mother had always changed the subject, so he had learned to turn a blind eye.

"Ma, what happened to my father?"

Mrs. Braverman was visibly upset. She knew she could not avoid the truth anymore. Her son had exceeded her and everyone's expectations. He deserved to know.

"Your father gave his life so we could have ours."

"Ma, what does that mean?"

She squirmed in her chair. She was beginning to sweat, and that nagging pain was back in her chest. She hoped it was just that annoying angina that seemed to creep up when she was losing at bridge with the other ladies.

"Your father was a hard man, but a good one. We loved each other. Ukraine back in the 90s after the Russians left was in chaos. Your father was in the Soviet Army, and after the independence the colonel came back. We were living in Mariupol, your dad wanting to start his own business. Wanted his own boat to get into shipping wheat. Of course, he knew nothing about shipping or wheat. Then the colonel came to him. Told him he could set us up in America. Your dad could learn to be an American businessman. So, we packed up and went to Brooklyn."

"Who was this colonel guy?"

"Your dad was Spetsnaz with him. They were in Angola together when he was younger. He looked up to him. Remember your dad was from a small village in Ukraine, and he admired this Russian officer.

"Why would you pick up and leave Ukraine? Your family?"

"To go to the states? We all had that dream. I was pregnant, and while we loved Ukraine, the chance to come to America was something we could not pass up."

"What happened to dad?"

"The colonel came back to us in New York. He told your father that he was recruiting for a special mission in Afghanistan, and he needed a soldier of your father's skill. Your dad was great with explosives. I begged him not to go. He told me, if he went, we would be set up for life. He did it for you, for us."

"Do you know how he died?"

"With honor, that's all I was told."

"Ma, why would the colonel be back?"

"I don't know. Your father paid the debt. I don't know."

"What debt, ma? Did dad owe money or something?"

"Not money, freedom. It wasn't like it is now. We were part of the Soviet Union and back then we couldn't just leave. They set us up in America, and we loved it here. We wanted to give you a new life. Your father made a deal: if he went to Afghanistan, we would be free."

"That was a huge price, ma."

"Your father would have done it every time," she insisted, her voice muffled with the emotion beginning to overtake her, remembering his sacrifice.

Charlie knew it was time to retreat. He had pushed too much. He picked up the menu on his mother's granite kitchen counter. The food at the cooperative was as good as anywhere in Providence, and it was time to start cultivating his followers. He knew seniors voted en masse.

"Ma, they've got tenderloin julienne tonight. Let me call Christine, and we'll dine together. You can introduce everyone to your future daughter-in-law," he invited. Charlie had learned from his mother how to change the subject.

7

Mayor John Campagna arrived at his office at Providence City Hall at the same time as the custodians. Every morning he chatted it up with the Portuguese lady who cleaned his office. He could only make out one of three words she said, and even though he arrived at 6 a.m. to get a head start on the challenges he faced, he understood that speaking to her every morning made her day. Campagna had not let the trappings of the office change him.

He looked at his calendar that had been left for him by his secretary. It was another full day, from his staff meeting at 9:30 a.m. to the school committee meeting at 5 p.m. and closing with a wake for a Silver Lake constituent at 7 p.m. Then it was home to have a late dinner with his wife and then tuck the kids in at 9:30 p.m.

And then he would do it all over again, different meetings, but all the same. Routine was working well for him, and the city as well. What Providence needed most after the tumultuous Mayor Jack Donovan was a disciplined administrator at the helm of the city. "Mr. Steady," as the press had dubbed him, was a tireless worker who,

while he appeared calm and serene above the water, was hard pad-
dling, making things happen underneath.

He looked at his watch, knew it was his cue, and began his walk
out of the office. He shuffled down the balcony stairs in the ornate
foyer of city hall, waved to the security guard at the front brass doors,
and navigated the marble steps. He strode down the streets he was
responsible for restoring until he arrived at one of the five coffee
shops within a ten-minute stroll of city hall. It was Tuesday, and
today's destination was the French revival coffee shop owned by a
Lebanese immigrant who had married a French Canadian. He loved
their French press coffee, and as he walked through the doors, he
could smell the aroma of his new day.

"Thank you, Ghasson. When are you going back to Montreal?"
Campagna politely asked the owner.

"Next week. I'm going to pick up my daughter at McGill. She'll
be working here this summer. Need the help, no one wants to work
these days," the shop owner admitted.

Mayor Campagna handed him a hundred-dollar bill, but the shop
owner demurred.

"Mr. Mayor, your money's no good here."

"No, please take the money, and keep the change. The coffees
are on me, you decide who gets them," he said as he offered the c-
note and then palmed his hand.

"Teachers, police, first responders?" he asked, having received
his offer before.

"And moms and dads and students too. It's up to you."

"I will, Mr. Mayor, have a good day."

Campagna said hello to everyone in the shop. He patted the construction worker on the back and listened to the proud father tell him
how his daughter had made the middle school soccer team.

"I'm going to make sure that the field she plays on is the best in

Rhode Island. All our fields in Providence, when the kids come up from Barrington and East Greenwich, I want them to feel it's no different here."

He politely excused himself and walked by the corner table where a young Latina student was on her laptop.

"You know I did the same thing. I studied before school, every morning," he told the young woman, who finally looked up from her screen when she realized the man before her had sincerity in his words, not the condescending tone she heard too often.

"Thank you, sir," she replied, not knowing who the polite man was, until the nice lady next to her told her.

"That's our mayor."

8

Jana Strakova was enjoying her sabbatical. Having absconded with nearly $2 million from the Donovan-Silberman racketeering ring in Providence, Rhode Island, she was settling into her new life in the Italian Alps in the village of Cervinia. After securing her future in Geneva, she made her way to Zermatt, having decided to keep moving in case Silberman's people were looking for her. She knew she could never return to her adopted hometown of Prague, so she was looking for a new place to settle. While in a cafe in Zermatt, she overheard a German couple talking about going over the Matterhorn to Italy, skiing the glacier, and then taking the tram down to a charming Italian Alpine village. Having never skied before, something that was out of her league as a working person from the Baltics, she took the tram to the top from the Zermatt side, and came down to Italy on a second line. It seemed like an idyllic place to settle into for some time, and if there was a European arrest looming, she could always retreat back over the border to safety in Switzerland.

Like any ski town appealing to a wide range of tourists, she made her way to a place she was familiar with, the town's only Irish bar. She ordered a shot of Irish Whiskey and raised a glass to her old friend Sean Murphy, the pseudonym of Mayor Jack Donovan, whom she had met, loved, and defrauded in Prague. Her heart still panged for her last lover, Danny Conroy, whom she left at the altar of their heist. She could have been on a honeymoon with him, but she made the existential choice to take her chances on her own rather than share her loot with her accomplice. Even though she had fallen for Danny like a precocious schoolgirl, her hardened life of countless men taking her body and mind for granted had led her to that fateful decision to take it all. Danny had become the unsuspecting victim of her calculated call to turn the tables on everyone.

"Can I get you another, love?" the burly Irish bartender asked her.

"Actually, bourbon," she replied, wanting something authentically American again.

"I've got Angel's Envy, straight from Kentucky. I think I'll have one myself." It was only the two of them at the bar. The students from Florence had left, after the bartender had convinced the brash Brit boy to have a shot of Milk of the Mother-In-Law, an alcohol like grappa distilled from the peels of grapes and mixed with cream. That would knock some humility back into him, he thought.

Billy the bartender, who introduced himself to Jana, was intrigued by this blonde beauty before him, who had a thick accent he identified as Eastern European. Jana had transformed herself from brunette to blonde in a salon in Geneva, shortly after she had landed from her flight from Grand Cayman.

"So, Billy, what brought you to Cervinia?"

"My parents own this place. They're back in Dublin, go back and forth. I stayed here to watch the place. It's off-season here, so it gives me some time to catch up on things. What about you? Didn't catch your name."

"Genevieve. I'm from Switzerland."

"Really? I would have thought Poland or Baltics by your accent," he said, showing he was smarter than he appeared.

"Originally from Latvia," she lied, figuring that was close enough, even though Lithuanians felt far superior to Latvians.

"So where to next?"

"Not sure, thinking of Cervinia for a while. Rented a flat in town."

"Well, there's one place open for dinner tonight. Ezio the chef came up from Abruzzo. Best food in Valle d'Aosta. You want to join me? I'm closing up and heading over there."

"When in Cervinia…why not." Two years on the run had seen little companionship, and she could use a reprieve from her life on the lamb. Some authentic Italian food with a jovial Irishman seemed like the right recipe.

"Ezio, this is my friend, Genevieve, from across the border. Can we give her some good food? She's used to the other side," he said, taking a shot at the Swiss.

"I just got some guanciale. I give you my best bucatini," the chef proudly announced.

"Do I even want to know what it is?" she asked.

"Let's just say that I could tell when you came in you were the type of cheeky girl who needed to find herself," Billy quipped, a little flirtation in his words. "Ezio is a character. He thinks of himself as a shaman, and by the end of the night he'll do a ritual on you to cleanse you of your bad luck. His grandmother had the gift, and she claimed it was passed on to him. Just go along with it; it's quite entertaining."

After two bottles of Barolo wine and the best dinner she could remember, she felt she could stop running for at least the time being. She had never really had a family, having left a drunken father and absent mother at eighteen to study in Prague. Her career in social work had never materialized, and low choices had led her to swindling both herself and her unsuspecting accomplices. Jana Strakova was finding a new family and home at the base of the Matterhorn.

9

Henry was at home in his new 3,500 square foot house in a leafy suburb outside of Providence. His new home had the tranquility of a stream running through the backyard. Its location also afforded him the ability to be anywhere in the state in 30 minutes. He was at his office in downtown Providence in 15 minutes, while Lyndsay was at the children's hospital in equal time. As she was learning to save children, Henry was building for generations. And he knew that part of his new job was convincing his entitled brother-in-law to accept a position on his right side in the new empire he was engineering. Brad and Bridget had returned from their two-week honeymoon on a cruise from Venice through the Greek isles, to Sicily and then Rome. Cranston, Rhode Island, was no Rome. Henry hoped to convince Brad that settling in Rhode Island was in the best interest of his new family, especially for his new wife, Bridgit.

Lyndsay was rolling out the pasta on their counter. She was in her happy place making homemade pasta while her sister indulged in a Super Tuscan red. She had met a resident in her program at

Brown who was first generation Italian, and she and Henry had been taught by him how to make traditional homemade pasta and gravy, which they called it in these parts.

"You're not drinking with me?" Bridget asked her sister.

"No, early rounds," she quickly replied.

"You want a cigar?" Henry offered his new brother-in-law.

"Would love one. Haven't had one since the wedding," he told him.

"Henry, you're not going to take him down your path, are you? He must take everyone down his path," Lyndsay joked to her sister and brother-in-law. Dumont followed Henry off the deck, across the lawn, and down a path he had carved.

"You're not going to believe this place. Fifteen minutes from Providence, but you're a world away," Henry acknowledged, as they descended down the path to a stream carved into the woods. "I made a path all the way down to the foundry that goes back to 1812. Even made cannon balls for the civil war."

"Probably some of the ones who took out my people," Brad jokingly replied, reminding Henry that he was from the South.

"Yeah, forgot about that. That was over 160 years ago. Hoping we've moved past that by now."

"I'm just messing with you, Henry. This place is really cool. Why did you really bring me down here?" Brad asked, sensing he was being worked.

"No agenda, if that's what you mean. I wanted to run something by you. We're doing big things up here, and I need someone I can trust. Family. Someone who understands what's at stake. We're trying to set things up for the next generation—our kids."

"Whoa, little too soon for that. It's funny, before, it was, 'when are you getting married?' Now, it's 'when are you expecting?' Man, we just got off the honeymoon."

Henry knew this all too well and retreated to common ground. "I know, I know, we get that all the time. I tell them, let Lyndsay finish her residency. Of course, we want to have kids, me especially. I'm going to be 33, and I don't want to be a senior citizen when my kids are going to college."

"I hear ya, Henry. What are you thinking?" Brad asked. He was a little intrigued by what Henry had in mind. He had heard the stories from his bride. Henry, according to her, had masterminded the election of the current mayor of Providence, and even more importantly, had earned the trust of her father. He was thought of as the heir apparent of the Sinclair dynasty.

"Not sure what your next step is, Brad. I need someone with your background to help me with these complex deals we're looking to broker. I didn't come from the M&A world. You do."

"Hey, I'm just a kid from the Carolinas."

"Who went to Duke, and got his MBA at Harvard," Henry recalled.

"Yeah, up here, they looked at me like an outsider. Nothing I wouldn't love more than to take the game to them. So what are you offering me, Henry?"

"Senior VP of Acquisitions. Front lines with me. We're going to be acquirers. And I'm about to take it to them. There's this company I want. It's based here in Providence. They make everything from helicopters to advanced weaponry. It was founded as a textiles company in the Industrial Revolution. We're taking them over, and I need a guy who thinks like them, as I move to take over the board."

"Ambitious, Henry. I like it."

"So, you in or what?"

"Yeah, why the fuck not?"

10

What seemed like ancient history for Henry was really only two years ago. He had battled for the future of Providence and won. It had not come without costs. Like everything he had achieved to date, Henry had gone all in, and it had almost consumed him and everyone around him. He had jumped into his next endeavor, wanting to prove that he was not Reggie Sinclair's sorry-ass son-in-law but a man who should be respected. One battle after the other was starting to reveal his battle scars. There was something about the fight. He loved it. He was good at it. And as long as he kept winning, he was in it for as long as he could last.

Now, he stood at the pinnacle of power, and understood that it was what he did with it that mattered. His mayor was now in city hall and had already done what everyone expected. He was steering the city in a new direction.

Mayor Campagna and Henry had a standing meeting once a week for breakfast at one of Henry's private clubs, and it afforded them the opportunity to keep tabs on each other's progress.

"Mr. Mayor, you're looking good. All that walking you're doing. Like it," Henry said, as he embraced him like an older brother he admired.

"Look at you," Campagna reminded him, giving him an up and down. "You're the man, Henry. Everything I knew you could be."

"Appreciate the boost of confidence, sir, but you and I both don't have time for fawning over one another. I hear the governor's not running. This could be your shot."

"C'mon, Henry, it's not even two years, and I'm just starting to make things happen again for this city. I'm not going to leave the people mid-term. Nor am I going to take the same failed shot so many of my predecessors have made. There's a reason why Providence mayors never make it to Smith Hill," he said, referencing the seat of power of the thirteenth colony.

"Yeah, that may have been the truth before. Things have changed. You've changed them. You'd have a free shot and would still be mayor if it didn't work. Just think about it," Henry urged him, knowing an opportunity to run for higher office while not risking your current seat that wasn't up for reelection for two more years was every politician's wet dream.

"I'll think about it. I will. I don't think that's the only thing on your mind, Henry."

"Well, there is something else," he admitted.

"There always is, just ask me."

"The Providence mayor gets an appointment to the RITECH board," Henry explained, revealing that the Rhode Island based conglomerate was on his radar.

"And you want it, Henry? You've never asked me for anything. So, this is what you want? What does it do, legitimize you or something? You can tell your father-in-law that you got this on your own? That you're in his league? Is that it?" Campagna asked, clearly talking to Henry like he was his little brother.

"The reason they gave the mayor of Providence a seat at their table was so that he would assure that a working-class person would have a seat," Henry replied with an admonishing tone.

"You want it, Henry, it's yours. You don't need to explain to me the 'why.' As far as I'm concerned, you've earned it."

11

Charlie Braverman's indiscretion in Prague seemed like a distant memory, and he had not heard from the shady Russian who had emerged onto the scene. Maybe he had crawled back into the darkness from where he had come. Charlie was a student of realpolitik and understood that Russian intelligence officers often had a shortened life span. For all he knew, this so-called colonel could be holed up in some CIA prison in Albania. He had more pressing matters at the moment, principal among them his new pending nuptials to his current chief of staff and fiancée, Christine. If it all timed out like they had planned, they would be married in six months, with plenty of time before he announced as a candidate for governor.

Before he could finalize his best laid plans, he needed to attend to his current duties, which once a week fell at lunchtime in the governor's office with the affable and supportive Robert Daniels. The old and the new were at work in Rhode Island, but never more divergent than in the governor's office. If the lieutenant governor and governor were able to run together, Daniels never would have picked

Braverman, who had taken out the term-limited secretary of state in the democratic primary two years ago. Here they were to do the people's business and banishing him to Europe to promote Rhode Island on the continent seemed like a fitting trip for his Ivy League educated junior executive.

He never thought he would bring back an offshore wind deal that could catapult the state into a new renewable energy revolution. Charlie believed that Rhode Island with its rich resources and prime geographic location could be at the forefront of an emerging Blue Economy. The state, which already had a strong defense industry that was only matched by its marine trades and fisheries, saw offshore wind as a critical driver for its new economy. The Blue Economy was already generating more than $5 billion a year and was projected to double annually in ten years. Charlie saw himself as the champion of this new economic revolution for the state. The current governor was happy enough to leave his progressive underling to focus on Rhode Island's idealistic economic dreams, while he dealt with the grinding day-to-day of budget fights and spending federal aid with the general assembly.

"Charlie, my boy, you did well, real well. Closing that deal with the Dutchman," the governor said to him, slapping him on the back like he was a coach encouraging his star player.

"Thank you, Governor, it's going to set up Rhode Island's future."

"That's what I want to talk to you about, Rhode Island's future."

"It's what it's all about, isn't it?"

"Yeah, but not for me, anymore. Look, you know about that FBI investigation. It's a big pile of dog shit. After Donovan, it's the last thing this state needs."

"Governor, everyone knows they're on a fishing expedition. You did nothing wrong. The optics are bad, that's all."

"Yeah, my so-called friends tell me they can handle the contract. Of course, I trust them, they wouldn't burn me. If I've learned anything in this business, Charlie, be careful of your friends as much as your enemies. At least you can see your enemies coming at you, but your friends…."

"Governor, you've done so much with what you were handed," Charlie assured him.

"Look, I got what I wanted. When the governor left for the Cabinet, I got my chance. I was just like you, trying to make something out of the LG office before I got the call up. I had my chance, and we did a lot of good with the ARPA funds. It's time for me to turn it over to the next generation. Your coup in Prague, that's going to help you unite the business side of the party. It's your time."

"I wasn't sure if you were running. Of course I was planning to be by your side whatever you decided," Charlie admitted. "I'm hoping I can have your endorsement." He had to ask.

"Not only my endorsement, I'm going to give you my fundraising list and introduce you to all the money people. I'll tell them that this liberal kid they fear will do what he needs to do once he's in office. You've gotta tell the old timers and the conservative wing that you understand their interests. That's what you gotta do to get elected. Once you're in, do what you want," the Governor reminded his lieutenant.

As much as Rhode Island was a blue state it had its own unique political slant. The Republicans had pretty much conceded power in these parts, with only a handful represented in the state legislature. Every decade a retired businessperson would run under the Republican mantle and achieve the state's highest office, but after the national party's recent flameout they had become an endangered class. That left the Democrat Party to fracture off into an ultra-liberal Progressive wing and a conservative Democrat faction. In fact, there was little daylight between a midwestern Republican and a Rhode Island conservative Democrat in terms of standing up against abortion rights and for limited government regulation in gun control.

This Rhode Island realpolitik made it difficult for a candidate like Charlie Braverman to win the chief executive's seat. Sure, he could win the do-nothing lieutenant governor's office, which had no constitutional responsibility other than to wait for the governor to die. In order to win the governorship, he needed the old swamp Yankees and ruling class who had governed Rhode Island for 250 years. Many of the state's elite had found a welcoming home in the state's Democrat party, which did not go unnoticed by the new Progressive movement. The conservative Democrats had their say for a hundred years, and a new aggressive and motivated movement was gaining momentum. They wanted to lay claim also on their first state house, demonstrating that a movement by the people and for the people was again the future of American politics.

And just because he was considered a Progressive did not mean that Charlie would not mire himself in the same type of hard-fisted political fights of the other political animals. His plight for the working man had not softened his ambition for achieving what he felt people needed from their government. To deliver for those people who had been forgotten by the system, or even exploited by it, he had to play by his own set of moral standards. And sometimes another true believer would need to be sacrificed during his pursuits.

Fellow state representative, Alondra Garcia, had witnessed firsthand what it meant to go up against her fellow Progressive legislator when she challenged Charlie for the open seat for lieutenant governor. Garcia had bootstrapped herself up to become one of the top Hispanic legislators on Smith Hill, fighting vigorously for her constituency on Providence's South Side. She had hailed from Cuba, coming to the mainland when she was just 12. Her family had left their Cuban community in South Florida to join relatives in Rhode Island, who were enjoying new-found prosperity. While she had not spoken much English before her arrival, her parents had been determined that she would learn the language of opportunity. Her dogged work ethic had catapulted her to graduate with high honors, attend two years of community college while working in a bakery, and then graduate from Rhode Island College under the state's free College Promise program. She then had been elected state representative as she worked as a paralegal and attended law school. After three terms at the state house, she decided to also throw her hat in the ring for lieutenant governor.

She had not anticipated what she would be up against from her own political brother, who had been one of her closest allies at the state house. She and Charlie had championed the Progressive causes —$25 minimum wage, predictive worker scheduling, and universal state health insurance. They had even slept out in tents on the lawn of the state house to raise greater awareness of homelessness. Charlie had known all along that there was room for only one dominant Progressive voice. So, he had taken her out.

During their hotly contested three-way primary that featured two Progressives and the establishment's water carrier, Charlie had not held back. He had simply discounted the moderate wing's attempt to hold power with their 70-year-old mayor they had brought out of retirement. He had launched his assault on his unexpected Progressive opponent, who received her baptism of fire in a 30-second television and radio barrage to ensure that the Rhode Island electorate had heard her in her own words. These were the very same words her consultants had begged her to refrain from in television and radio. Charlie capitalized and had aired a barrage of her top sound bites for her. While many of her words were echoed by Charlie in his own speeches, it was how they sounded, not their content, that he had wanted the electorate to hear.

Her broken English had been broadcast across the airwaves of Rhode Island, with Charlie opening, "Alondra Garcia does not want to debate me, so let's hear what she has to say about important topics in her own words." What followed had been her liberal leanings that had been delivered in her heavily accented voice. This had been followed by Charlie acknowledging in the ads, "While Rep. Garcia and I share many of the same values, I'm not afraid to express them." Charlie had known that it was how his words had been articulated that mattered to many of the Rhode Island voters outside the urban areas. While they also wore their liberal credentials on their sleeves, they were not ready for someone who did not sound like them. Charlie had won by 3 percentage points in the contested three-way race and had made it clear he had been in this fight to win. Sure, there were those Progressives who had thought what he had done to their sister had been downright ugly, the very entrenched tactics they had been fighting against. Charlie had known that in order to win the state he would have to leave his Progressive friends behind. He had always been in it to win.

***

As soon as Charlie returned home, he knew Christine would be all over him like an inquisitor. She soon lived up to his expectations, on him as soon as he opened the door.

"How did it go?" Christine asked Charlie.

"With the Governor?"

"No, with your priest. Of course the Governor; what did he say?"

"You were right. He's not running. Told me he'd back me, turn over his fundraising operation, and introduce me to his money people. It's a go."

"You'd be the youngest Rhode Island governor. You do it for two terms, then the senate or cabinet. I'm so proud of you, Charlie."

"It does mean…"

"What?"

"We've gotta move up the wedding."

"Yeah, I agree, we can't wait for the Fall. Let's do it this Summer in Newport."

"Everything's probably already booked. We're not the only ones who want to get married in Newport."

"You're Charlie fucking Braverman. The next governor. They'll find a way to accommodate us. Speaking of Newport, I want you to attend the New England bankers' convention this Tuesday. Just some opening remarks. We need to start getting you in front of as many business groups as possible," she told him. "Just focus on the off-shore wind deal. Show them that you're an innovative leader. Then stick to bread-and-butter stuff for them. Reduction of the state corporate tax to be more in line with Massachusetts. Expansion of the sales tax holiday. Shoring up the state unemployment trust fund."

"That's my girl, always thinking."

"And when we're at the hotel, I'll talk to the GM. I'll get us a date for the wedding."

"That's what I love about you, you take care of everything."

"My job is you, Charlie. Your job is to run for governor," she said with forcefulness in her words. Christine was a pro. She graduated top of her class at Brown University in political science. She came from California, and her parents were both lawyers. They wanted her to be educated on the right coast to broaden her perspective. Her mom and dad's dogged determination had been ingrained in their only child. She was a political animal, and she had attached her dreams to the boy she had met in International Relations her sophomore year. She had endured his many trysts, knowing full well that when he grew up, he would need a woman by his side that was not only his equal, but more likely his superior.

12

"Paul Mercucio to see Henry," the forty-year-old leading thoracic heart surgeon said to Henry's receptionist.

"He's expecting you, Dr. Mercucio, let me walk you down."

"That's OK, I know where to go."

"It's changed, Dr. He's now in the office overlooking the city. Let me take you to him," she said as she walked Henry's brother through the new maze of offices to Henry's new corporate lair.

"There he is," Henry put down his papers and embraced his older brother like they were returning home from war.

"I had to meet one of my colleagues at Brown. We're going to Africa to teach surgeons the new open-heart procedure we've been working on at the Brigham."

"Cool, I'm glad you could come, check this out. It's the model of the new public course we're building in Jamestown. See that, that's where those assholes had dad build their garage. I took care of it. That's where the kids' training facility is going."

"Always thinking of the people, Henry. Dad would be proud.

Can we sit? I've gotta tell you something."

"Oh, so this wasn't just a social pop-in. What is it? I'm not your fragile little brother anymore. You can tell me."

"OK, I'm just going to come right out with it then."

"Straight forward, that's all I've ever wanted."

"PJ Roberts is dead."

The name lingered in silence for the moment, and Dr. Mercucio could see the effect of his words on his little brother. He needed to look into Henry's eyes when he told him the news, to make sure it did not trigger Henry into a spiral he had worked his whole life to prevent.

"Good, I hope the fucker burns in hell," Henry said, breaking the silence.

"He hanged himself in prison."

"A fitting end, since he robbed so many lives."

"Look, Henry, I want you to talk to someone at the Brigham. Harvard guy, leading expert on Complex PTSD."

"Paul, I'm fine. It happened 10 years ago. I don't need another shrink to tell me what I already know."

"Henry, the repeated trauma, it's taken its toll. You don't realize it, but people like you who have been repeatedly traumatized can internalize it. I didn't want you to hear about Roberts from anyone else. These things tend to be triggers."

"Paul, it's not your job to protect me anymore."

"I'm your older brother, Henry. That'll always be my job."

"You did your job. You and Sinclair got me the care I needed."

"Yeah, we did. I'll never forget what they did to you."

"I'm not going to let it dictate my life."

"What you went through is enough to take down most men. Not you though, Henry. No, you came out fighting even harder. I think it's why you do all this, to prove to everyone that you can build great things," he said to his little brother, pointing to the monument to golf he was constructing.

"I do this to make money, and to grow my influence and power, to do good," he sternly replied. "Not everything is about the past, Paul. Some things are just what they are."

"OK, Henry, I'm leaving the doctor's card. Just take it, and give him a call. Next time you're in Boston, just go see him. Can't hurt."

"Digging up the past, Paul, sometimes these things are better buried for good."

"Or understand them, free yourself, and no one will ever be able to stop you, Henry."

***

Henry had to tell her. He couldn't hold it back any longer. If anyone could understand, it was Lyndsay. Ever since the other doctor in his life had reminded him of his devastating experience suffered on the streets of DC when he and Lyndsay had been assaulted and himself viciously beaten, Henry finally mustered the courage to tell his wife how he felt. She would understand, he knew. If anyone could help him through, it was Lyndsay. As he turned off the TV, the only thing that calmed his mind to put him to sleep, he called to her. She was doing her evening ritual in the bathroom, which seemed like an eternity as she took out her contacts, brushed her hair, and decompressed from the day of taking care of other people's children. She came out in her sweatpants and oversized shirt, and right away she could see something was unsettling. Henry was sweating even though the room was a cool 68 degrees. Trained to read a patient in seconds, she knew that something was just not right with Henry.

"Henry, you're shaking."

"I have to talk to you."

"What is it. Can you tell me anything?"

"My brother, he came to see me."

"Your mother, is she OK?"

"She's fine; that's not why he came. He came for me."

"I don't understand."

"One of the gangbangers who assaulted us, he hanged himself. My brother wanted to tell me in person."

"That's awful. I'm so sorry, Henry."

"I hate the fucker; he's the fucking antichrist," Henry yelled. He never swore in front of Lyndsay. This was one of those rare occasions.

She hugged him, and he cried like she had never seen him cry before. She had been trained in trauma and understood not to say anything. Her job was him right now, and what he needed was comfort, not words. "I've got you, Henry," she assured him.

"It's not fair."

"No, it never is. We were just on a date."

"I mean it's not fair to you, you didn't sign up for this. I buried it so deep. If the fucker hadn't killed himself, I wouldn't have thought about it again, I would have kept it buried."

"Of course. you can tell me, and I'm not leaving you. I love who you are."

"My brother thinks I have Complex PTSD, whatever the fuck that is."

"Your brother's a great doctor, but he's a better brother. He cares about you. He sees how you do everything like it's your mission. I think he's just watching out for his little brother."

Lyndsay's training took over, and rather than probe and risk Henry shutting down, she continued to comfort him. She could see his need to get everything out.

"I've always been this way. It didn't just happen after the incident. Varsity soccer, hockey, tennis, class president, 13th in my class.

I bomb my SAT's. They took me anyways."

"You're talking about BC and the Jesuits," Lyndsay understood.

"Yeah, the Jesuits are the Marine Corps of the Catholic Church. They're badass priests. Committed to education."

"Henry, you can't blame yourself for the assault," she called it like she saw it. "The man I see right now is someone with incredible empathy, a man who fights for what he believes in. A man who can literally make things happen."

"It's made me into a radical. I take no prisoners. You know my brother fought his way into medical school. He didn't get in right away. Had to get his Master's Degree first. Now he's the best heart surgeon in Boston. We both understand that no one was going to give us anything in this world. We had to take it."

"People need you, Henry," she said, no longer holding back.

"When does it end, Lyndsay? When does it stop?"

"When you're ready to let it stop, Henry. When you're ready."

"I'm so close. I just have a few more moves, then it's over. The things I'm about to do will change everything for us. Our kids someday, they'll never have to do what I had to."

"The thing is, Henry, I've heard these same exact words from my father. 'Lyndsay, you and your sisters can be anything. I've already paid the price, so you don't have to.' Sound familiar, Henry? Different, I know, but parents always want better for their children."

"Let me tell you, Lyndsay, our kids, they'll be able to do whatever they want, just like you and your sisters."

"You know what I want, Henry. I want you, in the present. Here, now, with me. Just us. Not our pasts. Not what our future will be. Just us, now."

13

Charlie couldn't stand these things. He promised Christine he would play nice in the sand box and tell the bankers what they wanted to hear. Now he needed a reprieve, and when one of the bankers invited him to Casablanca, a cigar bar on the harbor in Newport, it was an offer he couldn't refuse. The bankers liked their cigars, and politicians who understood them, so Charlie was happy to oblige their schooling of him on their issues on their own turf. The bar itself was true to form, down to every detail of Rick's Café Americain, complete with a baby grand at the center and tuxedoed players.

"Hello, Charlie," the man in the dark corner said to him, as he walked by on his way from the bathroom. "Don't be in such a rush. Have a Cuban with me."

"You know they're still illegal here."

"A small technicality. Sit please, I came down from Boston to see you."

"Boston?"

"Yes, my new post, cultural affairs director at the Russian

consulate."

"Is that where they retire old spies?"

"Yes, for my dedication to the motherland, I got my pick of consulate jobs, and I chose to be closer to you. Your father asked me to look out for you, his last words to me as I held his hand in Afghanistan," Antipov said, understanding which buttons to push with his new asset.

"You say you knew my father. My mother tells me you recruited him. He bought us our freedom. He paid for it, for us, so why don't you just tell me what you want," Charlie said as strongly as he could without raising attention. He was already taking a longer time in the bathroom away from his guests and didn't want them to think he was abandoning them for a networking upgrade. The bankers wanted their time with the favorite to be Rhode Island's next governor. The bankers were not the only ones interested in having unfettered access to one of America's fifty states.

"I just wanted to give you something. I came across some interesting polling from the *Boston Globe*. They just polled the race, and I have all the cross tabs that they didn't release. You have some work to do with the establishment, so go back to your guests. Take this little gift from me, from someone who respected your father and only wants to help his son."

"What do you want, Mr. Antipov?"

"To see my comrade's son rise to the highest office in this state. Consider me a friend, or as they say, your guardian angel. I held your father in my arms when he passed. To see his boy all grown up—the lieutenant governor, soon to be one of America's fifty governors. Quite a feat for the son of a Ukrainian merchant who didn't even speak English. You are the American dream, Charlie," Antipov told him, almost believing it himself, and knowing Charlie certainly would.

"I appreciate it, Mr. Antipov. Thank you for the cross tabs, but

I'm my own man," Charlie said with conviction in his voice.

"You don't need to sell your soul to those bankers, Charlie. I know your campaign needs financing. I have money from your father, considerable amounts, for his service to Russia. It's yours, Charlie. You don't have to worry about money, ever."

"I'm not taking Russian intelligence money."

"It's your father's. He earned it, and you're his son. I promised him I would give it to you when you were ready. You're getting married, you could use it. It's not my money, it's not Russian money, it was your Ukrainian father's, for distinguished service to the Soviet Union," he pleaded, as he handed Charlie a slip of paper with numbers on it. "This is your account number at First Suisse. It's in your name, under your social security number. I'm just a former soldier honoring his comrade's service."

"No strings attached?" Charlie asked. He needed to hear him say it.

"Just want to be your friend."

"That's all?"

"And I will always be looking out for you."

Charlie, somewhat satisfied, palmed his hand and took the paper slip. Charlie never had money. He went to public school in Providence, got a scholarship to Brown University as one of Providence's top public students, and his lieutenant governor's six figure salary was the most money he had ever earned. He wasn't sure how his mother was able to afford her apartment at Providence's exclusive senior living cooperative, figuring she had some family money from Ukraine she cashed in to live comfortably during her golden years. He graciously left his benefactor and returned to his guests, not quite realizing he was one of the wealthiest men at the table.

***

"How did it go?" Christine asked him as soon as Charlie arrived at the apartment she had rented for them on Providence's tony East Side.

"Interesting," was the first word that came into his head.

"What? What happened? Please tell me you didn't share your Progressive propaganda with them."

"Nope, told them what they wanted to hear. How I want to cut the corporate tax, so we can attract more offshore wind. Their eyes lit up, because they know that they'll be funding a whole new industry and all the spillover they'll see with the whole infrastructure that will need to be built. Yeah, they're on board."

"That's awesome, Charlie. You did it."

"I got the cross tabs from the Globe poll."

"How do they look?"

"What we expected. They perceive me as too left."

"We knew that. That's why you're moving to the center. Wait, how did you get them? They're not public?"

"A friend I know in Boston knows someone at the Globe. Wants to get in my good graces."

"Awesome, I've been trying. Couldn't get them."

"There's something else," he told her, then handed her the paper slip.

"What is it?"

"It's a bank account with First Suisse. Apparently, I'm rich. My father's money, I'm told."

"Wait, what?"

"Yeah, when we were in Prague, a guy came to see me while I was having coffee. Said he knew my father. Told me this story about how my Ukrainian father was in Soviet Special Forces and died in Afghanistan. I thought he was a joke, but my mother knew who he was. She didn't tell me much. What she did tell me confirmed he's legit."

"Why didn't you tell me about this, Charlie?" she asked, clearly annoyed.

"I thought he was just another crackpot until I heard from my mother. That was last week. Then he shows up in Newport and hands me that account number to First Suisse."

"Well, let's look at it," she said as she grabbed her computer, Googled First Suisse, and entered his name and account number into their online portal. "OK, give me your social, and your mother's maiden name and birth date," she told him, and after his compliance, she looked at him and whispered, "Charlie, you have $11.6 million dollars."

"What?!"

"Look," she told him as she pointed emphatically at the screen.

"That's impossible. I can't have 11 million dollars."

"Eleven million, six hundred thousand, Charlie. I mean, what's an extra six hundred thousand dollars?"

"I don't get it. My father was a Ukrainian merchant, no way he had that kind of money."

"It's right there, in your name, your social security number. It's your money," she said, her voice rising, no longer a whisper.

"What do we do?"

"What do you mean?"

"I mean, do we move it, keep it, use it. What do we do with it?"

"I think we sit on it, for now. We do nothing," Christine insisted. She was overwhelmed by the magnitude of their fortune and could see Charlie was not concerned with its origination.

"We don't do anything?" he questioned. "I mean, it could fund the whole campaign. It means I could be my own man, not have to take any money from the rulers. I won't have to sell my soul."

"That money could be used for our future. Our kids, a house," she reminded him that there was a life outside of politics.

"Our future is in politics. C'mon, Christine, you know our future is all about this election. We can go all in with this money. I won't be beholden to anyone."

"In politics, you're always beholden to someone or something, even if it's your virginal belief that you really can do this all on your own. That goes against the very nature of this business," she told him, her practical, realistic self taking over again.

"My father, a guy I never knew, he gave his life for this money, so his son could make his own path. That's exactly what I intend to do with it. This money also buys me freedom, from those I would have had to bend a knee to. Now, I get to call the shots."

"It just seems too good to be true, Charlie. A guy just appears in our lives and all of a sudden you have 11.6 million dollars. He has to want something."

"Have you stopped to think, maybe I finally got what I deserved? All those kids who got to play with their dads growing up, teaching them how to catch a ball, how to shave, this is what I get."

"I know, Charlie, you were robbed. You really think this is your payback?" she asked, hoping he could see that the truth he wanted to believe was not based in any factual reality.

"All I know is that I have 11.6 million dollars from my father. That's all I need to believe in right now."

14

Henry took the elevator down from the 36th floor of the Bank of America building in Boston, departing the Boston College Club, which he liked to visit once a month to remind himself where he came from. He was a Bostonian at heart, having grown up in the wealthy Boston suburb of Wellesley. He was anything but wealthy. His mother was a teacher in one of the state's top school systems, while his father bounced from job to job. His maternal uncle, an attending physician at Tufts Medical Center, always loomed behind the scenes, ready to step in if his nephews needed what their own father could not provide.

Like most Rhode Island carpetbaggers from Boston, Henry had to earn his way into the insulated culture of his adopted state. Rhode Island may have left the Massachusetts orbit in 1636, but the two states were interlocked. Many Rhode Islanders commuted to Boston for jobs, taking advantage of a 25% housing deduction, beautiful beaches, and fine cuisine in the Rhode Island area. Mass-holes, as they were affectionately known by their compatriots, enjoyed a more puritanical lifestyle than their little brother state.

Henry's driver was waiting for him as walked out of the office tower in the Boston financial district. Richard, who ran his own car service after a career in high tech, was Henry's go-to driver for trips to Boston, so Henry could speak freely on the phone while conducting what had always sounded like important business. Richard assumed they would be going back to Boston's burgeoning seaport for Henry to look again at office space. He was surprised to be directed to the Brigham Hospital. He dropped Henry in front of a brownstone near the Brigham and was directed to pick him back up in an hour. Richard took out his Uber sign and figured he could earn an extra c-note while his primary client took care of whatever business he was up to at the moment.

"Henry Mercucio for Dr. Kelleher," Henry said to the secretary. She was hovering near 70 years old and appeared as any grandmother, revealed by the many photos on her desk. Henry could see she was very well cast for her role.

"Could you fill out this form, Mr. Mercucio. Lou will be with you shortly," she said, referring to Dr. Kelleher by his first name.

Henry went down the list in 30-seconds, checking "no" across the board, and handed it back within a minute. Dr. Louis Kelleher revealed himself from his office, welcoming Henry inside. He was closing in on sixty years old, was slim and balding, wore thick black glasses, and donned khakis and a blue button-down shirt.

"Lou Kelleher, come on in," the doctor announced.

"Where would you like me to sit?" Henry asked.

"Wherever you like, make yourself comfortable," the psychiatrist offered.

"That's not going to be easy."

"Why's that?"

"Getting comfortable. I'm only here because my brother asked me."

"Yes, Dr. Mercucio reached out to me. I told him I would be happy to see you."

"So how does this work?" Henry asked, never having been to a psychiatrist, only having spoken to a counselor one time while a student at BC when he was suffering from one of his many insomnia bouts.

"Well, your brother filled me in, told me you're recently married, you're a lawyer, political consultant, and now a business executive. He also shared with me his concern for you after someone from your past recently committed suicide."

"You mean the fucking guy that beat me like a dog." And there it was, the icebreaker, the trigger that caused Henry to reveal it. It hadn't taken long. Some things just needed to come out.

"Would you like to talk about it?"

"No. What's the point, I'm sorry I didn't mean to swear. Very unprofessional of me."

"You can express yourself to me however you like, Henry. I have the whole afternoon, so take your time." For a professor of psychiatry who supplemented his salary with private practice with time blocks filled out every hour on the days he saw patients, his afternoons were rarely free. This was a professional courtesy, so he had traded one of his research afternoons to see the brother of one of his colleagues.

"I just don't know if I understand the point of this. Why should I open up old wounds, torture myself again. To what end?"

"You're a busy guy. You didn't need to come here today. You chose to. Maybe you're ready to talk. As to what end, or what this may accomplish for you, it may help you understand how your past affects the decisions you make today. You're a practical guy, I can see that. A man who understands his past, and for you, someone who can put it behind him, well that man would be very formidable."

"Ok, let's do this then." The doctor struck a chord with Henry. If Henry could slay his demons, even control them, he may have a leg up on his opponents. The doctor was on his level, Henry surmised.

"Are you ready, Henry? Tell me about your life today."

"My life today, well I married the girl of my dreams. She's a doctor too. She does God's work. My angel, Lyndsay," he said, starting to tear up. "I almost fucked that up, excuse me, I almost lost it all. I turned the tables on everyone and beat the best at their own game. The game, though, it runs me. I'm no longer the master, the game is my master now."

"This game, what do you mean?"

"You want to hear about how I tricked the campaign that was blackmailing me—my own fault by the way—how I turned the tables on them, how I made them think I was throwing the Providence mayoral. I won the whole fucking thing, and now the righteous man sits today in city hall."

"And what are you doing today?"

"Today, I was working a deal to move my whole operation to Boston. My wife finishes her residency in May, and I'm going to encourage her to take a job at Dana Farber."

"Looks like you have everything planned out, Henry."

"Well, someone has to be in charge. Someone has to make the tough calls. Who's it going to be? I've seen the people in power. I've been at their table. No, someone needs to fight for the little guy, the one not in the game, the pawn who gets fucked every time. Nope, not me, I'm not going to do it to them. No, they have a warrior, finally on their side."

"Very Shakespearean, *Hamlet*," the doctor replied, trying to make a deeper connection.

"No, the warrior for the working man, *Henry V*."

"Oh yes, Prince Hal, I remember him from college. I recall his father was…"

"A usurper," Henry interrupted. "He was busy fighting his civil wars, just like my father."

"What civil wars was your father fighting?"

"He would say to us, 'At least my sons won't be like me.'"

"That's quite a burden for any son to carry, his father's failures, a son's need to right the sins of the past."

"So, is that what it is? I'm some sort of crusader, or something?

"Your brother told you I study Complex PTSD."

"Yeah, I looked you up. You're the best. My brother told me he thinks I may have it. I know about PTSD. What's this Complex PTSD?"

"When traumatic events happen to young people, their self-confidence can be altered as they get older. Adults with Complex PTSD can lose their trust in people."

Henry did not say a word. He listened, not feeling the need to establish control. The doctor continued, "Feelings of shame, guilt, difficulty controlling your emotions, removing yourself from friends and family, difficulties with relationships, and destructive, risky behavior—this is what people with Complex PTSD experience."

"OK, in some respects that's me. I lash out. I'm very difficult to be around sometimes. I've worked very hard to control my emotions, but the sheer magnitude of the stress I'm under, sometimes I just can't control it. It explodes out of me, and those around me are devastated from the fallout. So here I am, all my scars. So where do we go from here?"

"Well, that's up to you. People with Complex PTSD often have difficulty trusting people. You seem to have a loving wife who you adore. Your brother thinks the world of you. He spoke with the love of an older brother who fought to protect you, and still wants to today. What he told me about you, what you have accomplished, your resilience, it's truly impressive."

"So, what do you think, doc, am I broken? Can I be saved?"

"You already have, Henry. You saved your own world from crumbling, now you seek to change others' lives from crumbling. It's very noble of you. What about you? What do you need to do to be happy?"

"Happy, that's for children."

"Interesting."

"What?"

"You went back to childhood, Henry. It's where your innocence was taken from you, so you try to restore a sense of justice. Your own form of it, I may add."

"If not me, then who?" Henry asked. "Who will stop guys like Silberman and Donovan from fucking the people?" Henry added, referring to his ridding Providence of its unholy actors.

"Yes, Mayor Donovan's antics were well documented in Boston. You were the guy, I understand, who helped bring in the new mayor."

"John Campagna, a good man."

"So, is that it, Henry? Without you, a man like Campagna would never have made it?"

"Not a chance. They would have destroyed him."

"Who are they?"

"The machine, it would have grinded him. It doesn't want honest men. It wants men it can control."

"And you can stop this machine?"

"I'm going to tear down the whole fucking thing."

The doctor retreated after Henry's declaration. He could see before him that Henry's mission had driven him. He did not want to derail him, but he wanted to help ease his pain.

It was Henry who broke the ice after the silent pause. "I'm not here to wallow, I'm here to move forward."

"Henry, the question is how do you want to move forward? Will taking out your anger on the people you feel are taking advantage of others bring you the happiness you seek?"

"If not me, doc, then who? I know what's going on behind the scenes. I've been there. I actually can do something about it. Isn't it then my responsibility to step up? If I actually can do something to make life better in my little world, shouldn't I?"

This one was hard for a doctor as talented as Kelleher. Henry could easily have appeared as a classic narcissistic personality who believed he alone had the power to change things. From what he had heard and what he could clearly see, the man before him may have the actual talent and power to effectuate real change. The question was how medically he as a physician could help him. His obligation was to his patient and easing his pain, not for changing a world of politics and business he did not fully comprehend.

"Yes you should, Henry. You should help bring about this change you seek if it actually brings you the peace you are seeking in your life. I just don't want to see you also tear down all you care about in the process."

"That almost happened last time, and I won't let it happen again. This time I have deep resources, doc. Last time it was just me, but this time they're not going to know what hit them."

"I hope this has been helpful for you, Henry," the doctor acknowledged he also was unsure if their session was productive.

Henry stood up, offered his hand, and said, "Thank you." He had a glimmer in his eye again with a confident stride as he exited the office.

Dr. Kelleher asked, "Will I see you again?"

"I think you will."

15

Henry decided to make his rounds. Having arrived at 5:30 a.m., he already had four hours of highly concentrated work under his belt, and now was the time to walk the expansive office floor to check in with his staff. His office suite was housed in the penthouse of the Superman building, the twenty-six story art deco Industrial Trust tower originally erected in the 1920s to mark Providence's commercial might. Having rescued the building from its ten-year dormant state, Henry's masterful moves to obtain historical tax credits, secure state and city funding, and provide financing from the Sinclair Group had catapulted the former political consultant and lawyer to the top of the New England business elite. Before their eyes they witnessed the rise of a new business titan and power broker, and at thirty-three years old, Henry Mercucio had many more moves to make during his time in the sun.

Henry did not let his recent trappings of success change him. He was still that same scrappy, persistent grinder who was at his desk hours before his employees and worked for hours after their jobs were complete. His work ethic was infectious, and he noticed a number of his co-workers arriving as early as 6:30 a.m. for the same jump-start on the day. No matter how engrossed he became in his work, he held sacred the 9:30 a.m. time slot.

His first stop was his new assistant. Tommy was twenty-two years old and a recent graduate of Providence College, having studied political science like Henry. He was from Warwick, Rhode Island, and had put himself through school. He had emailed, called, and even shown up at the office to ask for an internship. Having interned for Henry during his Summer after college, Henry put him at his desk to work as his personal assistant.

"Hey Tommy, looks like your Friars are going to make the NCAA's. They could match up against my Eagles in the Frozen Four. It's in Boston again, and we have to go if they make it."

"That'd be awesome, Henry. There's a hoops game tonight. Playing Villanova at home. Going to watch it with my dad," Tommy told him.

"Actually, I hope you two will watch the game from my seats," Henry offered, placing his center court tickets on his desk.

"Thanks, Henry. I've only been to the student section a couple of times; just didn't have the extra cash."

"Well, get used to sitting center court with your dad any game you want. You're going to do great things, Tommy," he said, wearing the biggest smile across his face.

Henry walked to the next desk in the open floor plan that he had designed to promote collaboration and innovation. He stopped in front of Haley's desk, a twenty-five-year old analyst whose big wide eyes were engrossed in a spreadsheet. She looked up when she saw her boss coming toward her. They all knew the Henry routine. He would shake it up each morning, checking-in with different people from different starting points.

"Hi Henry, been doing a deep dive into RITECH, and I think you're going to like it. You were right, the efficiencies you're proposing by selling off some of their divisions would improve profits by two-fold."

"That's great, Haley. I'm really interested in their new anti-submarine missile system. I know it's their flagship, so to speak, but I think if we move it out of here and to the Naval Underwater Warfare Center, RITECH would make a handsome profit, and the combined resources of their team and NUWC would leapfrog us ahead of the Chinese."

"Alright I'll start running the numbers so you have this in your back pocket for your board meeting," she told him.

"Thanks, Haley," he said, and then turned back to her, "Oh hey, you know *Hamilton's* back at P-PAC," he said, referring to the Broadway show at the Providence Performing Arts Center. "I can't use my tickets. Why don't you and your boyfriend take them for Saturday night? And I've got this gift certificate I just can't seem to ever use for Capricio's. Maybe the two of you could take it off my hands. They'll actually take you over to the show in their limo. Make it a date night."

"Thanks, Henry! I've always wanted to see *Hamilton*. I can't thank you enough."

He could see a tear forming behind her thick-rimmed glasses, and when he looked up he saw his old mentor Congressman Ray McNally storm through the front door, walking with urgency to his receptionist. He retreated back to his office to prepare himself for whatever brought McNally to him.

"Good morning, Congressman."

"I need to see Henry, right now," Ray McNally demanded.

"Let me see if he's available," the receptionist said as she had been trained.

"Don't bother, I know my way," he said as he blew right by her and headed to Henry's office."

"Ray," Henry said to his former boss and mentor as he looked up from the papers on his desk. "Didn't know we had a meeting. What's up?"

"The implosion of our party, that's what's up, Henry."

"C'mon, Ray, Charlie Braverman is not the Progressive boogeyman you and the boys think he is. He'll come to the center. He's got the governor's endorsement, and he'll come over to the right side with you guys. Don't worry about it."

"Easy for you to say, Henry, you're on your big stage now. The rest of us are still left to fight for our piece right here in little Rhody."

"Hey, Ray, I'm still here, aren't I? I'm very much invested in what goes on here."

"Then show it, Henry. You gotta talk to Campagna about challenging Braverman in the primary. I tried, and he told me he's staying put. Every Providence mayor's dream is to be governor, but not your guy."

"I think he likes his job, he's doing great, and he made a commitment to stay for a full term. He's not moving," Henry told McNally.

"Henry, do you have any idea what a disaster Braverman will be if he gets elected? He's to the left of Lenin for God's sake. He wants a $25 minimum wage. That would decimate our economy."

"I think he's come back to reality on those issues since he's seen how things work," Henry reminded McNally. "Hey, it's a new generation of politicians. He'll fall in line just like all the others have."

"Henry, even the unions are scared of him. He's too much of a maverick for them. And our top companies could all leave if that corporate tax hike that he tried to pass ever saw the light of day."

"Well, here you go. You always wanted to see Big Labor and Big Business united, and now you'll get your dream, Congressman."

Even though McNally was no longer in Congress, that's how Henry would always know his mentor. "I think your union friends are concerned that they won't be able to control him like all the other candidates they've elected and gotten to do their bidding."

"Don't forget, Henry, they backed Campagna for mayor."

"Oh, I know, and I understand how powerful they are in local elections. Hey, I'm more closely aligned to their issues than anyone in the business community. And as for our top companies, they all say they're going to move out and go to the South. They're not going anywhere. The talent pool up here is too strong, with Boston and everything, they're not leaving. Plus, even if Braverman does make it to the governor's office he won't go after them like Roosevelt did to DuPont and Morgan in the '30s."

"Look, Henry, I'm asking you to talk to Campagna one more time for me, and see if you can persuade him to jump in. I can get him the union backing, and we can secure all the big money if he gets in now. We need to stop Braverman in his tracks before he starts building momentum. He's already been meeting with the banking community. He's making a lot of noise."

"Yeah, I'll talk to him. I'm not promising anything. I actually like Braverman, and I'm not convinced he's the liberal antichrist you all are making him out to be. And do I think Campagna should run for governor? Absolutely. Look what he's already done in Providence. He'd be exactly what we need, but my influence only goes so far," Henry admitted.

"Really? I heard Campagna got you a seat on the RITECH board. I know you, Henry, you're up to something. I know their CEO. I can help you," McNally offered.

"Congressman, you know the importance of giving back by serving on boards. I'm just there to learn how a major conglomerate like RITECH works. And give them the local feedback, which was what the board seat was intended for. Not everything I do has an angle."

"OK, Henry, sure. Just know my offer to help stands. And do us all a favor and talk to Campagna," McNally said as he retreated, knowing his influence over Henry clearly wasn't as strong as it once had been.

**

Freed from his demons and with clarity and focus, Henry had used the last two weeks to put in motion a move for the Sinclair Group to acquire a controlling interest in RITECH. He would have to give up his board seat on RITECH. He always saw it as a means to an end to use his father-in-law's fortune to acquire a company that could catapult the Sinclair family into the stratosphere of American business fortunes. His father-in-law, Reggie Sinclair, was thrilled that his son-in-law had turned his focus toward winning on a playing field worthy of his talents. And when his people reviewed the plan Henry had orchestrated, they too saw that Henry was truly a once-in-a-generation transformational leader. There were just a few more moves Henry intended to make before his showdown where he planned to unveil his ambitious takeover plan in the next board meeting.

As Henry contemplated his next move, he was asked by his top lieutenant, Danny Conroy, if he could have a word. Never one to raise an alarm, Danny was the type who only came to Henry when matters warranted his utter attention. And this was one of them.

"What's up, Danny?" he questioned him before he was even fully in the room.

"Boss, you asked me to keep an eye on Brad. I gotta talk to you about something," Danny told him, clearly uncomfortable as evidenced by his less than confident tone of voice.

"Tell me, what has this little silver spoon gotten himself into now?"

"Well, I think that's the problem, he's gotten himself into a lot. He's been enjoying himself in the Providence clubs a little too much."

"He likes to go clubbing, so what?"

"No, not those clubs, the other ones," Danny told Henry, referring to the underbelly of the Providence nightlife that included its many notorious strip clubs where the rules had always remained relaxed. It was only 10 years ago that a loophole in the law even permitted in-house prostitution, before it was closed for good by a morally outraged legislator, but the legacy lived on. Basically, everyone in the Northeast knew that Providence was the Vegas of the East for its hands-off approach toward its strip clubs, which resulted in a very hands-on experience.

"Oh man, what did he do? He hasn't even been married for three months."

"He wanted to go to Chateau, so I took him, and I waited for him at the bar when he went off with one of the girls."

"So he gets a lap dance, big deal. Wouldn't be the first married guy to do so," Henry rationalized.

"He's then gone maybe for an hour, Henry. I know a lot of the girls there, having worked for Donovan and Silberman. Donovan always had me fetch girls from there," he admitted, referring to his prior work for notorious Mayor Jack Donovan.

"Well, an hour's a long lap dance," Henry said, suspecting they both knew what his brother-in-law was doing.

"Yeah, I talked to one of the girls. He's got quite a reputation. Throws around a lot of money. He's with two to three girls a night. And they're not just dancing."

"Oh, man, this is what I fucking need right now. I'm about to make my biggest move and my brother-in-law's banging strippers two at a time. Alright, I got this. Thank you, Danny, I'll take it from here. And I appreciate your discretion on this one. I'm going to need you to do something for me, and you need to keep him out of the clubs next week."

Henry knew it was time for another strip club sweep. Anytime a major politician got in trouble with the FBI, or a major government scandal broke, a change in the local narrative was needed. And often Providence's strip clubs were the natural target. After Henry got Danny to convince one of the Chateau girls to make a statement, one that cost $2,500 cash, Henry called his friend at the Attorney General's office. There now was a first-hand account of prostitution taking place at Chateau's.

Henry's call resulted in a Rhode Island State Police raid not only at Chateau, but across the whole city landscape. Five of Providence's strip clubs were found to be engaging in prostitution, and the whole underground flesh trade was shut down for a fortnight. There was a laundry list of businessmen, gang bangers, and lonely divorced men who no longer had an outlet for their desires for the rest of the month.

It would be back up and running after the lawsuits began flying and the public was distracted again. Few things really changed all that much. Henry was not relishing the conversation he needed to have with his brother-in-law, Brad Dumont. Brad had been used to a life of people cleaning up his messes, and Henry did not want to be just another one of his enablers. He called Brad into his office and didn't waste any time getting right to it.

"What are you doing, man?" Henry came out and asked.

"What are we talking about, Henry?"

"Your little brothel there, Chateau, it's closed down," Henry came right at him, wanting to see what his reaction would be.

"What, that strip club? So what, I got some lap dances, like you haven't. I know you're not a boy scout; I saw your pictures."

"Yeah, nice try, those pictures were fake," Henry attempted to cover, not wanting to let Brad use his own missteps from a former life.

"Look, I don't know what this is about. I'm not going to let you accuse me of cheating on Bridgit. I was just blowing off some steam."

"Look, I honestly don't care what you do. I just don't want it to become a spectacle. You gotta clean up your shit. They just raided all these clubs and imagine if your face and name were all over the 6 o'clock news. We can't have that, so get your shit together," Henry fired at him.

Having not been talked to like that before, Dumont was stunned. Henry was only seven years his senior. And sure, he looked up to Henry for all he had accomplished, but Henry was some middle-class kid and should not be talking down to him, Dumont believed. He had been caught literally with his pants down, and the only option he knew at the moment was to beg for forgiveness so he could live to fight another day.

"You're not going to tell Bridgit or Lyndsay, are you?" he asked, his defiant tone changing.

"No, this one's between us. Look, we all fuck up. Me too, almost took me down. You need to be smart. You can't be hanging out in places like that anymore."

"I was just so stressed out, I was looking for something to distract me from all of it. Bridgit's all over me, wants to get pregnant. I'm not sure I'm ready, clearly, right? Then, I'm up here all by myself, don't know anyone, trying to prove I can do things on my own. I'm sorry, man, I just lost it."

"I get it, I know. I've been through it. You can't fuck up like this. You were lucky this time. This shit's gonna catch up with you. Just go home and be with your wife," Henry told him, knowing he needed to heed the same advice.

"We good, you and me, Henry?"

"Yeah, we're good, Brad, just understand I know what you're going through, and you can always confide in me. I mean that."

"Thanks. I appreciate that, Henry," he told him as we walked out his door.

16

Charlie and Christine had it all planned out. The first ads were scheduled to hit broadcast and cable television, backed by a digital barrage on YouTube, Facebook, and Instagram. For the next two weeks ahead of the filing deadline anyone considering running would have to think twice if they wanted to go up against the political machine that Charlie had engineered. His newfound fortune of $11.6 million was bankrolling the best Democrat consultants out of DC, and his initial $250,000 ad buy would paint a whole new picture of him for the electorate.

He needed to change the conversation that he was a Progressive candidate looking to impose his liberal views on working class Rhode Islanders. His money had helped build a new image of an innovative leader bringing a new renewable wind economy to Rhode Island. Inking the Dutch Wind deal to bring offshore wind turbines to Block Island Sound had transformed this once anti-business crusader into the new commerce maverick. No longer was he remembered for testifying at the House Finance Committee for a $25 minimum wage or before the Senate Labor Committee for wanting to subject small business owners to predictive scheduling. Delivering a new industry to a state that was usually first into recessions and then last out had absolved him of all his past sins against the business community. The Dutch investment in Rhode Island's future was not the only deal he had inked in Prague. Christine had brought all her talents to enhance his team.

As his *de facto* campaign director, Christine was calling all the shots from behind the scenes. The triumvirate of Charlie, Christine, and Ernie, his long-time seasoned political advisor who was providing adult supervision to this loosely run campaign, was corralling a team of DC advisors and local operatives riding the Charlie Braverman gravy train. They all wanted to be first in the handout line when the state contracts and appointments were doled out.

Christine was first on that list and already had proved her mettle. Her payback was the two-carat ring on her finger, which they had used some of their new-found fortune to purchase. Most of the Russian money had made its way into his campaign account by a scheme that Christine had carefully orchestrated. She maxed out donations from Charlie's personal account to every Democrat candidate in the northeast along with top liberals from around the country. With a wink and a nod, they returned the favor and maxed out to the Braverman Campaign for Governor. Friends and family, from college roommates to staff members for local lobbyists, were given small increments of $500 to $2,000. For their donations back to the campaign, they were rewarded with a commission for just making a deposit and writing a check. It was an easy way to make a c-note. All that a twenty-two-year old employee for a lobbying firm needed to do was write a check to a campaign for $500 after depositing $600 from their boss. The only problem was that it was illegal.

Even though Charlie Braverman was a new politician, he played by the same old political rules that the local culture had tolerated by its willful disengagement in the political process. And while he relished the limelight on the campaign trail, he was fortunate to have Christine as his stage manager behind the curtain. She knew that politics was really just show business for ugly people, and even though Charlie had the looks of a good b-movie actor, that was as far as he would go on stage in New York or on screen in Hollywood. In politics he could become the youngest governor in the country.

Christine often felt limited by the talent around her. She was tired of having to explain herself to the campaign staff and would have preferred that they just do what she asked. However, this was not an absolute dictatorship, and Charlie had built a team atmosphere in which everyone's opinion was encouraged.

"Look, just put a red box around his picture on the media page," she told the web designer.

"Why would I put in a red box? It looks gaffe," insisted Mark Renard, a thirty-something web designer who had left his contract job at a major retailer to make some quick cash on a campaign that was paying top dollar for talent.

"Can you just do it? I know it doesn't look pretty. That's not what this is about," Christine fired back, not really asking.

"Maybe if you tell me why we're doing this, I can give you some better advice," he replied, holding his ground, and realizing he may need to retreat from his boss, who was also the candidate's fiancée.

"Look, just do it. Put a red box around his photo so the PAC's know to use this image in their ads. We can't coordinate directly with them. We can make it very clear what assets we want them to use."

"Oh, OK, got it," he said, realizing she was way above him.

"I want you to do the same thing on the section of the website where we go into the details about the new energy economy. Put a box around these two paragraphs," she told him, pointing to the sections on the screen that detailed Charlie's vision for turning Rhode Island into a staging ground for a new burgeoning offshore wind industry.

"So now I'm ruining this page with this gauche red box?"

"It's not about looking pretty. That red box is going to tell the SuperPACs, who you'll remember we're not coordinating with, to use this exact wording in their ads," she told him, giving air quotes around "not coordinating."

"Wow, OK, I'll put in the red lines."

"Good. Remember I'm not just a pretty face," she said, using her feminine charms on a man she assumed hadn't been laid in years, if ever.

"I need to talk to you," Charlie said, rescuing her from the awkward silence that followed the void look on the designer's face. "Hey, Mark, can you give us a minute?" Charlie asked, watching him get up and scurry out of Christine's office. "Love the website, you're doing a great job," he told him, watching a smile envelope his face.

"I swear these people are driving me nuts. They just don't get it. I want a fucking red box around some words and they keep questioning me, worried about how it looks. It's how we get the Super-PACs to do exactly what we want."

"Look, Christine, I love what you're doing, how you figured out a way to use our cash. And what you're doing with the SuperPACs, I'm glad I have a pro like you, but I'm just not sure about this," Charlie confided in her. He felt he could tell her exactly how he felt. She had become his sounding board, and it did not take a therapist to see that his constant rantings about the money were revealing the underpinnings of the stress he had inflicted upon himself. He was crashing on the couch at 9 p.m. the nights he was not at events, and regardless of what time he went to bed, he was up wide eyed at 3 a.m. It was the same repeating drama every night for the past two weeks. Sometimes she could get him back to sleep after giving him the only remedy she knew to calm his racing thoughts.

"Charlie, we've been over this how many times," she told him, calmly rubbing his shoulder. "We've got the best DC consultants.

They're Lorie's people," he told her, referring to Rhode Island's first female governor who now was serving as United States Treasury Secretary. During her Rhode Island reign, Lorie, affectionately referred to by her first name by all the political insiders, had exiled current Governor Robert Daniels to Siberia while he was lieutenant governor, something Daniels refused to do to Charlie as the state's current number two.

"I know we have the best. It's not them; it's *how*?"

"Whadaya mean, how are they running things so far?"

"No, I mean, how we got it. How we got the money," he said more emphatically to her.

"Charlie, you worry too much. Who cares how we got it? We now have it, and we can win with it. By showing our viability with all this cash, and then the governor's people lining up, and now Lorie backing us with her people, we're creating a sense of inevitability."

"Ya know, when I'm lying there awake in bed, I just keep thinking about that Russian. He's literally keeping me up at night."

"Charlie, your mind is playing games on you. He's just an old man who honored his comrade by giving you what you're owed. Your dad sacrificed for that money. And you sacrificed too, never having a father."

"I would've rather had a father, to be honest."

"I know, sweetheart. Look at what he has given his son, the chance to be one of fifty governors."

"You're right, I just need to chill. It's all the pressure. We're out every night. It's just been getting to me," he admitted.

"How about just you and me tonight. We'll make a pizza, have some wine, and watch Netflix like a regular couple."

"Actually, a little normalcy sounds pretty good right now."

"Then it's a date, just you and me tonight, Charlie."

"Love you, Christine."

"I know."

17

"Moscow is all over me. They want a full debrief," the Russian Consul General told Antipov. While his day job was overseeing the Russian consulate in Boston, his nights were running special operations in New England for the GRU. He had active measures with Antipov in Minsk, Belarus, and a stint in Riga, Latvia, but this operation was like nothing they had ever attempted. He also knew of Antipov's legendary feats in Belarus and his failure in Ukraine to prevent that country's current leadership from sticking a thumb in Moscow's eye. He understood that was why Antipov had been sent to the United States. Partly it was to get him out of Eastern Europe before he was purged from his distinguished Russian service. The other reason he was operational in this new mission was to lash back at the Americans for all their interference in Russia's greater European ambitions.

Infiltrating elections had become an art for the Russians, their type of asymmetrical warfare to compensate for their considerable shortcomings on the traditional battlefield. Like any true virtuoso,

Alexi dreamed of his big score. This was his great symphony, orchestrated by the master himself. He had fine-tuned his operation for twenty-five years, and now it may start paying back for his beloved homeland.

"Tell the bureaucrats back home to leave me to my op," he said to his old comrade as they sipped their vodka.

"We just gave you $12 million, and now you want $10 million more? Not to mention all the money over the last 25 years to get this whole thing going. We must have $100 million all in on this."

"That's a minor investment to infiltrate American states. Think about it. I bought him pretty cheap for $12 million. Now he's got the PAC money coming in. It's a small price to buy a state. The governor's race in Wisconsin was $55 million. We can have Rhode Island for $12 million. He shows the early money, and the rest will flood into his campaign," Antipov explained.

"Still, you want another $10 million on top of what we've given you," the consul general reminded him.

"The money we used initially was to set up the larger operation. If it works, this will set the stage for how we do all political infiltration campaigns in the future."

"Look, I know the initial funds came from the president himself when he was at KGB, and I know what he thinks of you. The vultures are circling around him, and therefore us, so we have to be careful."

"They're busting my balls over another $10 million I need. It's one less yacht for our president, a small investment to prove we can buy a governor."

"Oh Alexi, you make me laugh," he said as he stared him down and pointed up emphatically, reminding him that the room was bugged.

"We always need to spend the motherland's resources wisely, comrade, not foolishly like we have in the past," Antipov brazenly shot back, sending a message back to whomever was listening. If Russia was truly to compete, he understood it needed to act like a responsible nation state, not a kleptocracy. He knew there were others who felt the same way. But, he realized that change would have to wait. One day the new Russia would be the envy of the world. Right now he needed to wreak havoc on her number one enemy, the United States of America, and undermine the very institutions that were the bedrock of its misguided idealism. Antipov's father had been slaughtered by the Germans in World War II like so many other Russians who were used as cannon fodder as the Americans played their war games in North Africa. He was not alone in a sentiment that was shared among many of the Russian elite. The Americans needed a reminder that while they were the biggest bully on the block, they too were vulnerable. Anitpov simply wanted to knock them down a peg, and he was just the David to poke Goliath's eye.

18

Henry had prepared for this moment pretty much his whole life. This was his opportunity to prove that he was a true business maverick. Certainly, to this point he had proved his mettle, having rescued Providence's largest building from the trash heap of corporate downsizing and restructuring. His deal to build a destination golf resort that was accessible to anyone who wanted to play, a rival to the state's most elite courses that shut out the average working man, was also transformational to the landscape. Acquiring a controlling interest in one of Rhode Island's leading conglomerates, that would not only earn him the reputation he so sought, it would cement the Sinclair dynasty for generations.

Henry had reviewed this deal from every angle. He typically would ask his father-in-law for advice and counsel, but he wanted to do this one on his own. Sinclair knew what he was up to, supported him, and also gave Henry the space he needed. If Henry were to command their fortune in the future, Sinclair understood he needed to let him fly on his own at times. He had bailed Henry out before, and sometimes he knew that the greatest learning experiences were from the failures. Henry had painstakingly considered every move that the RITECH board could throw at him to thwart their takeover. He had researched the company and its competitors and had completed his homework the same way he performed in college and law school, over-excelling his classmates. Henry was doing it the only way he knew how. It was go time.

"I'm sorry, Mr. Mercucio, the board meeting has been rescheduled for tonight. Mr. Teller asked that I escort you to his office," Teller's executive secretary told Henry. As the CEO of RITECH, Timothy Teller, affectionately referred to as TNT by his peers, was a maverick himself. As the CEO of a conglomerate that made advanced weaponry, he enjoyed the perks of his profession, and after receiving flight training, he flew his own helicopter to Providence when he was in town. Today was such a day he needed to make a grand appearance.

"I should have been told the board meeting was moved. Can you tell me why at least?" Henry asked the secretary. She was skilled enough to dodge his question with an evasive response.

"I believe Mr. Teller wants to tell you in person."

"Come on in, Henry," Teller offered, motioning Henry to take a seat on his coach. "Coffee, Henry?"

"No, thank you. Just some answers please," Henry replied, his tone showing he knew something was amiss.

"Thank you, Justine, we're all set," Teller said to his secretary and turned his attention back to Henry as the door closed.

"Yes, Tim, looks like things are all set," Henry knew, revealing he understood that his plans had been uncovered.

"Ya' know Henry, I remember you from the Campagna campaign. What you did, exceptional. It's why when the mayor came to me, wanting you to have the board seat, I was excited. Someone with your talents is what this board needs."

"Tim, just give it to me. You don't need to butter me up."

"OK, Henry, I respect that. So then let's get right down to business. Your board seat was a favor, not a real one. And the board voted earlier this morning to eliminate the seat."

"Of course they did."

"You don't seem surprised."

"No, I'm not," Henry told him, then stood up and buttoned his suit.

"It's just business, Henry. I like you."

"Yeah, just business," Henry countered as he walked out of the office. He wanted to tell him that this day was not the end of it. He could have reminded him that this was just one counter strike in a longer offensive, but Henry realized he was defeated this time. He wanted to preserve himself to fight another day. This one cut deeply. He had worked this deal for six months, had invested considerable resources of the Sinclair company, and now he would have to return to his office with his tail between his legs, defeated, no longer the golden boy with the Midas touch.

Henry had never felt so low. Not even in the depths of the Campagna mayoral campaign when he had risked his conscience to preserve himself had he felt such crushing defeat. Not since before Lyndsay had the pangs of self-doubt come crashing down on him. His self-worth was predicated on his success. Without it, a girl like Lyndsay would never be with him, he surmised in his head. Because without his unbridled success, he was a nobody, just another average guy, certainly not worthy of his fiancée who was an up-and-coming pediatric oncologist who also happened to be an heiress of a great American fortune. How could he look her in the eye, and then her father, and admit he had been duped by a sharper and savvier businessman? It was supposed to be him. Henry was to be the next coming, the new business phoenix rising from the ashes of obscurity to take his place next to the father.

Henry looked as he felt, a man beaten down. He was able to muster enough dignity to walk himself out of the RITECH tower. As soon as he exited the building, his driver Rick pulled up the black Suburban beside him.

"I wasn't expecting you so soon, boss," Rick admitted.

"Neither did I, Rick. Just take me home."

"Not back to the office, Henry?"

"Actually, yeah, Rick, take me back to the office, I gotta find who just fucked me," he blurted out, knowing he could speak freely in front of Rick. He then reached for his phone and called another man he knew was always with him. "Danny, it's me. Listen, you need to do this discreetly. Go over to Haley and ask her to look to see who else has accessed the RITECH merger files in the last 48 hours. I'll be there in 15 minutes. You gotta do this delicately. If she has any questions, have her call me directly on my cell. She knows that if it's coming from you, it's from me. Thanks, buddy," Henry hung up before Danny could even get a word in.

"You OK, boss?" Rick asked him, looking through the rear-view mirror at someone he did not immediately recognize. Henry's calm temperament had been traded for a fast talking, agitated, and frantic man, who exhibited the look of a zealot about to make a rash decision. Rick pulled the car over and turned to Henry.

"Boss, never seen you like this. You don't look good; you're sweating," he told him, feeling the need to interject, risking his job, but just being a responsible human being. Henry was obviously in distress.

"I'm OK Rick, really, and I appreciate your concern for me, I really do. I just realized how the deal I've been working on for the last six months was pulled out from under me by someone close.

Yeah, I'm pissed, fucking livid, and if you really do care about me, you'll take me back to the office right now so I can get to the bottom of this."

"You got it, boss, I just…"

"Rick, I appreciate it, I do. You're a good friend."

Rick pulled off from the curb and darted through traffic, equally driven to help Henry get to the bottom of what had transformed this once enthusiastically positive human being into a visibly beaten down man. Before the Suburban had even fully stopped in front of the Superman building, Henry had jumped out and made his way to the ornate entrance. He brushed by the security guard, not saying his usual "Hi, Manny," and pressed the button to the 26th floor. Everyone outside the elevator knew who he was, and they could tell from his demeanor that something was amiss. They backed away, not hearing on this day the jovial Henry make a comment about the Red Sox starting rotation or the latest play at PPAC. Henry had not even noticed that no one had joined him in the elevator. As he rode solo to his destination, thoughts of betrayal raced through his head.

He quickly strode off the elevator, opened the glass doors into his palatial office suite, and brushed by the nice new receptionist he had usually made a point to stop over to make polite conversation upon every entrance. This was no day for trivial office decorum. Henry needed to flush out a rat. He knew it as soon as he saw Danny and Haley look up at him from in front of her computer.

"It was fucking him, wasn't it," he said as he approached two of his most faithful disciples. Haley could not look up, and a tear was already rolling down her cheek.

"Let's go in your office, Henry," Danny said, using his own personal experience as a handler for the former mayor to his benefit. Once he had Henry in his office, he told him, "Yeah, it was Brad. He accessed the files two days ago. He must have downloaded the whole thing and given it to the CEO of RITECH."

"That fucking bastard. If you just looked at those files blindly, without my explanation, of course they would kill the deal. I needed to walk them through it."

"I don't get it, Henry, he's your own family now. Why would he do this to you?"

"He's not family, he's fucking one of them," Henry fired back, demonstrably pointing to Providence's tallest tower in the financial district, which at this moment represented the elites Henry fought so hard to be part of, but who continuously had shut him out of their exclusive club. "You know where he is?"

"I bet I can find him. He's all too predictable."

"I want you to grab him and bring him back to me. Will you do that for me?"

"Of course, Henry, anything."

***

Danny knew where to go. It was Thursday evening, and if Danny knew Brad as the creature of habit that he was, then he would be off celebrating his perceived victory in one of Providence's gentlemen's clubs. He had shadowed Brad on many an afterwork jaunt at Chateau's, and he still knew all the bouncers by name. None of them ever wanted to give up one of the more lucrative gigs in Providence, where politicians and businessmen always paid well for discretion.

"My boy in there?" Danny asked Pat the bouncer, who had worked the door for what seemed like a generation.

"The Southern dandy, yeah, he came in with a bunch of other suits, they've been here for a couple of hours."

"Thanks, Pat," he said as he cupped a hundred to him.

"Danny, you don't need to give me this," Pat told him. He

thought of him more like a compatriot than one of the other assholes who paid him to look the other way.

"No, Pat, I'm going to need to give you that," he admitted as he brazenly pushed open the doors to see the menagerie of naked women, gang-bangers, the socially-awkward young and old, and the businessmen in search of distractions.

He saw his favorite bartender, Samantha, and put down a fifty-dollar bill. "Hey Sammy, you seen the Southern gentleman I've been in here with before?"

"Yeah, he's been back in the private rooms for about an hour."

"Who's working the door, anyone I know?"

"Yeah, you know Pat's little brother, Paulie."

"Of course I do, thanks Sammy."

Danny walked back to the private rooms and saw Paulie standing guard. Though he was the little brother to Pat, he was not very small, and in fact his chest and forearms far exceeded his brother's imposing stature.

"Hey Paulie, I'm Danny Conroy. I'm friends with your brother, Pat."

"Sure, Danny, I know you. You used to watch the mayor. Miss him, he always tipped us good."

"Yeah, that was me. Listen, I got to talk to one of your guests."

"Let me guess, the Southern fucker I've seen you in here with. Be my guest, he's a fucking asshole. Tips good. Thinks he's better than us."

Danny handed him a hundred and asked him which room he was in.

"Number four, and I think he's onto his second girl by now."

Danny opened the door to number four, and as soon as the door busted open the twenty-something blonde jumped off Brad's lap like she had been thrown from a bull.

"What the fuck? Oh, Danny, it's you. I thought you were a cop."

"You wish you were getting busted, you fucking little douche bag," he told him as he grabbed him from the ear lobe. He told the girl to grab her things and handed her a hundred for her troubles. He turned back to Brad, "Get your clothes on, and man, cover yourself up," he said as he turned away from the scene of a married man with a condom dangling and little dignity left.

He gave Brad a minute to gain his composure as he guarded the door like he was on a secret service detail. As soon as Brad came out, he grabbed him by the arm, only to have him fire back, "Don't you put your hands on me. I'll fucking have you fired."

Danny replied with a stiff jab to his stomach. Brad buckled over, and Danny escorted him out past Paulie and Pat the bouncers and on to the waiting Suburban. Rick the driver helped Danny put Brad in the car, appearing like just another businessman who had too much fun in a local strip club.

Danny sat next to Brad in the back of the Suburban as they made their way back to the Superman building. Brad had reached for his phone, but Danny slapped it out of his hand. "What the fuck, man?"

"You're not calling anyone until you talk to Henry first," Danny admonished him. What felt like a silent ride with your angry parents after catching you in a lie at your teacher's conference was only a ten-minute drive back to Henry's office without another word said in the car. Rick parked the car right in front of the building and backed up Danny as he walked their guest past security and deposited him into the elevator. They rode in silence to their destination and walked into the empty offices where the employees had returned to their families and loved ones for the night. The only ones left were Henry, Danny, and Brad.

"Whadaya gonna' do, Henry, whack me? No, you wouldn't do it yourself, you'd have your goombah do it," Brad fired at them, the first to break the silence.

Henry understood that the first to speak often lost, so he held his tongue. He let Danny respond to the derogatory comment aimed at him.

"I'm Irish, you asshole," he said, responding with a backhand to the face.

"You're all the same," Brad defiantly shot back. His cocky grin gave way to a red welt forming on his face.

"Brad, we're all done. I know it was you, but why?" Henry asked.

"Because, Henry, you don't play in our game, we play you."

"Is this a Southern thing?"

"No, it's you, Henry. Sure, you can play up here in Providence in your politics. You're way above your pay grade. Leave the big business to the professionals."

"We could've had it all," Henry told him.

"Why would I share anything with you? Your daddy was a drunk. Mine built a fortune. You're just lucky you were able to trick Lyndsay. Everyone knows it, you're a fraud."

Henry was stunned. It had been a long time since anyone had spoken to him like that. He was used to people fawning over him with praise for his political and even business genius. He knew he needed to control his emotions, make a measured response. His strategic reasoning gave way to the sheer emotion that was boiling his blood inside. The self-doubt fueled by a history of abuse erupted as he lunged at Brad. Danny, sensing his boss's visibly changing emotions, blocked him like a linebacker, so Henry could not sack Brad.

"You're all fucking done, you little shit. I'm going to enjoy watching you squander your daddy's money and fuck up everything," Henry fired back at him, his words more bruising than any punch he could throw. His verbal assault continued, "You think because you were born into privilege that you have the right to treat people like you do. To treat women in your life like objects for your pleasure. You look at me like I should be thankful to have the privilege to work with your family, like I'm some landed gentry to your royalty. Let me bow down to 'Brad The Great,'" he said, genuflecting to drive home his point. He was not done though. "You may not have realized this while your daddy was buying your way through life, but the aristocracy is over. Welcome to the meritocracy here in America where people who actually have talent succeed."

Danny had let go of Henry, seeing his words were more lethal than his fists. He too hoped to one day master the oratory arts, and saw that Henry was truly masterful in this discipline. Brad was left dumbfounded and picked up what was left of his dignity, retreating from Henry's office. Henry had discovered the traitor in his midst. Treachery had a way of rearing its ugly head again.

19

Home was Henry's refuge. After his battle with Brad, he had waited before returning home, much to the urging of his most trusted lieutenant, Danny. They had 18-year-old scotch in Henry's office, discussing their next moves. Henry did most of the talking, and Danny saw the benefits of serving as Henry's sounding board. He was truly now in the inner circle and had a front seat to Henry's thinking. Now it was time for Henry to leave his office in downtown Providence and return to his suburban bliss with his wife.

Having already fought one fight for the day, Henry was relishing the calm confines that only Lyndsay provided him. These were extraordinary times for Henry, and when you fought as hard as he did, there was the danger of unexpected collateral damage. That was the problem with war. Once it was unleashed, it was difficult to contain. It too often consumed the innocent.

Henry often exhibited relief when he walked into his new home, a symbol of what his talent could build with the Sinclair family's backing. His pride diminished from the sound he very rarely heard in his home. It was not soft whimpering, but harsh cries that often only come from betrayal. The only one home was Lyndsay.

Henry walked up the stairs as the cries grew louder upon each step he took closer to their bedroom. He opened the door only to see Lyndsay throw herself off their bed and run to their bathroom.

"Lyndsay, what is it? Did someone die?"

"Us." At least that is what Henry thought he heard from the muffled cry from behind the closed door.

"Lyndsay, what's going on?"

"Everything I feared," she told him, as she stormed out the door, throwing his toiletry bag at him. "Get out."

"What do you think I've done?" Henry asked, clearly startled. Lyndsay was not easily rattled. She was a trained physician who dealt with the most stressful situations. Telling a mom and dad that their child had cancer and calmly explaining a course of treatment took a high level of ingrained empathy and professional skill. Henry knew his literature, and "Hell hath no fury like a woman scorned."

"I've always been here for you, Henry. Stood by you, helped you through whatever shit you're going through at the time. Calmed your doubts, eased your fears, always taking care of you. Because you're so special, so talented. Henry's going to do great things, so I've got to be there for him. You're so damaged, and I thought I could be the one," she said, her resignation revealed as she turned away from him.

"What is this, Lyndsay?" he pleaded with her.

"My sister called me crying. Brad came home with a welt on his face. She asked him what happened. Usually, your husband does not come home from his downtown job with a bruise on his face. He wouldn't tell her anything but then he broke down. You had your thug, Danny, beat him. Why would Henry do that? He was in politics and it can get dirty. He'd never have anyone beaten up, or worse, or would he? I don't know anymore. Why would Henry have his brother-in-law beaten like an animal?"

The usually eloquent Henry could not find any words, and he himself was even beginning to question how he had handled Brad. He did not have a quick retort for Lyndsay's accusations, and simply listened as she continued. "Of course, Bridgit couldn't believe it either. Not Henry. Everyone looks up to Henry. He's our dad's golden boy. Our family's savior is fucking strippers, Henry?"

"What?!" While Henry had stood silently as Lyndsay justifiably berated him for how he had Brad man-handled, this accusation was too much for him. "That little fucker," he uttered.

"Of course, you deny it. Not the great Henry."

"Lynds, you really think I'm out fucking strippers? Exactly when would I have the time to be doing that? I've been working on the RITECH deal. You know that; your dad's involved. Want to know what really happened? That little fucker, Brad, goes to their CEO and reveals my plans before I had the chance to walk their board through my restructuring plans, the ones your dad vetted with me and has been working on side by side with me for six months. It was your dad who warned me about Brad in the first place. I never thought he would do this to me, and to us."

"I don't know if I believe you anymore, Henry. This is all too much. I've been through all the political shit with you. You promised me this stuff was over. I just don't know if I can do this anymore. You promised me you were out, but you're clearly fully back in."

"Yes, I am all in, Lyndsay. I'm in an even more difficult world today that is even more treacherous than I could have ever imagined. You're what keeps my sanity. Knowing that what I'm doing will someday help make a better world for us, and our kids."

"And that's how you do it, by fucking strippers?" She couldn't hold back, since the thought was so horrifying to her, especially in light of her own secret she was holding back from him.

"Lyndsay, please listen to me, I haven't been in a strip club in years, I swear. It was Brad. Yes, Danny did rough him up a little bit. He pulled him out of a strip club in Providence after I discovered he had betrayed us. The truth is Brad's been going to these places two to three times a week. And he's not just watching. He's in the back room, sometimes with multiple girls, and he's cheating on Bridgit. I just found out myself, and I wasn't sure what to do. Then he literally fucked me over. When Danny brought him to me, he said some vile shit, and Danny whacked him, because that's what guys like him do. You know Danny, he's a good kid. When he heard Brad talk to me like he did, he responded the only way he knew. That pales in comparison to what Brad did to me, and to your sister," Henry told her, trying to help her see the truth within the chaos.

"I don't know anymore, Henry," she said as she brushed by him walking to their guest room.

"Where are you going?"

"I want to be alone," she told him.

***

Henry wasn't sure how much he actually slept. When he saw the clock next to him strike 4 a.m. he decided to hit the shower and begin his day. With both his business and family now in doubt, he reacted the only way he knew. He was going to work.

Toiling away at his desk from 5:30 a.m., he started to plot his comeback. Henry's turnaround was interrupted by a call to his cell. Few people called him this early. His brother, for one, knew Henry was always up this early and often tried him as he went into rounds at the hospital. The only other one up this early working was Lyndsay's father, Reginald Sinclair. The last person who needed to rise before dawn to work was Sinclair. He had already earned his fortune, but habits that built greatness were not easily shed.

"How's the boy?" It was how Sinclair referred to Henry, and though it could have been perceived as condescending to Henry, he never felt that way.

"You know about RITECH I'm assuming, that's why you're calling me."

"Yes, Henry, I know, and that it was Brad. I told you to watch him."

"Not like that, never knew he would go around my back like he did."

"You'll learn there are few you can trust outside of family."

"I thought he was family."

"Not our family, Henry."

"I thought it was going to be different than politics," Henry admitted.

"That's why I knew you would be so good at this. Politics is war, and business is the new battlefield. It's still the same fight between families, even today," Sinclair reminded him.

"I just don't know if I'm cut out for this anymore."

"Pick up the pieces of your pride, Henry, and get back in the game. You can't let an amateur like Brad derail you. He's an imposter just like his old man."

"Funny, I thought I was the imposter in your world," Henry revealed to his father-in-law.

"You've got to leave this imposter syndrome bullshit behind you. You are a real player in our world. You lost this round, but there are many more rounds to play. This is not the end of the RITECH deal. We're still a major shareholder, you and me. Let them think they have us beat for now," Sinclair told his son-in-law, reassuring him in an attempt to build him back up.

"And that back-stabber, Brad, what do we do about him?" Henry asked.

"You mean that little shit who's cheating on my daughter."

"You know?"

"Of course I know. It's my business to know." Henry let those words sink in for a moment before he responded. *How did Sinclair know*, he pondered to himself. Before he could utter a response, Sinclair added, "His father was a degenerate too. Like father like son, in this case," Sinclair said, covering himself at the end, knowing Henry's own father was a sore subject for him.

"So, what's next?" Henry asked.

"That's up to you now, isn't it, Henry?"

"It always has been," he quipped.

"That's right, Henry, you have to act like you're in this alone, but you're not. You've got me, Lyndsay, all those devoted disciples around you."

"I've got you, and maybe my team. Not sure I've got Lyndsay anymore."

"Henry, you think Mary just stood idly by while I was off making my moves? There were struggles, and yes, there were times she doubted me. She always came back, and so will Lyndsay."

"I hope you're right, Mr. Sinclair, I hope you are."

"It's dad, or Reggie, not Mr. Sinclair, and I would love for you to call me dad sometime."

"Someday. We good?"

"We're good, Henry."

And so, the day went on with the call from Sinclair giving Henry a brief reprieve from his self-masochism. Henry hunkered down in his office, silenced his cell, and put his office phone on do-not-disturb. Through the glass walls of his office, he could see his co-workers walk by and stare in and quickly look away to avoid his glance. He only imagined what they could be thinking. He had so much invested in the RITECH deal, and he expected resignations and a mass exodus to follow. Henry could not recall ever feeling so down. When in such a state, he realized it was hard to remember any other time of despair where he felt so dire. His mind even took him back to his past that had been robbed by a boy on the street. Why his mind had turned to his darkest memory he could not understand. He picked up his head and turned back to his computer screen. He desperately needed to find a way forward. For Henry, it started with a knock.

"Boss, you alright?" Danny asked him. Little did Henry know that his co-workers had nominated Danny to deliver the message from them all.

"I'm good, buddy, just figuring out my next move."

"Henry, we just want you to know we're all with you. The entire staff, in fact. They asked me to come talk to you. We had a meeting, a Captain's meeting like you told us you wanted us to do when you couldn't be with us. We just want you to know that every one of us—Jenny, Tommy, Haley, Sarah, Paulie, Alex—everyone on the team, they wanted me to let you know we're here for you."

"I appreciate that, Danny, I do. I'm supposed to be the one that is here for you guys, not the other way around."

"That's why we're now here for you, because you're always here for us. Now it's our turn. Tell us what you want us to do. The people here would walk on hot coals for you. I would pretty much do anything for you. Just tell me."

The depression that was suffocating Henry was lifted as Danny spoke his feelings. It was like Danny's words had turned a switch on in him. One of the analysts, Haley, then appeared in the doorway next to Danny and whispered in his ear. Danny nodded to her, and she turned to Henry.

"Lyndsay is out front," she said. Henry was not sure what to expect. Lyndsay rarely came by, more comfortable on the floors of the Children's Hospital than in corporate offices.

"My wife doesn't need to wait for me, she can come back. Wait, let me go," Henry reacted. He walked down the hallway at a frenetic pace for a pivotal meeting. Lyndsay was still in her blue hospital scrubs and was making small talk with the receptionist. As soon as she saw Henry reveal himself from around the corner, she lit up like she had after he had walked her home from their first date. She gave a polite goodbye to the receptionist and moved to Henry, clutching his hand.

"Can we talk?" she asked.

"Of course, let's go to my office."

"I forgot how nice your office is. I love the light," she told him as she looked out over the sunsetting skyline. "I'm sorry," she told him, before he could even speak.

"I would never, Lyndsay."

"I know, that's what I'm sorry about, that I ever doubted you."

"That's OK, I often doubt myself," Henry admitted.

"My sister, she called me at the hospital, crying. She found a condom wrapper in Brad's jeans. They've been trying to have a baby, so why would he have a condom? She confronted him this morning. He was all hung over. He told her that she's no different from the strippers he's with, that my dad whored her out so he could take over their business. She's crushed, I had to leave work, and I just calmed her down and had to come see you. I'm so sorry, Henry."

"You don't need to apologize to me. I love you, and I would do anything for you."

"I know that, and I've been racking my brain trying to figure out how I could let my emotions affect my judgment. I know you, and that it's not in your character to cheat. So, at the hospital I took another test. I want to wait the full 12-weeks before we tell my parents."

"I don't know what you mean, took a test. You've already passed your boards."

"I'm pregnant."

20

"Hello Charlie," echoed from a side room off the hallway. Charlie was making his way to the bathroom, having just come down the stairs from a fundraiser held by an influential union lobbyist in Camille's Italian Restaurant on Providence's Federal Hill.

"Antipov? You have a funny way of appearing in my life. What do you want?" Charlie asked, his annoyance clearly evident.

"Come sit with me and have the veal chop. It's the best in New England," Antipov offered as he poured a glass of Caymus. "You Americans make the best Cabernets. Much better than the French."

"I've already had lunch, and the last thing I'd have is a baby cow."

"Ah, yes, that would not sit well with your Progressive friends," he chided.

"Yes comrade, my liberal friends once looked to you for your idealistic views. Now, you've become worse than the greediest capitalists, and certainly more corrupt."

"Oh Charlie, I'd love to sit with you and wax philosophical about the sins of both our governments. Let's focus on the present. You have a race to win, Governor Braverman, and I have something that will interest you."

"I don't want anything from you or your people," Charlie insisted.

"Indulge me, Charlie, one last favor from the friend of your father, who is honoring a debt to look after his only child."

"You love to always bring my father up. Did you really know him?"

"Your father was a hero of the Soviet Union. He was my friend. You dishonor his memory with the mere suggestion," Antipov fired back. He was highly skilled in the art of deception, and he could tell that his conviction had convinced his mark.

"I just didn't know if this was another GRU plot."

"I'm the Russian cultural attaché, Charlie, nothing more. I'm retired."

"So that's why you're here, you want to experience our Italian-American cuisine here on Federal Hill. You figured it out like so many in Boston that our food is better."

"Yes, your city is a culinary gem, and this is from someone who spent years in Paris."

"So, you're not here to talk about cuisine. Why are you really here?"

"I came across some information on your opponent you may find interesting."

"There's nothing you can tell me about Stevens that my team doesn't already know. He's just another carpetbagger investment banker who thinks he can just waltz back into our state and take over our government." Chad Stevens was a forty-five-year-old, Harvard educated multi-millionaire, who realized he could spend a small portion of his fortune to capture the governor's office as his first step to achieve higher office and real power and influence in America.

"Do you know he has ties to the Gaspee Militia?" Antipov asked him, referring to a homegrown right-wing group that had pledged to protect Rhode Island's upcoming elections. These self-proclaimed new Patriots were hoping to spark a new revolution and had been inspired by the 1770 burning of the British tax collection ship, the Gaspee, in which Rhode Island rebels rounded up the crew, shot the captain, and burned the vessel.

"C-mon, really. He's an evil bankster, not a right-wing nut-job," Charlie countered, but the information was enough to make him stop and listen. He sat down in the booth in the private dining room with Antipov.

"Look at this," Anipov told him, sliding over an envelope with photos and text message transcripts.

"How did you get this?"

"What matters isn't how I got it, Charlie, but what's in it. You've got a serious candidate for governor meeting with a group that has a stated mission to overthrow your government. When I learned of it, I had to do something about it. You know we were the ones who warned your government about the Tsarnaev brothers," he told him. While Russian intelligence had been in contact with their counterparts about the Kyrgz-American brothers who perpetrated the Boston Marathon bombing, they were also running multiple operations targeting both the far left and right groups to undermine the American political process. Antipov's rival at the GRU was in charge of the right-wing operation, and if he could one up his competitor while at the same time strengthening his own mission, then that was a double-win for him.

The Russian government through the GRU had been meddling in elections throughout the world for decades. From bankrolling Brexit to backing fascists in Italy, and even a successful foray in the 2016 US elections, this once perceived powerful military foe was playing by a new set of rules. While their conventional forces were no match to the American and even European technology, their asymmetrical warfare made up for their shortcomings on the battlefield.

Democracy by its very nature was vulnerable, and often all that was needed was a spark to ignite the fire that would engulf it. In its ashes a new authoritarian model was planned, predicated on a get-it-done-at-all-costs mindset that preyed upon the inherent fears and ingrained prejudices of the masses. It was why many right-wing groups gravitated to the strongman model propagated by the Russians. While they once had championed communism throughout the world, their new cause was aimed at liberal democracies falling like dominoes.

Charlie's turning stomach wasn't from the antipasto salad he had devoured or the influence he had been subjugated to during the lobbyist fundraiser upstairs. It just didn't add up. Oftentimes those things that seemed too good to be true were just that. His own unique history made him vulnerable. It did not take a clinical psychologist to understand that a fatherless child would romanticize about a heroic father who gave to a cause bigger than his son. The whole situation was beginning to become unsettling for him.

However, his sneaking suspicion did not stop Charlie from taking the information Antipov had volunteered. It was evident on his face as he walked out of Camille's and was picked up by his waiting driver. He asked his twenty-five-year-old political wannabe chauffeur to take him home. He needed to see Christine, calling her cell and asking her to meet him at their apartment.

Christine understood Charlie enough to realize that when he called her after an event in distress, her most important job was to meet and calm his nerves. While the campaign employed an official campaign manager and a cadre of consultants, they all understood that she was calling the shots. The most important person in the campaign needed her, and Christine superseded everything else on her plate for the day.

"There's something really rotten in Rhode Island," he told her as she entered their living room, which had been converted into a war room. Antipov's pictures and text message trails were strewn across their coffee table.

"What is this?" she asked, as she picked up the photo of Chad Stevens meeting with the scraggly bearded head of the Gaspee Militia.

"There's more. Check out these text messages. It ties him to the group, the same ones who have vowed to guard our elections in November. Their stated goal is to overthrow the Rhode Island Constitution. Stevens has denied any contact with them, and this clearly proves it."

"Then we got him in a lie. We need to leak this," she told him.

"Wait."

"Charlie, we've got to. People need to know that the Republican candidate is meeting with a right-wing militia that's pledged to overthrow our government."

"I really don't think Stevens is working with them, but just the appearance alone is disturbing."

"He's giving credence to their claims. His meeting implies it," she reminded Charlie.

"There's something else you need to see first," Charlie told her, handing her another envelope. It contained the photo of the two of them during what they had thought was just a fun, distracting tryst with a girl in Prague. Christine's confidence was shattered by the realization that what she thought was a drunken induced sexcapade was now documented for distribution.

"What is this, Charlie?"

"It's blackmail."

"Why would someone want to blackmail us?"

"They wanted to show me that they could get to us. I think it's to be used to hold over our heads."

"What do they want?"

"This may be bigger than us."

"The money."

"Yeah, I don't think the money is really from my father."

"If it's not from your father, then who's it from?"

"The Russians."

"The Russians, but the Ukrainians hate them."

"My father apparently fought for the Soviet Union. I think it's a lie," Charlie realized.

"Oh my god, we got played. They set us up, and we're implicated. I moved all that money around. The Feds got us on a thousand counts of wire fraud and campaign finance violations. We're fucked."

"I think it's bigger than us," Charlie admitted. "I think the Russians are making a play at our local elections, not just in Rhode Island, but everywhere. This goes way beyond us."

"What are we going to do?"

"We need to expose it."

"How, without destroying us?" she asked him.

"I don't know, and right now we play along. There's still a week before the filing deadline, and we need to think."

"We need someone who gets it. We can't go to the Feds yet. We need to cut a deal," she told him, her strategic thoughts replacing her desperate despair.

"I think I may know who to talk to. There's only one guy who can navigate both worlds of politics and power, who can handle something like this."

"Mercucio," she knew.

"Yup, Henry."

"He's not in politics anymore," she reminded him.

"You never really get out. He's using his political connections to build his power base."

"Yeah, from his wife's money, something you and I have to earn."

"No, he's just like us, Christine. He may have powerful backers, but he's just like us."

"He's got talent."

"Yup, and if anyone can help us, it's Henry."

"I've heard the story. Is it true?"

"Yeah, they had something on him, but he turned the tables on everyone. He was the mastermind of getting Campagna elected. In fact, I thought he was going to be our likely Democratic opponent, and I figured we would have to go up against Henry. I'd much rather have him in our corner."

"With what we're up against we need everyone we can get. These people are not like the typical political hacks we can outmaneuver. We're going up against Russian intelligence."

"Didn't think this would be my call up to the big leagues. My very own trial by combat," Charlie admitted.

"Big times call for big players. Time to make the call," Christine told him.

👑
21

Henry was still not right. Certainly, Lyndsay's realization of Brad's treachery had provided him a needed respite from his self-loathing. Of course, the scuttled RITECH deal paled in comparison to the possibility of losing Lyndsay. It still cut deeply into his psyche and fragile ego. To Henry, so much of who he was as an individual was centered around his work and what he could win or achieve. How could he not have seen Brad's treachery, how could he let this happen, why had he not been prepared? These were the thoughts that echoed in his head as he endured another sleepless night. It's not that he did not receive any sleep. While Lyndsay was working the night shift at the hospital, he was sacked out on the coach, out cold by 8 p.m. Then he was up by 2 a.m., tossing and turning until 4 a.m., and then out the door at 5 a.m. His tailored Italian suits had been traded for jeans and a golf shirt, and his two-day stubble revealed a bit more about a man who was always well manicured. Henry was at his best when he was competing. The fight prevented him from having to deal with his past and his own insecurities. However, his current plotting for his business comeback would have to take a back seat to more pressing matters.

"Henry, It's Charlie Braverman."

"Charlie, I think I'm already maxed out to your campaign," Henry reminded him.

"No, it's not about money. Well, actually it is, but I'm not asking you for money. This is not a fundraising call. Any chance we could meet? There's something I need to talk to you about."

"Sure, always happy to meet with the next governor. Where do you want to meet?"

"I'll come to you. You're still at the top of the Superman building?"

"Yup, top of the world."

Charlie was at Henry's office within 15-minutes. He was a bit taken aback from what he found. Henry no longer looked like the buttoned-up political maverick who was taking on New England's business titans. He was disheveled with bloodshot eyes from multiple sleepless nights. He was still Henry, and even though he was half the man he once was, he still towered over most.

"Sorry, been pulling some all-nighters working on a new deal," Henry admitted.

"I appreciate you seeing me," Charlie responded, looking past the obvious shortcomings of a man he once admired.

"So, what brings you out here? You should be out shaking hands and raising money."

"That's what I gotta talk to you about."

"I have to admit, I was surprised you were able to raise so much so quickly. You scared everyone else out."

"Even Campagna?"

"No, Campagna wants to finish the job he was elected for. Believe me, there's plenty of people who wanted him to jump in.

They're scared of you, Charlie."

"They're scared of change."

"Yeah, that too. Charlie, you're not here to talk politics with a former political hack. Why don't you tell me what's up?"

"You're hardly a hack, Henry. Campagna would be toiling away on the city council if it weren't for what you did."

"You're gracious, Charlie, appreciate it. You don't want to reminisce about the political battles of the past. Why don't you tell me what's going on?"

"I don't even know how to start," Charlie admitted.

"Whatever it is, there's always a way forward. Trust me on that, from someone who's been knocked down more times than you wanna' know, and has come back swinging," Henry told him, reminding himself as much as trying to ease Charlie from whatever he was enduring.

"I think I'm getting played by the Russians," Charlie admitted, the weight of it lifted by actually saying it aloud.

"Wow, we've come a long way from Smith Hill, Charlie. What could the Russians possibly have on you?" Henry asked him, the revelation sounding outlandish to him. As someone who had been extorted himself in previous elections, he could understand how nefarious actors could play a role in local elections, but the Russians in Rhode Island, that was foreign ground.

"I met this Russian who told me he served with my father in the Soviet Army. My father was Ukrainian; I never met him. This Russian tells me my father was a hero of the Soviet Union. Gave his life in Afghanistan, and for his service his so-called comrade tells me they have money set aside for his son."

"So, this Russian tells you he knows your father and gives you money, and you don't question where it really is coming from. Really, Charlie? How much are we talking about?"

"About 11 million dollars."

"That's real money, Charlie, and you didn't think…."

"Look, I never knew my father. My mother told me he died in a car accident back in Brooklyn. I wanted to believe he was a hero. Doesn't every son want to think that about his father?"

"There's always going to be someone who preys on our insecurities. What did you do with the money? I hope you parked it somewhere?"

"We used it for the campaign. Created a SuperPAC too: Progress First. My girlfriend, Christine, I mean, she's my fiancée now, she, well, we, donated to campaigns throughout the country and to friends who then donated back to our campaign."

"You know you broke about a hundred campaign finance violations, and you could go to jail for that. I'm going to stop you right here, Charlie. Do you want to hire me as your legal counsel? Because that would mean anything you now tell me is privileged."

"I think we're at that point, Henry. I'm fucked, aren't I?"

"Well, it's not good. There's always a way though, we just don't know what it is yet. Who else but you and Christine know about this?"

"Just us, and, well, of course the Russian."

"Who is he?"

"His name is Alexi Antipov, claims to be the Cultural Attaché out of the Russian consulate in Boston."

"So the Russians are here. Thought I'd seen everything in Rhode Island," Henry pondered, realizing he was now entering a new, uncharted place. Little did he know at that moment the places it would take him.

"The Russians are in Rhode Island," Charlie responded, almost not believing he was uttering it himself. "So, what are we going to do about it?"

"They think we're some sort of backwater state that they can just roll. They have no idea who or what they're fucking with," Henry fired back, his confidence returning with the blood rushing to his head.

"What are we going to do, Henry?" Charlie asked, witnessing the change before him in the man he always considered the best political mind in the area.

"We've got to get you out of this. You can't run; you need to pull out," Henry admitted to him.

"My whole life is in this."

"Yeah, and it's led you here, to this point, and if you stay on this course, you'll either end up in jail, dead, or you'll compromise our entire state. You bowing out is the lesser of the evils," Henry told him, his rational political mind clearly in charge.

"I can't believe I fucked up my whole future. I could have been someone," Charlie lamented.

"You are someone, and you can recover. If we do this right, no one will ever know. Let me tell you something, Charlie, we all spend so much time wanting to be someone or something. It's all bullshit. Just start with being a good man, husband, father," Henry sermonized, the words sinking in for himself. Having been through the political grinder, he was one of the few who could in fact dish out that kind of advice to Charlie.

"How do you see this playing out?" Charlie asked him, his curiosity about what Henry had in mind overtaking his self-loathing.

"I don't know yet. I have to think about this. It's gotta be something that comes along that is so enticing that you would pass on running for governor. There's really only one thing that would get a would-be governor out."

"Congress, maybe. Even McNally wanted to be governor. Of course, the Senate, but no one's going anywhere in our state. They're elected senators for life here."

"McNally is the key here," Henry admitted, referring to his former boss who had served multiple terms in Congress only to be thwarted by a failed run for the governor's office.

"You think McNally would run for governor?" Charlie asked him.

"No, he makes too much money now," Henry acknowledged. "No, he won't run for governor. He would like to see someone else in there. Sorry, Charlie, you have not exactly endeared yourself to the power brokers in our state."

"No offense taken, Henry. We all know who the real power broker today is anyways," Charlie informed Henry, recognizing what so many understood, but what Henry could not see through his own current fog.

"McNally still has great contacts in the administration," Henry told Charlie. He knew McNally had strong ties to the current Democratic machine in Washington, which was principally responsible for his steady stream of income.

"Why would McNally help me? As you pointed out, we're about as far apart as Democrats can be."

"Because he's pragmatic, and he knows what having a governor close to him means to him both financially and politically. Trust me, he'll play ball."

"If I'm compromised with the Russians as governor, wouldn't it be worse if I was in the Cabinet?" Charlie realized.

"Yeah, I figured that, Charlie," Henry told him, one step ahead of him. "The Cabinet's out, but there are places just as prestigious."

"What's bigger than being governor or in the Cabinet?"

"It's not what's bigger. We just need something good enough for you to save face, and for you to use your talents. Consider it a placeholder for a while, and then you can run again down the road. I'm thinking of academia, and you becoming the head of the new Center of Politics and Policy at Brown."

"Professor Tolman is an institution at Brown. He'll never leave. Plus, I never really thought about going back to Brown. Sure, I love Brown, but I always thought I'd make a difference in government."

"Make a difference? How's that working out for you right now? You'll make more of a difference effectuating real policy and helping mold future leaders, like you. This is your lifeline, Charlie, and I can probably make this happen for you," Henry told him, understanding that Charlie did not realize how truly compromised he was. "And as far as Tolman's concerned, if a big policy job in DC is dangled in front of him, he's out of here."

"OK, Henry, that's why I came to you. If you can get me out of this, I'll do it."

"I've got this, Charlie. Go home and spend some time with your fiancée. This will all be taken care of. We've got a week before the filing deadline, and I've got a few things I gotta do."

22

"Congressman, it's me." Henry's first call was to McNally.

"Hey buddy, sorry about the RITECH deal."

"Yeah, I didn't watch my left flank, didn't see it coming. It won't happen again. Listen, can you meet me? I'll come to you."

"Of course, Henry, people would love to see you. Come on down."

Even though he was still a partner, Henry hadn't been to the offices of Warner & Isikoff in six months. As soon as the Industrial Trust building, colloquially known as the Superman building, had been habitable again, he chose his penthouse over his ten-by-ten office next door. Henry took the elevator down from the 26th floor and walked out through the ornate foyer that was being turned into a Michelin restaurant in the former space that once served as a shrine for Providence's own gilded age. He only had to walk one building over to One Financial Center Plaza, formerly known as the Hospital Trust Tower, which reflected the significance of the medical community in the state.

"Hey, Billy," Henry said to the security guard in front of the elevators.

"Henry, it's been a long time. How are you?"

"Living the dream," Henry quipped, wearing a smile across his face. He picked up his stride heading toward the higher elevator floors. Warner & Isikoff had not changed all that much. In fact they took great pride in helping to preserve the status quo.

"Henry! I heard the conquering prince was returning," said Emily Rousseau, one of the associates Henry had mentored. She was standing at the reception area, chatting it up with the receptionist about who was leading in the rumor mill to make senior associate.

"Hardly a conquering prince, more like a ronin."

"Yeah, we heard about RITECH. The one thing I know about Henry Mercucio is there's always a second act for him."

"Ah, Em, how ya' doing? See you still have a finger on the pulse of what's happening here."

"You know Henry, we all gotta' use our God-given talents to get through the day."

"Speaking of local gods, how's the Congressman?"

"He misses you, Henry. You know where to go. He's waiting for you."

Henry walked down the same hallway he had rushed frantically down on numerous occasions. McNally was Henry's go-to for problem solving, from how to turn a councilman to vote for tax credits to helping him walk the tight-rope on the last mayoral election. While in many respects the pupil had surpassed the professor, Henry knew there were certain circles where McNally still eclipsed him.

"There he is," McNally announced as Henry turned toward his door. McNally's office was just as Henry remembered, a virtual shrine to his power and influence.

"Congressman," Henry still addressed him with his official title, even though he hadn't served in Congress in six years.

"C'mon in and sit down," McNally offered, motioning Henry to the leather chair in his sitting area.

"Thanks, Congressman, appreciate you seeing me on such short notice."

"Henry, I think we're on first name terms, don't you think?"

"OK, Ray."

"And you don't need to call to come see me. You're a partner here and can pop in any time. Look, I know the RITECH deal hurts. Trust me, there'll be others."

"Thanks. Appreciate that, Ray, but that's not why I'm here."

"Oh, just assumed that's what you wanted to talk about. I know you started working on that deal while you were here. So, what's up?"

"The governor's office."

"What about it? We're all fucked if that kid gets in," McNally echoed what many others in the political and power establishment felt.

"There may be an opportunity to get him out, but it's a difficult one."

"There's nothing more important than getting him out," McNally admitted.

"I'm going to need your help."

"Consider it done."

"Professor Tolman, over at Brown, you know him?"

"Know him, he and I grew up together in Elmhurst. Went to LaSalle together. I went to PC; he went to Brown. He worked on my campaign. Of course, I know him."

"The head of the Brookings Institute is retiring. I need you to use your contacts to get your friend, Tolman, to take over at Brookings."

"How do you know the Brookings job is open?"

"Just like you, Ray, it's my job to know these things. You think you can get Tolman to go for it?"

"That's a dream gig for him, of course he'll go for it. I mean he'll hem and haw at first about not wanting to leave the kids at Brown. This is a once in a lifetime opportunity for him. He'll go for it," McNally confidently assured Henry.

"And can you make some calls to some of your pals over at the House and Senate to make sure he secures it?"

"That goes without saying, Henry, of course. What does this have to do with Braverman?"

"I need an offramp for him, and I'm going to try to slide him in over at Brown. The new director of the Center for American Politics and Policy."

"Better place for him, let him live in his imaginary perfect world over there," McNally did not hold back from saying what he really felt.

"He's a good guy, Ray, just a little over his head right now. Didn't realize what he's gotten himself into. You and I both know what the political machine does to honest souls. And it's worse than when you and I were doing it. There're new players, and they operate by a whole new set of rules."

"There may be new players, Henry, but the rules haven't changed that much in a thousand years. It's all about power. That doesn't change. If you're getting Braverman out, we can't just hand the governor's office to that Republican fascist. You know what you gotta do, right?" McNally asked Henry. He was really reminding him of what he should have done earlier on in the political discussion for governor.

"Yeah, I know. He's going to fight it. He'll tell me his work isn't done yet. With Braverman out, and the prospect of Stevens getting his hands on the reins of our government, he has no choice."

"He has to now, there's too much at stake, and he'll get that. You want me with you when you go see him. I can assure him that the money will follow if he jumps in," McNally offered.

"No, I better go see him first. I'll tell him you're ready to jump on board, and you'll be Chairman of the Campaign."

"Of course, the party will line up behind him. Braverman did us a favor by clearing out the field. And that's what I just don't get, what did he do that he's gotta get out? He was probably going to win the thing."

"He's had a change of heart. He's allowed that. He's a young guy, and the timing just isn't right, he realized. Better to preserve him. He's got a great future ahead of him," Henry told McNally. He wasn't ready to let McNally know the extent of Charlie's transgressions.

"You've always seen the better angels in people. OK, I'll convince Tolman, and I'll make sure he has some powerful backers on the Hill to get him in over at Brookings. I think I got the easy job though, Henry. You gotta convince your boy scout Campagna to go back on his promise to serve the full four-year term and jump in for governor. Good luck on that one. Just the whole state of Rhode Island is at stake. Kinda makes your RITECH deal really not that important anymore."

"Yeah, they're all just deals, aren't they, Ray? They come and go like thoughts in our head. Some stick around and are worth concentrating on, but right now I need to focus on what really matters. Like you said, our whole state's in jeopardy if the wrong people get in power," Henry admitted.

"Glad you're seeing that, buddy. I know you want to be this great business success. That's what RITECH was all about for you, wasn't it? That's a big shadow to have to live under, your father-in-law. Maybe you should just be Henry. I gotta tell you, that guy is pretty impressive."

"Thanks, Ray, I appreciate that, I do. It wasn't that. I wasn't trying to prove anything, or make up for my father's failures, or any of that bullshit. No, I just thought I could get my hands on this company and could turn them in a new direction. I saw an opportunity, I thought I had everything lined up, and I lost. That doesn't mean I'll miss out next time. In fact, it's made me better. And like you said, we've got bigger issues now that need my full focus. I've got this."

"You always have, Henry. Few people can rival your talent. Time for you to shine again," McNally told him, returning to the mentor he was to Henry.

"I just don't know why this hit me so hard this time, Ray," Henry admitted.

"Doesn't matter, buddy. What does is climbing back into the saddle and getting back into the fight. You've got a difficult path ahead of you. You need to be all in for what you're going to do next. I'm not telling you anything you don't already know, nor am I giving you advice you wouldn't say to a client yourself."

"Ironic, isn't it?" Henry pondered. "Easier to spout out advice to others than give it to yourself. I've been listening too much to that little dictator in my head," Henry confided.

"Yeah, I've got one of those too, Henry. And I'd never let him talk to you or anyone else I love, not even my worst enemy either," McNally admitted.

"Gotta slay that internal demon first, I guess," Henry realized. He felt he had a receptive audience in McNally for sharing his deepest insecurities.

"I think you already have, buddy. And now you're really dangerous."

"Dangerous?" Henry asked.

"Yup, a man who has slain his biggest enemy is truly formidable. A hard man to beat, the man who knows himself. A man who understands his limitations, who is loyal to his friends and to himself, who places truth and honor above all else, that man is unstoppable."

"The higher I climb though, Ray, the harder it gets. It makes guys like Beako look like the JV."

"What did you expect, Henry? The Beakos of this world, they're small-time players. Sure, big up here in Providence. You're on a new stage now. I got a sniff of it while in Congress. I saw how things work. You just adapt. They're all just like you and me, the high achievers. You need to stay true to yourself, always, that's the key," McNally tutored his mentee.

"You miss it?"

"Do I miss Washington? Being at the pinnacle of power, yeah, I miss it, sure I do. We got a pretty good thing going on up here. And it's real. The people are real. That's who you need to fight for again, Henry."

"Looks like I'm back in."

"You were never really out, Henry. Just be who you are. Always."

Henry needed to hear his words. As Rhode Island's resident power broker, McNally would not immediately appear as a grounded guru, and no one was better to coach Henry on how power really worked than a man who had achieved it, lost it, and reclaimed it. Henry knew what he had to do next. He walked out confidently from McNally's office. It was time to make his way to city hall across town. There was only one man he knew worthy to take control of Rhode Island, and his very reluctance to do so only reassured Henry. A man who did not covet power was the ideal candidate to wield it.

The power dynamics had changed with an unsuspecting public unaware of what was really at stake on their own little island. Henry took it upon himself to be their selfless champion, and while his political machinations may never be uncovered or recognized, his actions would affect countless people who just wanted to put in an honest day's work and enjoy a day in the sun. They needed Henry, and

Henry needed them.

Henry Mercucio was back.

.

23

"Can you get me in to see him today?" Henry asked Kristen, Campagna's secretary and official gatekeeper.

"He'll always see you, Henry, you know that. He's got Public Works at 11, E-Dev at one. I blocked out lunch for him at Noon. He's walking across the street to Haven Brothers. Don't tell his wife, it's his little guilty pleasure—hot wieners once a week, so I indulge him. He deserves a little something. So, why don't you join him?"

"Thanks, Kristen, I'm so glad you're with him."

"No, thank you, Henry. I won't forget how you got me the job. I love it and love him. There's really no one better, and we all know you're the reason he's here. We all owe you."

"I think the entire state needs him now, Kristen."

"Don't take away our mayor, Henry, but I agree, the whole state needs him. Is that why you want to meet him?" she asked.

"Just want to see a friend, that's all."

"Sure, Henry," she understood.

Henry met Campagna in the hallway outside the executive suite, with the Mayor's uniformed police officer in tow. The six-foot two burly officer towered over Campagna by a good six inches, and his imposing presence was always a few steps behind. Campagna's own appearance was captivating, and his radiance was infectious to all around him. Even Henry, who had orchestrated his election and understood his shortcomings, equally gravitated toward his brightness.

"I didn't think you ate hot wieners, Henry," Campagna could not hold back.

"I'm open to new things. You know what's in those things?"

"Sometimes you just don't ask, you just go with what you know is good," Campagna countered.

"Yeah, I agree. I'll take it all the way," Henry told him, referring to a hot wiener with a steamed bun, mustard, meat sauce, onion, and celery salt.

"You're not here for hot wieners, are you, Henry?"

"I wouldn't be here if it wasn't really important."

"I figured you wanted me to get you that board seat back at RITECH. Sorry, that's out of my control. Didn't think you were doing McNally's bidding anymore," Campagna told him, revealing his own political savvy.

"Can we talk in your office? Please just hear me out. I'm assuming your office is still secure?"

"I have the Providence Police sweep it once a week, not that I have to worry about what I say."

"What I have to tell you is going to blow your mind. It changes everything."

Campagna's additions to the mayor's office reached further than the wall art and gaudy furniture from his previous predecessor. Former Mayor Donovan's extravagance had been showcased in his office, with the walls cluttered with photos of dignitaries and signed autographs of New England sports stars. All of it had been packed away for safekeeping to return to him after his sabbatical in Danbury Federal Penitentiary. While the strait-laced Campagna replaced the wall hangings with pictures of his family, he kept the former mayor's desk, chairs, and couch, simply because he did not want to incur the expense of refurbishing the office. With a grossly underfunded pension liability, crumbling schools, and pothole-filled streets, the last thing he wanted to do was spend the hardworking people's money on office cosmetics.

"Have a seat, Henry," Mayor Campagna graciously offered.

"I like what you've done with the place," Henry sarcastically said.

"Yeah, my wife tells me I need to paint it and get rid of Donovan's stuff. It doesn't bother me. It reminds me why I'm here, to clean up this mess."

"Look, Mayor, I'm just going to come right out and tell you why I'm here," Henry told him, quick to get down to business. While the men were friendly, they both understood that there was little time these days for idle chit-chat.

"OK, Henry, then tell me what's on your mind."

"We need you, and I'm not just talking about the Party. The whole state needs you."

"We've been through this, Henry. There's too much work here. I made a promise to the people of this city. Plus, we have a candidate for governor. Braverman will do a good job. He's a bit to the left. If he gets in he'll move to the center. He'll have no choice. Sure, he's lieutenant governor, but he hasn't seen what it's really like to be in charge, when it's all on you. If he wants to govern, he'll have to work with the legislature, and they'll roll him if he doesn't play ball. I'm not telling you anything you don't know."

"Braverman is dropping out. He can't run."

"So, they got to him. What did they offer him, a big corporate job?"

"No, it's not what you think. It wasn't McNally. In fact, he's helping me bring him in for a soft landing."

"Oh, I just figured McNally and the boys were scared of a Progressive like Braverman in there. They just wouldn't have the leverage over him."

"Yeah, change is a scary thing, but that's not what this is about."

"Then who? Who could get Braverman to pass on the chance of a lifetime?" Campagna asked, fully acknowledging that the governor's office was the job coveted by everyone who sought power in the state.

"The Russians are here."

"What?"

"Look, I'm operating under attorney-client privilege here. He expressly wanted me to talk to you about this, because he thinks you can help," Henry told Campagna. "He's compromised. A Russian agent told him he knew his father. His dad died as a kid, and the Russian made him believe he was a hero of the Soviet Union. The kid grew up without a father, so he wanted to believe. The Russian gives him money that he says his father earned as service to the country, for his sacrifice. The kid's never had real money, so he takes it. He and his fiancée, she's running his campaign, make straw donations to raise money for their own campaign. You know the drill, they donate to you, then you return the favor and donate to them. They also created a SuperPAC. They laundered millions. That's where the financing came from. Then everyone else jumped on board because they looked like the presumptive frontrunner with the early fundraising lead and with the backing of Governor Daniels."

"Jesus, Henry. What have you gotten yourself into?" Campagna asked him.

"I certainly didn't seek this. Braverman came to me. What am I going to do?"

"If anyone can figure it out, it's you, Henry," Campagna admitted.

"There's no good option here. If he comes clean, he goes to jail and we hand the governor's office to that fascist Stevens. Or he runs, wins, and we have a compromised governor beholden to the Russians."

"Neither is a good option. You have something else, don't you, Henry?"

"Well, there's only one Democrat I know who could jump in the eleventh hour, has the gravitas, the message, who is turning around Providence and can do the same for the state. McNally and the boys will back you, and money won't be an issue."

"And Braverman, what happens to him?"

"He goes over to Brown to head up the Taubman Center. He donates all the money to Rhode Island non-profits. We preserve a promising future and protect our state from outside influences that could affect us for generations."

"So, I either hand our state over to a fascist or the Russians, or I run myself, that's what you're telling me?"

"Yeah, pretty much. Desperate times call for heroic figures."

"OK, if I'm going to do this, I want something," Campagna told him. He was not someone who traded in political favors, but this was already uncharted territory.

"What do you want?" Henry asked him.

"You."

"What?"

"You run my campaign. That's the only way I do this."

"I've been out of the game for two years. You wouldn't want me, I'm a has been," Henry revealed to him. He had not fully come out of his doldrums, and his pessimistic perception of himself was on showcase. But, he was talking to Campagna, who himself had battled depression and had emerged even stronger.

"You're the best around. I wouldn't be in this office if it weren't for you, you and I both know that. And if I'm going to run for governor, there's no one I want by my side more than you, Henry. It's a non-starter. If you don't run my campaign, I don't do it."

"Then I guess I really don't have a choice either."

"We both have choices here, Henry. What are we going to do? Our actions could affect over a million people. It's our time to step up."

"I was supposed to be the one convincing you, now you've turned the tables on me," Henry said to Campagna, clearly kidding him and bringing a bit of levity to an otherwise difficult situation.

"You think it's difficult right now, just wait," Campagna acknowledged.

"Yeah, I gotta tell my wife, and her father, who thought he rescued me from politics."

"Yeah, I gotta tell my wife and kids that we're going to go through this rollercoaster all over again," Campagna thought aloud, not relishing the new political storm he was about to unleash on his family.

"You gotta wonder if this is worth it, and why we're the ones who have to do this," Henry pondered.

"The times have chosen us, not the other way around. We did not seek this. That's probably what qualifies us," Campagna admitted.

"If not us, then who?"

"Yeah, that's exactly the problem here, isn't it? If not us, then we hand things over to people who won't put the people's interests first. I'm in, Henry. I'll jump in the race," Campagna told him.

"And I'll run your campaign."

Campagna's campaign for governor was not a foregone conclusion. He had to file his candidacy, make an announcement, build a team, and raise four million dollars in a matter of months. Campagna started with universal name recognition in the state and a war chest of over one million dollars. Even though the Providence mayor was one of the most recognizable and powerful politicians in the state, the governor's office was often denied to the Providence chief executive. The powerful suburbs around Providence often dictated who ran the state. Campagna would need to reach beyond the urban core to appeal to suburban mothers and fathers who wanted to make sure their governor shared their core values.

As a new suburbanite himself, Henry understood the power dynamics in Rhode Island and how Campagna would need to modify his appeal across the state. While the bluest of Democratic states, Rhode Island still had a conservative streak especially within its more rural communities. With its high proportion of French Canadian, Irish, Italian, and Portuguese ethnic groups joined by an active Latino community, the state was heavily influenced by Catholic traditions. While Campagna was a Democrat, he was pro-life, though he was in favor of ensuring that women were responsible for the ultimate decision on their bodies. He also bucked the powerful labor unions in the state, making uncomfortable cuts to city pensions to ensure its solvency.

Timing was not on their side and if Henry was going to pull off another Hail Mary pass, he had considerable work to accomplish. He needed to rally McNally and the Democratic establishment to really fall in line behind Campagna. They wanted Campagna because they hated Braverman. They also knew they could not control him. That was probably the easiest task to cross off his list, keeping the party together. Before he could make Campagna's announcement, he had to exit Charlie Braverman out of the race while still preserving his career. And then he had to tell his father-in-law he needed to take a sabbatical from the firm to reenter a world he had once rescued him from in another lifetime. And then of course, there was Lyndsay, to whom he had promised to swear off politics. It was not that she hated Henry's work, although her family perceived it as a dirty business. It was more the intensive all-consuming nature of the work any spouse detested. In order for Henry to win this race, he needed to be all in. With Lyndsay pregnant, there was no worse timing for him. Like Campagna, Henry understood that this was their calling, and if they did not seize this moment the unintended consequences could be too devastating for everything they believed in. The future of their state was at stake.

24

Jerimiah Dexter's life was complicated. His family were some of the original pioneers of Scituate, Rhode Island, and he could trace his mother's family back to the Mayflower. To keep her happy, he proudly displayed his certificate from the Mayflower Society on his office wall, next to his diploma from Yale. The scion of one of Rhode Island's original families who followed Roger Williams from the Massachusetts Bay Colony to build a new state based on religious freedom, Dexter still fought for religious, political, and economic justice throughout the world. While his day job was investment banking, managing a fund that invested some of New England's oldest money, he followed the other tradition of his forefathers in the dark arts of the intelligence trade.

A Dexter had fought alongside Nathaniel Greene, one of Washington' top generals, uncovering secrets of Tory loyalists and informing on British military control over Newport, Rhode Island. Jerimiah Dexter's grandfather, his namesake, served in the Office of Strategic Services, or the OSS, the famed predecessor of the CIA, and had helped recruit and organize the French resistance against Hitler's domination. And his own father had planned the Panama invasion and helped set up the Colombian intelligence network that caught Pablo Escobar. Intelligence was in Dexter's blood, and protecting the nation from enemies foreign and domestic was their calling.

Dexter's four children, ranging in age from fourteen to twenty-two, did not know that their silver-haired father had himself run operations in Venezuela and Iran. They had become conditioned to the comfortable lifestyle in their five-bedroom colonial that overlooked the Scituate Reservoir, the state's primary source for drinking water and a pristine setting free from the noise pollution of motorboats and beach goers on Rhode Island's other busy shorelines. His twenty-two-year-old daughter, Emma, was a senior at Yale, and he soon would need to explain to her that her family's comforts came at a cost. His seventeen-year-old son, who also shared his name, was already six foot two, two hundred fifteen pounds, and had been recruited on his own to play for the Yale Hockey team. His imposing presence and frenetic skating had earned him the name "Wild Bill" in youth hockey. His second son, sixteen-year-old John, played hockey and also excelled in lacrosse, likely becoming the family's second division one athlete. His youngest, Ava, could rival her brother in lacrosse and also was coached by her mother, Jennifer, who herself was considered the Bill Belichick of high school cheer.

Jennifer Dexter had her own unique story. Convinced she was half Italian and having embraced the Neapolitan traditions and cuisine, a home DNA test revealed that her Italian ancestry was actually Lithuanian. Two hundred years ago, her seafaring Lithuanian ancestors had followed the trade winds to Naples, Italy, and settled there to build a new life. This revelation had led her to take her family, including her eighty-year-old mother and eighty-five-year-old great uncle, on a summer cruise to the Baltic states. This could not have worked out any better for Dexter, known by his company colleagues simply as "Dex," to check in with his Lithuanian assets on Russian border movements. While intelligence experts rationalized that the Russians would not risk an incursion into the Baltics that would bring out the full wrath of NATO, they had been wrong about Ukraine, both in the Russians' decision to actually invade and in the quality of their forces.

While his family was sleeping in at the Grand Hotel Kempinski in Vilnius, Dex met with his Russian asset, who was still able to cross freely between the borders. Vlad was a university professor in St. Petersburg, who wasn't in it for the money but more for the hope for change in his country. This is what motivated him to work for the Central Intelligence Agency. He represented a growing number of intellectuals in Russia, primarily in St. Petersburg, who no longer could turn a blind eye to their leader's transgressions in Ukraine. Their Faustian bargain, economic prosperity in exchange for totalitarianism dressed in democracy, no longer was sustainable with the economic sanctions imposed on them by the rest of the free world. Vlad's generation no longer stood idly by while Russia was robbed of her resources by a select few who continued to sacrifice Russia's future for their self-preservation.

Dex was a highly skilled operator in running agents. This was hardly his first rodeo, and while assets had their different reasons and motivations, it was his job to uncover what made these people choose to risk their lives for a greater cause. Vlad had earned a Ph.D. in Physics, so he was not easily susceptible to Dex's traditional tactics. His motivations were pure, to ultimately transform his country. He still took the American money and stashed it in Switzerland, as his insurance policy if he ever had to quickly flee his country. It's why they still took precautions for their clandestine rendezvous, meeting in an American safe house rather than in the open where peering Russian agents made little effort to hide their surveillance.

"You had no problem finding this place, Vlad?"

"No, your directions were clear."

"It's just not safe for you to meet with me in the open," Dex explained.

"I appreciate your concern for my safety," Vlad acknowledged.

"I have about an hour before my family wakes up and wonders where I've gone. So why don't you tell me what you have that made you want to meet with me in person."

"My associate and her husband have fled. Alana Turgenev, she's a professor in molecular biology at the St. Petersburg State University. Her husband, Yuri, runs the St. Petersburg chapter of the Anti-Corruption Party. He has a bomb he's sitting on."

"We got wind of something. There's been a lot of chatter we've picked up, but we don't have the details."

"There are rumors all over the university," Vlad told him.

"It's got the Russian leadership in a panic, so it must be good," Dex figured.

"You would think using our poorest citizens and youth as cannon fodder for your Western weapons would be enough to cause a more serious uprising. It's not enough, yet. You know we turned a blind eye when he took Crimea, many even in my circles see it as Russia. Same thing when he went into Georgia. But all the atrocities. These are people who are no different than us. What we have done to the civilian population, it's just not who we are as a people, or who we want to be. It's enough."

"Change is not an easy thing. It takes time. Look at the Russian Revolution. It took many attempts," Dex reminded him.

"This one goes right at the heart of our leadership. Their greed, it's no different than what the Tzars did to our people. This scandal could be the needle that breaks the camel's back. Once the floodgates open, there's no stopping what's coming next."

"We have ways of making sure the message gets out to the right people. We're in for the same reason you are. We want to see a free and open Russia that is part of the world community again," Dex told him.

"I know what I'm doing here," Vlad fired back. "Don't try to play me with your democratic and free market bullshit. As you Americans say, 'desperate times call for desperate measures.' We all know you're doing this for your own self-interest."

"Our self-interest is to make sure that my kids grow up in a world where the specter of nuclear war is no longer held over their heads. That's what I'm fighting for, so that your kids have the same opportunity as mine, to live in a world where they can be whoever they want," Dex countered. He hadn't devoted his life to the cause of freedom to allow this Russian professor to question his motives.

"I didn't mean to insult you. This is just really difficult for me, to be meeting with the CIA. I feel like a traitor."

"No, your leaders are traitors to their people. They have brought your country to the brink, and it's heroes like you who are stepping up to save her. Don't forget that," Dex assured him.

"I appreciate that. The scandal that Turgenev will break is going to have its own nuclear fallout."

"They've survived plenty of corruption scandals," Dex reminded him.

"Not like this one. It's at every level of our government and touches the political and business elite. Corrupt judges, bankers, government officials. They've been diverting funds for roads, bridges, and hospitals. This is the kind of stuff that brings people out to the streets. You add this to a battered military that has been embarrassed, and the whole establishment could come crashing down."

"We just need to help push it along. You have to understand

toppling governments takes time. You need to be patient and in for the long haul. And there will be setbacks. There always are," Dex reminded him.

"I'm here for the long game, and so are the people with me. We don't want to replace the current regime with another incarnation of the same. We need full comprehensive change, and we're going to need the West as our partner, not as our adversary. That's really why I'm here. Not just for the revolution, and it's coming, but for the aftermath," Vlad told Dex.

"My country may not be as rich in history as Russia. Our own legacy is helping to bring the light of freedom to the darkest corners of this world. Have we made a few, well actually many mistakes, during our fight for freedom? Yes, we have. My family has stood against oppression for four hundred years," Dex told him, stopping himself before he revealed anything more. It was important to reveal some personal facts to build a connection, but he also needed to protect his true identity.

Dex was not manipulating Vlad when he told him that his family had been promoting freedom since his country's inception. His forefather, Gregory, had been rumored as a close friend to the very founder of religious freedom in the United States, Roger Williams. Gregory's descendant, Ebeneezer, was a child of the Revolutionary War, which saw much of his state controlled by the British until it was liberated by the colonists and French. Ebeneezer eventually prospered in the mercantile trade that would make Massachusetts' appendage on the Atlantic the envy of the original states. In addition to the generational wealth he created for his ancestors, he also passed on his pious Baptist faith that inspired his ancestors to continue his righteous legacy.

Like other elite American families, Dex went to the same prep schools and Ivy League institutions as the rest of the American aristocracy. He remembered the day his father came to him while he was a junior at Yale, explaining his family's role in preserving the American social experiment. The Dexters had sworn themself to protecting American freedom and spreading the light of democracy around the world. The Central Intelligence Agency provided the toolbox for them to apply their trade. Things had gone off the rails in the past, even gotten a little messy in Guatemala and Cuba, but that was the nature of the business. The work for freedom required committed actors and true believers who were willing to do the necessary things in an imperfect world.

Dex was willing to do whatever it took. There was just too much at stake.

25

There was much to do for Henry. Organizing and winning a campaign for governor usually took two years, to lay the foundation, raise the money, organize the team, and refine the winning message. Henry had six months. The first thing he had to do was pave the way for Campagna, and that involved how he properly exited Braverman from the campaign. How Henry orchestrated the Braverman departure not only helped preserve a promising career for a candidate manipulated by a foreign power, but it also set the direction for the Campagna campaign. Henry could not afford to let the Democratic Party be perceived as fractured with Campagna only running as a last-ditch attempt to maintain their hold over the statehouse.

McNally had delivered on his end. He had convinced Professor Tolman to leave Brown University for the Brookings Institute. He traded favors with a few of his former Congressional colleagues, and with his long list of corporate and union contacts in New England and around the country, they knew McNally understood how to return the favor in campaign contributions. Danielle Monan, the

President of Brown University, who had cemented her own power base in the state, was more than happy to add another high-profile public figure to head up one of Brown's most outward-facing political institutions. Well regarded in public health and medicine, Brown needed to take a more active role in the national and international political debate, she believed. Charlie Braverman was just that kind of dynamic, young political voice that could help place Brown at the center of the discussion.

What was billed as a special announcement on the main green on the Brown University campus caught the Rhode Island press off guard. Seeing Mayor Campagna with the president of Brown and the leading candidate for governor, the press assumed that the university had made some major Payment In Lieu of Taxes (PILOT) compact with the city. Serving as the master of ceremonies, President Monan had not realized her role in the coronation of the next governor. She graciously gave the stage to Braverman to allow him to make the announcement of his new position, which traditionally would have been part of her protocol.

Braverman delivered the speech of his lifetime. Standing in front of the podium with Mayor Campagna to his right, he spoke without a written speech or teleprompter, and his remarks were well prepared and received.

"We stand at the precipice," Braverman started, capturing the attention of everyone who had gathered on the campus green. "Never before have the actors of darkness invaded our political system. Whether it's the dark money influencing our system, or the hateful rhetoric that has overtaken our political discourse, we have a choice before us. Do we make a stand for all we believe in or continue down the road that will sow our own destruction? It's why I have made the decision to end my campaign for governor and instead focus my entire energy on fostering a new constructive political discussion, both nationally and internationally, as the new Director of the Center for Politics and Policy at Brown University. This was not a decision I made lightly. And equally important to me is the future of our state. It is why I am throwing my full support behind the only candidate who I feel rises above the political turmoil that has invaded our country. It is why I am pleased to introduce Mayor John Campagna."

Campagna shook Braverman's hand as he exited center-stage. Campagna pulled down the microphone so he could speak more clearly. "Please join me in congratulating Charlie Braverman as the new Director of Policy and Politics here at Brown University. I am confident he will be a leading voice in helping us build a more constructive conversation in our political discussions today," Campagna delivered with eloquence. He then sought to address the issue of why he had not announced earlier and waited until his primary challenger had opted out. "The primary reason I was reluctant to run for governor is that I did not believe I had finished my job as mayor of Providence. I realized that in order to fulfill my commitment to the people of Providence I can better serve them as the governor of Rhode Island. Providence is central to the future of our state. It is our cultural and economic hub, and a vibrant Providence is central to a brighter Rhode Island. I sincerely believe I can bring the Providence turn-around to our entire state. It is why I have decided to announce for Governor of Rhode Island," Campagna delivered, showcasing his political acumen, turning his perceived liability into his greatest asset. He was no longer abandoning the people of Providence for higher office but helping to shine the Providence light over the entire state.

"Looks like you've pulled off another coup," McNally whispered to Henry as they stood alongside the other dignitaries.

"You know, Congressman, when you're on the right side of things it always makes it easier."

"Ain't that the truth, buddy."

"The real issue is what comes next. As good as this is, we both know it never lasts."

"Yeah, you won today. Tomorrow is another fight. Just enjoy this one. You earned it."

It was not all smooth sailing for Henry's political coup. The issue of Braverman's multi-million-dollar political war chest had not been lost on a suspecting Rhode Island press. Henry had a plan for that. Campagna needed to steer clear of Braverman's tainted funds, and Rhode Island's non-profits were the major beneficiaries. After paying his staff in full, many of whom went over to the Campagna campaign, he transferred the millions in his campaign account over to the Rhode Island Foundation to administer the funds to area nonprofits. The Russian blood money that was intended to purchase a governorship was now funding homeless shelters, stocking food bank shelves, and extending after school programs. Instead of supporting their own people, the Russians had unexpectedly strengthened Rhode Island's social network, a fitting ending for Charlie's flirtation with power politics.

The announcement was only the beginning. McNally again lived up to his commitment to the Campagna campaign for governor by helping to deliver the vast Rhode Island Democratic machine to line up behind the presumptive front runner. Rhode Island's public sector trade unions and big Democratic corporate donors were unifying their financial and organizational support for Campagna. Braverman also turned over all his opposition research on his Republican opponent, investment banker Chad Stevens. However, he did not include the photographs the Russians had unearthed connecting him to Rhode Island's far right militia. Braverman did not want the Russians to have any connection to his fresh start. Even with his late emergence into the race, Campagna was well positioned to keep Rhode Island a blue state.

26

Traditionally the national Republicans wrote off Rhode Island every election cycle. Their hope for a red wave flooding the entire country was too enticing, yet never realistic. When a Republican operative saw that Rhode Island did not have a minimum residency requirement for governor, they saw an opportunity. The incumbent governor was not running, and an open seat could be purchased for short money, compared to other large states and big media markets that cost hundreds of millions. Relatively speaking, Rhode Island could be bought for $10 million. The Republicans just needed another ego-laden multi-millionaire to cast his lot in the elected office sweepstakes.

They had their man in Chad Stevens. A Harvard law graduate and Rhodes scholar, Stevens was not your typical forty-something investment banker turned politician. He was the son of an Irish immigrant father and second-generation Italian mother, who had put their son through Providence College by working as a janitor and cafeteria worker. In fact, all three of their children attended the Dominican college in return for his mopping the floors, which the father did with a huge smile on his face. His mother worked in the PC cafeteria, serving other students so her own could afford room and board and enjoy the full college experience, something denied to both her and her husband. All three children—their investment banker son, dermatologist daughter, and lawyer second son—came together to buy their parents a beach house in Narragansett's Bonnet Shores for a retirement they had earned.

While at Harvard, Chad earned a joint MBA in the business school along with his JD. His MS in Financial Economics from Oxford University in England had provided him an entree into the world of mergers and acquisitions and leveraged buyouts. He could have worked for any white shoe Wall Street firm, but he chose to ply his trade in investment banking. Earning over fifty million dollars before he was forty years old, he sought new worlds to conquer. There was philanthropy. There was golf. There was travel. He did all that. It was time for a new challenge.

He already had a summer home in Watch Hill, Rhode Island, and had successfully convinced many other Manhattan socialites to abandon the Hamptons for his Rhode Island refuge. During one of his Gatsby soirees, his law school classmate, who now worked as a legal counsel to the Republican National Committee, had told him they were looking for a well-funded business maverick to shake up the political status quo in the Northeast. There was a quid pro quo. If Stevens took one for the team, when the Republicans returned to the White House, Stevens could find himself on the short list for, at the very least, Commerce Secretary. If he was ever able to pull off the upset, the Treasury Secretary was in play in the middle of his term.

It did not matter that Stevens was actually a registered Democrat only two election cycles ago. He was also listed on the voter rolls in New York City for the last election, and only registered in Rhode

Island at the beginning of the year when he had the first whiff of a potential run. Rhode Island law did not require him to register to vote in order to declare for governor, another loophole he planned to exploit. In Rhode Island, a candidate only had to live in the state for thirty days, so Stevens simply moved into his Watch Hill waterfront estate and again became a "Rhode Islander" in a month. It was like they were almost inviting an outsider.

That was not how Stevens planned to cast himself. He was the triumphant returning son, coming back to his native land to rescue her from the corrupt career politicians. He had a great success story to sell, from the college work study student who served alongside his mother in the dining hall, to the financial whiz kid with the Midas touch on Wall Street. His Horatio Alger story resonated with a Rhode Island electorate in search of new answers to old problems. Some red meat Republican rhetoric along with rising grocery costs and high gas prices made him an attractive alternative. He would even go as far as to meet with right wing wingnuts, whom he would have crossed a street to avoid in lower Manhattan. If an unholy alliance was needed to achieve the same office his childhood hero Alexander Hamilton had risen to, then it was worth the shower he would need after the meeting he attended.

He had not expected to meet a supporter in the woods only 20 minutes from his house on Rhode Island sound. He had befriended a member of the Westerly town council, who was serving as his local political advisor. Through a friend who knew a friend, a typical Rhode Island experience, his de facto advisor arranged for a private sit down with the head of the Gaspee Militia at a private hunting club in rural Rhode Island. Stevens may have been wet behind the ears as a politician, but he had not risen to the pinnacle of the business world by being careless.

Stevens had committed nothing more than a cursory look at the

Gaspee manifesto after he endured the conspiracy rants of his tat-
tooed, bald, and bearded guest, with whom he graciously shared pints
of Sam Adams beer. Stevens had been more comfortable arguing
Karl Marx with his left leaning friends at Oxford than with this neo
fascist who offered to protect Rhode Island polling places from what
he perceived was to be another stolen election. After downing his
beer, Stevens had felt he had given his troubled, delusional self-proclaimed patriot more time than he deserved, enough for him to feel
properly respected. Stevens had jumped into his Chevy Suburban to
return to his posh shoreline villa in civilized society. He had not realized his lapse of judgment to even meet with someone so vile would
end up in the hands of America's real enemies. The Russians had
always liked to play all sides.

27

Charlie had plenty to contemplate in the middle of the night as he stared at the ceiling in bed, alone. Christine had left him, returning to the West Coast, after realizing the political star she had latched onto no longer had much luster. A university instructor and policy director's salary could not afford the life she had planned. The recurring nightmare of Christine leaving played in his head, fading like a dissolve in a b-grade movie into the recollection of a conversation he had with Alexi Antipov.

Something just wasn't right for Charlie. He questioned how Antipov had information tying his opponent to a right-wing militia group. They clearly had spread their tentacles beyond the shores of Rhode Island, and the question persisted about how many other politicians they were looking to infect. He knew of two in Rhode Island alone, but he contemplated how widespread their infection might be. The dreadful thought of the Russian infestation in Rhode Island's political system caused him to jump out of bed to tackle his demons head on. It didn't matter that it was 3 a.m. This was one of those moments that could not wait for the light of day. He called the only other person he trusted, and the only one he knew would take his call at this hour. He reached out to Henry.

"It's 3 a.m, Charlie," Henry answered.

"You up?"

"I am now, what is it?"

"I think our little problem is bigger than we thought. Something occurred to me. The Russians also have the goods on Stevens. Pictures that tie him to the head of the Gaspee Militia."

"Jesus, how could Stevens be so stupid to be seen with them?"

"Yeah, that alone should disqualify him. That's not it. If they're funneling money to a Democrat, then extorting a Republican, both here in little RI, what else are they doing? How widespread could this be?"

Henry shot up in his bed, startling Lyndsay. Up until this point he had been whispering, figuring it would be a quick call or even a wrong number. This news was alarming. "Holy fuck," was all Henry could muster, which caused Lyndsay to give him a glaring look.

"You know anyone at the FBI we could talk to, someone who could leave me out of it for coming forward?"

"I know a guy we can talk to. He's kind of a rock star. I'd have to go to McNally to get to him, and he'll have to be brought in," Henry admitted.

"I don't think we really have a choice. This is too big. Can you arrange it?"

"Meet me at McNally's office at 9 a.m. We gotta get out in front of this."

Getting McNally in the office before 10 a.m. was no small feat. Unlike Henry, he was a late starter, mostly because he was out at multiple functions most evenings and usually wasn't in bed before 2 a.m. That was the time Henry was starting to fall out of his REM sleep to begin seizing the day.

"What have you boys gotten yourselves into that you had to see me first thing this morning?" McNally asked the two thirty-somethings before him who wore their anxiety on their faces.

"Are you still in touch with Jimmy Callahan? Didn't he move over to the FBI?"

"Jimmy, yeah, he's senior legal counsel now at the Bureau. That's what you get for bagging America's most wanted mayor. What do you want with him?"

Henry looked at Charlie, who answered with a nod.

"The money that Charlie raised, it came from the Russians," Henry told him.

"It's not what you think," Charlie insisted.

"Then what is it?" McNally questioned.

"I thought it was from my father. The guy told me he served with my father in Afghanistan and that the money was for his service. I wanted to believe."

"That's why I told you there was no way this kid could be governor," McNally turned and said to Henry.

"Look, I know how it seems. I really didn't think it was intelligence money," Charlie pleaded.

"Ray, it's worse, and it's not just Charlie. We think Stevens is compromised too. There are photos of him meeting with the head of the Gaspee Militia."

"Do you have them?" McNally asked. Henry understood why he was asking and knew that McNally would release them even if they came from a compromised source.

"No, I refused them. It's what made me realize that I wasn't talking to my father's friend from the service and that I may be caught up in an intelligence operation. It's why I came to Henry."

"And it's why you orchestrated the Brown job," McNally turned to Henry, understanding how Henry had played him. "Shit, you guys have gotten yourselves in way over your heads. Glad you came to me. Makes your mayoral maneuvers look like child's play, Henry. You've now graduated to international intrigue. Bravo."

"I didn't seek this, Ray. It's here now, and we have to do something about it. The Russians are literally in our own backyard," Henry reminded him.

"Alright, we need to fly down to Washington and see Jimmy right away."

"I already booked us on the Noon flight to DC," Henry told him.

"Now you're a travel agent, too, Henry. You should have just been a lawyer; you were a good one."

"You got me back into this game, Ray. I'm hoping you can get us all out," Henry reminded him.

***

"A former congressman, gubernatorial candidate, and political consultant all flew down from Rhode Island to meet with me. This has to be a good one," senior legal counsel to the Federal Bureau of Investigation, James Callahan, said to his guests.

"You got a place we can go that is secure?" McNally asked.

"We're the FBI. We're secure."

"You know what I mean."

"Yeah, I reserved one of our SCIFs. I figured it was sensitive."

"Mr. Callahan, we appreciate you meeting with us on such short notice," Henry opened, showing his respect.

"Henry, you don't need to be so formal with me, I'm the same Jimmy you met back in Providence when I was about to take down the mayor. As far as I'm concerned, you're as much responsible for bringing good government back to Providence as I was. I think we're on a first name basis by now."

"We didn't fly down here for your boys to have your little reunion, so why don't we get right to it. We got Rome burning here, and Jimmy might be one of the few people who can help you boys without you ending up in a CIA black site in Romania," McNally reminded everyone.

"Jimmy, I'm Mr. Braverman's attorney, and Ray is also here on his behalf, but we're hoping we can keep this off the record initially and that Charlie ultimately can be a confidential source," Henry began the negotiation.

"Like I said, we've got three heavy hitters walking into the FBI. I don't know what you guys got, but I know you. I got to hear what you have, and I give you my word if you say anything that I think is prosecutorial I'll stop the conversation, and let you know it's time to lawyer up. Fair enough?" Jimmy asked his guests.

"I told you he's the guy you needed to talk to," McNally assured everyone.

Henry gave Charlie a glance, and his nod back provided the go ahead. Henry started, "Jim, I know how this is going to sound, and I didn't think it was really happening at first either. There is something really rotten in Rhode Island right now."

"I know Hamlet too, Henry, so why not get right to it," Callahan told him.

"The Russians are in Rhode Island. They attempted to compromise our leading Democratic candidate for governor and we believe they're going to blackmail the leading Republican," Henry revealed.

"OK, first, let me understand this, you say they've attempted to compromise the Democratic candidate, so that's Mr. Braverman here. So what did they do?" Callahan asked pointedly.

Charlie knew that revealing the information could land him in legal jeopardy, but his strong belief in the American political institutions prompted him to risk his own future.

"Mr. Callahan, I got in way over my head. I wanted to believe that my father was some war hero. So, when this Russian came and saw me after I inked a deal in Prague with a Dutch energy firm, I fell for it. I've always had to scrape by, and all of a sudden the father I never knew had come through for me with millions of dollars."

"Classic Russian intel move," Callahan interrupted, not necessarily easing Charlie's moral crisis, but attempting to explain that his situation was not truly unique either. As a senior legal counsel, he was privy to classified counterintelligence cases that involved unsuspecting Americans manipulated by foreign adversaries with a whole host of enticements.

"This Russian, Alexi Antipov, claimed to have served with my father in Afghanistan. Told me he was with him when he died. I confirmed with my mother that my father had served with him. I didn't think he was Russian intelligence. It was not just the money. He started feeding me information, like polling data. When he said he had pictures of my opponent, it just didn't add up for me anymore. That's when I came to Henry."

"What did you do with the money the Russians gave you?" Callahan asked. He had not missed that fact.

"This is where we need your discretion, Jimmy," Henry interjected.

"Like I said, if what you say starts to incriminate you in something we would pursue that could lead to an indictment, I'll stop you."

Henry again looked back at Charlie with a signal to continue to move forward. He hoped he could trust Callahan, and he also realized there was no better option in front of them. This was their only way forward.

"We, well I, used the money for my campaign," he admitted, deciding not to divulge Christine's role in the scheme. His guilt surrounding her departure prevented him from implicating her in a campaign finance fraud that was her brainchild.

"Look, Charlie, I don't care about campaign finance violations over here. I'm much more interested in what the Russians are up to. I need to know what they have on you."

"I used the money I got from the Russians to donate to campaigns across the country. All these other campaigns and candidates, in turn, gave me donations to fund my campaign. A lot of the donations were made to the other candidates through straw donors."

"Is that it? Is that all they have on you, that you used their money to jumpstart your campaign?" Callahan asked.

"They've got some pictures too."

"You mean the ones on your Republican opponent," Henry chimed in, in an effort to help clarify.

"Well, those too, but they got pictures on me too."

"What do they have on you?" Callahan asked again.

"The night I closed the deal with the Dutch energy company in Prague, my girlfriend and I met a girl at the bar. And well, you know, we went back to her room. Next day, the Russian showed me the photos. Told me they were to get my attention. That he really wanted to protect me and that he knew my father."

"Who cares if you were with a couple of broads together while out of the country?" McNally could not help himself from saying.

"Well, I was there in my official capacity as Lt. Governor of the State of Rhode Island, and she was a member of my staff," Charlie admitted to them.

"Oh," was all McNally could say.

"Again, classic Russian operation. They honey-potted you," Callahan explained. "They're always looking to compromise our diplomats and agents overseas. Someone like Charlie, who doesn't have the training and wouldn't see this coming, is innocently going to think the hot woman at the bar is looking for a fun night with an

American. That's how they get you."

"So, Jimmy, can you help him?" Henry asked, cutting right to the chase. His client and friend had spilled enough of his guts for one day, and he needed to give him some sort of relief.

"Jimmy will do whatever he can to help, I told you that," McNally again interjected.

"Yeah, he's right. Nothing Mr. Braverman's done here is anything we would really be interested in, and I can shield some of the details, like the campaign finance stuff," Callahan told them.

"If it's any consolation, Jimmy, we're donating all the money to the Rhode Island Foundation," Henry told him.

"Not really to the FBI, but to me personally, it just shows me that he's generally a good guy that got taken by some very bad people. Him being here and then giving away all the money, that goes a long way in my book. He wants to do the right thing, and I want to help him," Callahan said. That earned him a fatherly pat on the shoulder from McNally and an expression of thanks from Henry. Charlie still wore the look of a man who had revealed his deepest insecurities and own moral failings in front of an unbiased arbitrator who also understood his own failings. "I heard you're the new Director of Policy and Politics at Brown. Just go do your job up there," Callahan assured everyone.

28

No matter how involved the Russians were in the Rhode Island gubernatorial race, Henry still had an election to win. And he was going up against an opponent who had an unlimited war chest to buy name recognition, though he was still a bit wet behind the ears politically. He was unlikely to make the same mistake twice and meet with any other self-proclaimed freedom fighters. Henry suspected the revelation of the infamous meeting may never see the light of day and even questioned whether photos really existed. The FBI took meddling in the electoral process seriously these days and would more than likely be launching an investigation.

Henry had written Campagna's first TV commercial on the shuttle flight from DC to Providence. He had chosen local talent to shoot and produce the spot, something Campagna was adamant about instead of turning to DC or New York like so many other politicians. "The local ad agencies are perfectly qualified to produce our own TV ads for our own people, don't you think?" Campagna had reminded Henry in the last campaign and in his new bid. Henry understood that every local art director, videographer, editor, and producer also talked to family and friends, who were all potential voters.

As much as he appreciated local talent, Henry would not leave the concept and copywriting of Campagna's entry into statewide elected politics to any consultant or ad executive, local or national. This was the defining moment for Campagna, and Henry wanted to be the mastermind to announce Campagna to a statewide electorate.

"It's morning in Rhode Island," the spot opened, a playoff of Ronald Reagan's "Morning in America" ad. The opening shot featured the sun rising over Narragansett Bay with waves crashing and birds chirping. "A new day for our state has emerged," was voiced over the visuals of the wind turbines turning in Block Island sound, and then dissolved into a drone shot flying toward a large green road sign at the highway intersection that showed an arrow pointing North for Boston, and an opposite arrow pointing south toward New York. "We stand at the intersection of our future, a state with unlimited resources and untapped human capital, a state with a proud tradition and legacy. We need a Rhode Island that works for all of us. I'm John Campagna, and together we will build a prosperous Rhode Island where our children will choose to raise their own families."

Campagna's ad was echoing a theme everyday Rhode Islanders feared. The state had seen a brain drain of its top talent for greater economic opportunities. If the state could tap into its potential, a thriving Blue economy built on its vast resources and proximity to the ocean and top metropolitan areas, then Rhode Island children may choose to stay and raise the next generation in the state. At the same time the ad positioned Campagna not as a Providence politician out of touch with the rest of the state but as an innovative leader ready to tackle a broader mission.

Chad Stevens did not leave Campagna alone to define his message. He too came out with his own one-minute profile video that pervaded the Rhode Island airwaves. You could not switch a channel during morning or evening primetime without seeing Stevens' portrayal of his life's rags to riches story. He argued that his lesson could be extended to Rhode Island's other children, who could be equally lifted up to rise to limitless success.

At the same time that he was extolling his exemplary story, he sought to eviscerate another. Yet he did not directly have his fingerprints on the character assassination of his opponent. He left that to Political Action Committees that flooded the race with their dark money. They spent five times as much for their negative onslaught on Campagna, and their money sustained the national media companies that had gobbled up local televisions stations and were delivering their national agenda to local audiences.

The first negative PAC ad against Campagna sought to advance an underlying theme present with the statewide electorate that a Providence mayor was out of step with average Rhode Islanders. It was nothing new for Campagna and an attack he had endured before in past campaigns.

"Another career politician," the spot opened with grainy shots from local news footage of Campagna heading out of city hall in step with his Providence police officer. "And another," the female voiceover continued as the footage shifted to Campagna's brother who served in the state legislature and was seen in footage shouting from the lectern during a heated budget debate. The spot neglected the fact that Rep. Campagna had been arguing for the restoration of food benefits for mothers and children.

"Rhode Island cannot afford Providence politicians using their insider deals to run our state," the voiceover from an audio voice bank in the Midwest said as old footage of Campagna with the notorious former mayor Jack Donovan reminded average Rhode Islanders of their state's greatest scandal, still an open wound in the public's consciousness.

"Rhode Island cannot afford another FBI investigation into public corruption. And how much do we really know about John Campagna? We know he's under psychiatric care, and do we really want someone like him running our state?" The commercial sought to tie Campagna in with the infamous case of the former Mayor who was serving a ten-year sentence for federal corruption and racketeering. He had fled to Europe to avoid charges and had even orchestrated a fake kidnapping to cover up his misdeeds. Also dredged up was the revelation from the previous mayoral campaign of John Campagna admitting he had been treated with antidepressants. While he had explained he had not experienced depression for quite some time, he had bravely admitted the truth, which instead of hurting him with the voters had actually further connected him. The consultants who produced the spot hoped a statewide electorate would not be as understanding.

"In November, Rhode Islanders have a choice—a corrupt career politician with questionable judgment or an accomplished businessperson with a new direction," the spot concluded, ending with the organization behind the message, "Paid for by Truth for America."

No television, website, or social media site was immune from the negative barrage that hit Rhode Island. From news and sports sites to lifestyle blogs, there was not a place in Rhode Island that the negative Campagna message did not hit. The ads followed visitors on social media and in their email. The hope was that the continuous, constant delivery would move voters to the right.

"Did you see it?" McNally asked Henry on the phone, breaking right in, not even with a "hello."

"Of course. Hard not to, it's on every channel," Henry responded.

"What are you going to do?"

"Nothing."

"You risk them defining Campagna. You know how it works

today. They just keep repeating the same thing over and over and people start to believe it. They don't need context, explanations, this is how it's done now," McNally told Henry, having fought and survived many political battles himself.

"Remember the crazies don't come out and vote, and that's exactly who this ad is appealing to," Henry explained. "The ad is meant to appeal to the lowest common denominator in the general population and what these national experts don't quite comprehend yet is that the conspiracy whack jobs don't come out and vote. They stay in their basements and fixate on the latest conspiracy, instead of coming out and participating in our elections. It's hard to mobilize them to get out the vote when they don't trust the process in the first place."

"There's still those voters out there who will start to question our candidate, who won't admit they wouldn't vote for someone taking antidepressants until they get into the voting booth," McNally reminded Henry.

"There are thirty-seven million people in the US on antidepressants, with the biggest percentage being women. Who votes? The largest percentage is suburban women. How many of them wish their own husbands, sons, fathers were being treated professionally rather than self-medicating? This whole political trope they're trying to sell that Campagna is unfit for office is going to backfire. You watch," Henry argued.

"Hope you're right, buddy, and I just fear you have too much faith in the electorate."

"Not just faith alone. I also need your insurance policy."

"You want my mail ballot guy," McNally suspected.

"I think his methods are a bit, how should I say, 'old school,' to be polite. I can't let the Republicans get him. It's purely defensive."

McNally wasn't buying it. "He works for the highest bidder.

Political ideology doesn't matter much to him, just the almighty dollar," McNally assured Henry.

"So, you think I can still get him?"

"He's already reached out to me. I just wasn't sure, since you were adamant about not hiring him the last time around for Campagna. The Stevens people don't even know about him. They're still amateurs when it comes to winning local races."

"There's just something not right about going into senior centers and having people who can barely even make out who they're voting for do so for your candidate. And he's just so blatant about it, he even signs as their witness, or has one of his family do it."

"Hey, buddy, those are the rules. We just play them better than the local Republicans. They can do the same thing and hire him too. In fact, he's worked for a couple of Republican congressmen. Sure, they'll say the mail ballots are corrupt. By the way, they'd do the same thing if they had the chance. You think if Stevens realized he could pay twenty-five grand to our guy for two thousand mail ballots in their favor he wouldn't jump all over it?"

"I know you're right. I don't have to like it."

"Hey, that's why your boy scout Campagna has guys like us, because if he didn't, he'd just be another do-gooder toiling away on the city council for another decade," McNally reminded his protege.

Henry's reality check was interrupted by another call. "Hey, can we talk later? We really could use your help in District 2, especially in Warwick and Cranston. They still love their congressman there."

"Yeah, of course, call me later," McNally said as he let Henry go.

Henry saw that it was his father-in-law, Reggie Sinclair, rescuing him from McNally. Henry did not need another lecture on how he was making a monumental mistake returning to politics and putting his new burgeoning career with Sinclair on hold. Sinclair was not one to lecture his son-in-law and understood that Henry had to chart his own path, just like he had done. In some respects, he actually respected Henry's decision and saw that he was honing important skills that could prove useful for their future.

"How's the boy?" Sinclair repeated a familiar opening when calling his son-in-law.

"Got a few balls in the air, you know," Henry replied.

"Well, that's the life you've chosen now, isn't it? The nine to five just doesn't suit you, Henry."

"You neither, huh,"

"I've been up since 4 a.m. with London. Opportunity does not sleep," he said, knowing he had a receptive audience. If anyone in this new generation understood the need to seize the moment, Sinclair knew that it was his own son-in-law, who equally demonstrated his own zealous ambition for success.

"So, to what do I owe this check-in?" Henry asked, getting right down to business, something Sinclair also appreciated about him.

"I'm going to be in town and want to get together with you and Lyndsay. I've got to go over the annulment with her sister and was hoping we could take Bridgit out to help distract her."

"Of course. You should check with Lyndsay about her schedule at the hospital."

"Funny, she said the same thing, to check with you and what you got going on with the campaign."

"Yeah, I'm doing double duty these days, running the campaign, and Northeast operations for you. Let's just say the final chapter for me has not yet been written."

"Doesn't surprise me, Henry. Winners always find a way. I've got something I need to talk to you about," Sinclair admitted.

"The annulment? I got this, already spoke with the Bishop's people, and they told me it's not a problem," Henry assured him.

"No, I knew you'd take care of that. We just want this abomination of a marriage to be like it never happened. Mary and I are really appreciative, and glad Bridgit's coming back home."

"Where did the little shit head go?" Henry asked, referring to his short-lived brother-in-law.

"Back under the rock he crawled out from under. That's not what I want to talk about. There will be a reckoning with the Dumonts at our choosing. Remember that the Sinclairs play the long game, and you're one of us."

"When it comes to Lyndsay and my family, I'm all in, all the time. You know that," Henry told him, although he also knew it did not need to be said at all.

"That's why I want to talk to you. It's time that we bring you fully in."

29

"I'm back."

"Happy to see you, Henry. When you left a message, I told my secretary to give you whatever time you could make it up to Boston," Dr. Kelleher told him.

"Last time I was in Boston I was looking to move my whole operation up here. Today, I'm fully engrossed in Rhode Island."

"Is that what you'd like to talk about?" the noted child trauma psychiatrist asked Henry.

"Every time I tried to get myself out, they pulled me back in," Henry admitted.

"This isn't *The Godfather*, Henry."

"Yeah, no kidding. *Godfather III* pales in comparison to one and two," Henry quipped, even getting a chuckle out of the stoic psychiatrist.

"While I'd love to debate with you what motivated Coppola to do number three, I'm not sure that would be a good use of your time," the doctor admitted.

"I just…want to put it all behind me once and for all."

"What is that?"

"The abuse, and not just the physical stuff from DC, but also the emotional."

The doctor just listened and could see Henry was beginning to open up. His training and experience guided him, knowing when to push and prod and when to listen and react. Henry did not wait long to fill the silence.

"Look, I know I can't be responsible. It was a random act of violence, I get that. Why me, why was I targeted? Other guys would have run away."

The doctor felt the need to interject. "Henry, it was an act of violence that you did not bring on yourself. It just happened, and there's nothing you can do about it. What you can do now is choose how you let it affect you now and go forward."

"I get it. I do, and to be honest with you, I've come to terms with it, I have. I've buried it for so long. These feelings wouldn't have come back if the fucker hadn't killed himself. Sorry, I didn't mean to swear."

"It's alright."

"I'm going to be a father," Henry told him, pivoting to another concern on his mind.

"Congratulations, that's great news."

"I just want to make sure I don't turn out like him."

"Who is that?"

"My father."

"You've mentioned your father before. He looms large in your life," the doctor said, seeing an opening.

"Yeah, he does, for me to not be like him. Everything I've done in my life has been to fight against everything he was…an utter failure. But now, I'm a grown man and I've failed. I know how it feels.

So, I think I now understand. He faced the same demons. I've just been able to find a different addiction. Mine is success."

"You seem to have done pretty well for yourself. Your drive for success is not the same as your father's issues."

"So, I'm just like him?"

"No, you're a different person, with different experiences, probably more susceptible to addictive tendencies."

"Great. Some fathers give their children their fortunes, I get addiction. Lucky me."

"Or you could look at it in a different way. I've known your brother since medical school. I was impressed by his drive and perseverance. You don't just become a leading surgeon without incredible discipline and drive. I see the same thing in you, incredible resilience. Perhaps that is the legacy your father left you, resiliency, that sheer will to pick yourself up when you've been knocked down and continue on."

"I'm just tired of always fighting. When does it end?"

"When you let it end, Henry. You've been fighting your whole life, and you've developed these habits and anxiety from these habits. Are you even sure you want to stop fighting?"

"I can't."

"You're telling me that no one else in the State of Rhode Island can do what you're doing? It has to be you?"

"I know what you think, this guy's delusional, has some sort of God complex or something, and yes, I am the only one who can do this," Henry said, his confidence clearly returning.

"Do you want to talk about what you're doing?"

"Well, like I said, I'm back in. I'm running the race for governor for Campagna, and at the same time trying to salvage what's left of my business. I really fucked up my business. Like Icarus, I flew too close to the sun. Just didn't see it coming, and it was right in front of me."

"So, you think your pride blinded you, that if you hadn't been overconfident, you could have seen the threat coming?"

"Yeah, I just didn't think it was coming from inside, that little shit. He then tried to make me out to be a cheater after he's been banging strippers while I'm trying to pull off the greatest deal the family's made in the last decade, something my father-in-law would have been proud of."

"Is that what this is about, Henry, making your father, and in this case, your father-in-law proud?"

"I just can't let this happen again. Too much is at stake. This time the whole state could be affected by the decisions I make," Henry continued on with his current train of thought, and he clearly didn't want to go in the direction the doctor was steering him. He didn't want to talk any more about his father.

"That's a large burden to carry. How is the sleeping going?" the doctor changed course too, sensing Henry was not willing to go down that road right now.

"I sleep soundly on a pillow full of money," Henry said half-jokingly. "I actually sleep until 5 a.m. like regular people."

"Regular people, as you say, don't get up at 5 a.m. if they don't have to. For you, that's better than 2 and 3 a.m., so we'll consider it a win for us."

"Lyndsay, she seems to like me better. I'm not on edge as much, much easier to be around. My anxiety, it's just not as bad."

"There's been a lot of research on anxiety, actually from a professor at Brown. The newer school of thought is that it's a learned behavior, and we can unravel it. I think you may have used your anxiety to push yourself. And in many respects, it worked. You got ahead. You achieved. Your anxiety fueled you. So, you used it to push yourself beyond your known limits. Now you have reached your true limit."

"Yeah, it's funny. I get myself all psyched up. I did it in college, would be up all night, couldn't sleep, because I worried about the test. Worried that I would forget the answers when I got in to take the test. And, of course, that never happened. Then I'd worry that if I didn't get enough sleep, I'd not be as effective, and then that kept me up. It was like a vicious cycle. I would even say to myself, if you get through this exam, and you don't blow it, then you don't need to worry. Now I tell myself, well, if you get through these next meetings, then you can relax. Leading up to the meeting, I worry about how I'll do. Each time, I excel in the moment. I don't panic, I just do it."

"It sounds like a form of performance anxiety, Henry. There's also such a thing as sleep anxiety. With your history, and your genetics, it'd be an extension of the trauma you went through. And don't dismiss it, it was trauma. OK, it wasn't like you got shot, or shot up people on the battlefield, but it's still trauma. The thing about anxiety, it's what kept us from being eaten by lions and tigers. Today, there are no animals chasing us."

"You haven't been in politics, doc. Trust me, they're animals."

"Yes, but they're not trying to eat or kill you."

"Well, maybe not eat you."

"OK, you get my point. Without definitive threats, our minds manufacture threats, help project them, and make them worse. The same way you learned to adopt this behavior, how you learned to harness your anxiety to motivate yourself, you began to realize that your success was your reward. So, you saw that the anxiety worked, it helped you achieve, so you kept doing it. The same way you learned to use anxiety to help get what you wanted you can learn to unwind it. You can understand it, where it comes from, how it's not real, and no longer let it run your life. You can do this. It will take time. It's not a quick fix, just like it took you years to learn this behavior, it will take some time to recover from it. You can, and you will. That same determination that has led you here, it can also help you prevent anxiety and its associated depression from overtaking your life."

"OK, so when do you think I can get off the medication? I mean, it's good, and I bought what you were saying about helping me get through this difficult transition. What's the plan here?" Henry asked the doctor, treating it like another negotiation.

"The sertraline seems to be working. It's a therapeutic dosage. And you seem to be handling your past. There's no shame in being on medication, Henry."

"It's just not for people like me."

"Didn't your mayor admit he takes an antidepressant?" he asked him, knowing the answer and looking to broaden the connection.

"Yeah, and I turned the tables on them, using our greatest weakness to make a deeper connection with the electorate."

"Henry, the fact that you called my office and asked me if you should be on medication is an indicator that you should probably be on medication. You told me you asked your wife, another doctor, if you should be on medication, and she told you 'yes.' So, what's the real issue here? It's OK to be vulnerable. It's not an indictment on your character. If a little pill could help you live a better life, why wouldn't you take it? You're a practical guy."

"If my enemies found out, they would use it against me, just like they tried to do to Campagna."

"And Campagna won. The voters in Providence didn't care. You know how many people are on antidepressants today? One in ten Americans. Let me ask you something. If you had diabetes, would you take insulin?"

"Of course, sometimes you can't help getting diabetes. It's not your fault."

"It's not your fault you have anxiety and depression. It's not your fault that you were assaulted. It's not your fault about your father."

"It's not my fault that my father told me he had one son who's a heart surgeon and another son who's a bum? What do you think that does to a young man, doc?" Henry asked, his voice cracking, beginning to break down.

"It's not your fault, Henry."

"It is my fault. It was all on me."

"We're not talking about your father anymore, are we?"

"The RITECH deal, it's all my fault. I wasn't paying attention. I should have known that little fucker would stab me. I trusted him. He was supposed to be family. My new brother-in-law, little fucking rich kid, who couldn't get ahead on his own, so he tries to bring me down. I won't let him win. They won't beat me."

"I think you are a very difficult man to beat," the doctor told him.

"You've got to get up pretty early to take me down. And I play the long game."

"I'm not sure if this is really helping you, Henry, the constant battle. It has its repercussions."

"Oh, you've helped me, doc. You definitely have. The man who has recognized and defeated his demons is a dangerous man."

"Indeed."

"And don't worry, I'm going to use my new-found powers for good," Henry said with a smile.

"Remember this, Henry, empathy is your superpower."

"We good, doc?"

"I don't know, Henry, are we?"

"Doc, how would you feel about sending a commando out to war?"

"I don't know, I haven't worked with the military. And I'm not so sure it's the same thing. You're not really at war."

"And that's the only thing you've said today, doc, that I disagree with. I'm going back into war, and I'm going to win."

Henry returned to Providence. McNally had called his phone three times while he was in therapy with Dr. Kelleher, and he called him back from his car. McNally had received a call from Jimmy Callahan in Washington, who told him he needed to see both of them immediately. He was on the shuttle from Washington to Providence.

30

Callahan was sitting in McNally's office when Henry arrived. He didn't even wait for Henry to sit down before he started.

"You guys have uncovered a hornet's nest, and it was about to sting us. We're unraveling the whole thing as we speak. Your buddy, Braverman, was just the tip of the iceberg. And he's not the only one. We've uncovered Russian plots in at least 13 states," Callahan told the stunned political operatives.

"What do you mean, Jimmy?" McNally asked the FBI senior legal advisor, calling him by the same name he had always used when Callahan was a kid coming up in the ranks.

"I mean, the Braverman plot was more widespread than we even realized. And if you two hadn't tipped us off, we wouldn't have known about it," Callahan admitted.

"So does that mean my guy has immunity and won't be prosecuted for any campaign violations?" Henry asked, putting his legal counselor hat back on.

"As far as we're concerned, he's our hero, so yeah, you can rest assured he won't be prosecuted. I'll make sure he's protected."

"Jimmy, are you saying that the Russians are here?"

"Yeah, they're here, and looks like for quite some time. We think this goes all the way to the top of the Kremlin, orchestrated by the big guy himself when he was in the KGB. They've been planting Russian children in the states with unsuspecting parents who thought they were just rescuing orphaned Russian children. They're approached with some bullshit inheritance story. The child was actually Russian royalty, or some other bullshit. The parents all of a sudden come into millions of dollars. The kids go to the best schools, get pushed up through the political establishment in an attempt to get them into elite schools. The goal is to put them into positions of power. The Russians get their tentacles into the family so that when they start to realize this is all too good to be true, they're too far in. And many of them never suspect it. Of course, the Russians are fueling anti-American views. They're pitching socialist ideology, and they encourage their new American kids to pursue a far-left agenda. In other states they push the right wing, anti-establishment agenda. If they see their kid is susceptible to racist tendencies, anti-gay, all that, then they push them in that direction."

"Jesus, Jimmy, this is some dark shit," McNally said, not holding back.

"The Russian agent that got to Braverman, what happened to him?" Henry asked.

"A ghost. We've been staking out the Russian consulate in Boston. Nothing. Like he was never there. No record of him. He's probably slamming back a bottle of vodka in the Kremlin right now."

"How did we let this happen?" McNally asked.

"It's our system, Congressman," Henry interjected. "It's always been susceptible. That's what happens when you have an open society and free and open elections. Not everyone is altruistic. They're not all Campagnas."

"So, what's next, Jimmy?"

"You guys sit tight, we got this. Keep doing what you're doing, running the election, like nothing happened. Your guy, Braverman, tell him to just lay low over at Brown. You'll start to see a number of raids and arrests. In fact, right about now," Callahan told them, looking at his watch. "We're raiding the Gaspee Militia, and they'll all be in custody. I know we've got some guys that hope they fire at our Hostage Rescue Team, who are chomping at the bit to take down a few white supremacists."

"I know the Russians are the real boogeyman here. They're just stirring up shit that's already here," Henry spoke freely.

"Yeah, we've got some issues here, not going to lie. The biggest threat to the FBI these days is the right-wing movement. You saw that the Germans just took down their own right-wing plot. It's not inconceivable it happens here again," Callahan reminded them.

"It's already happened here, Jimmy. We all know what January 6th really was. It was a coup d'état," McNally interjected.

"You know I can't really comment on what the FBI knows. Yeah, there's an organized right-wing movement looking to do some serious damage. Fortunately, they're loosely organized and not run by any Mensa candidates. We figure if we take down a few of them they'll scatter like rats. That's why we're happy to go in and take out these wingnuts camped out in the New England woods."

"Well, Jimmy, I appreciate you coming in and sharing with us what you could."

"The best thing you guys can do is just keep up business as usual. You've got Campagna, who's pretty much a boy scout. He'll be good for this place. You guys got this."

"Thanks, Jimmy. I'll walk you out," McNally offered as he put a hand on his shoulder.

Henry had been out of pocket for the morning with his side trip to Boston and return to Providence, and the anxiety was panging within him to check his texts and email. He scrolled through his dozens of texts to quickly see what may need his immediate attention before McNally returned to his office. He knew McNally would want to discuss strategy after this revelation. Other than the campaign texts from the pollster and media consultant, and a what-do-you-want-for-dinner-tonight from Lyndsay, there were no messages that needed his immediate attention, except for one. His father-in-law had texted him that he would be in town tonight and asked if they could meet at the University Club for a drink at 7 p.m. Most good sons-in-law would never turn down their wife's father for a drink when asked. For Henry, his new father figure had entrusted him with a multi-billion-dollar company, so he became the number one priority. Henry first had to deal with his other father figure.

"Can you believe this shit storm we're in?" McNally said to Henry after escorting their guest out and returning to the secure confines of his office. He had closed the door and really needed to process the whole situation with Henry.

"Yeah, we're not in Silver Lake anymore," Henry quipped, longing for what seemed like simpler days when the two of them were trying to wrangle votes in the top performing Democratic 7th Ward of Providence.

"And I thought Congress was fucked up. Sure, we had a few Communists and Fascists there too. Not like this shit. The fucking Russians here in our state running an operation, using us as a test ground to launch bigger operations against the American people? How did we let this happen?"

"We left our guard down. I'm off trying to conquer the business world and you're still playing kingmaker. We let a guy like Charlie Braverman get elected lieutenant governor even though we knew he was to the left of Lenin. He's a good guy, don't get me wrong. I like him. We had a chance to stop him in the primary four years ago. We could have the secretary of state in at LG, one of our guys, who would be governor now. Now, we have to take Campagna, who is doing a great job in Providence, and help us fix what we fucked up."

"I don't know if you can pin this all on us, Henry."

"I'm not. The blame is squarely on the fucking Russians. It's just that we have got enemies all around us, and we can't afford to let down our guard. And our enemies today are playing by different rules, where might makes right."

"That's what I love about you, buddy. You were classically trained. The Jesuits would be proud. I was a phys ed major who stumbled into politics. Remember I went back and got my law degree at night while I was teaching kids how to play basketball."

"You did pretty good for yourself, Congressman."

"Yeah, did alright," McNally said as he looked out over his ceiling high windows that could see as far as Narragansett Bay.

"Look, like Jimmy Callahan said, we don't need to do anything. We just got to go out and win this election. And we've got this," Henry confidently insisted.

"Yeah, those Russkies got nothing on us," the former congressman said, speaking like he was in the locker room with his quarterback. While he was a power player, he knew he needed his top performer to carry the day.

"We've got this in the bag. Just got the latest polling data, and Campagna's up by 15. I don't care how much Stevens spends. Let him blow $5 million. He'll be our poster boy for returning business executives who try to come back and think they can just buy elections."

"Yeah, we can't take this for granted. There's still plenty of time before election day and a lot can change. You know that."

"You bet. There's no way I leave my flank exposed again. I've got this."

"I know you do, buddy."

***

Henry had time to get back to his office before his drink with his father-in-law. Lyndsay was more than understanding that Henry was staying in the city for dinner when she realized he was meeting her father. She planned to use the time to spend with her sister, who was still recovering from the unraveling of her short-lived marriage. Henry used his afternoon to catch up on emails at the office, touch base with some key staff, and even get a short workout in before he grabbed a salad with seared tuna before his meeting with his father-in-law. Henry opted to dine in the University Club's locker-room after his workout, which was politely served by the locker-room attendant. While it seemed odd to be eating while seniors and Providence's business elites changed into their workout gear, Henry felt he needed some quiet time before his meeting with his father-in-law.

Henry walked into the dining room and saw his father-in-law sitting at a table near the fireplace. He was surprised to see he already had a guest with him. Sinclair's guest was a mere twenty-five years older than Henry, which meant that the two of them brought down the average age in the room by ten percent.

"There's the boy," Sinclair said. By now Henry was used to Sinclair's introductions and politely went along. Sinclair's guest stood up to shake Henry's hand. "Henry, meet Jerimiah Dexter."

"Mr. Dexter, nice to meet you."

"Please, call me Dex. That's what my friends call me."

"Henry, they still have that private room downstairs here? Let's grab you a drink and go down there," Sinclair suggested, but really told him.

"I didn't know there was a private room downstairs," Henry replied.

"It's secure, I had it swept," Dex assured Sinclair.

Henry was even more perplexed when they walked down the stairs to a room he didn't even know existed. He knew he needed to spend more time at the University Club if he really wanted to secure himself among the key power players in Providence. As he walked through the door, Henry could not help noticing the device on the floor emitting white noise to help ensure privacy in the room.

"Heard your meeting with Congressman McNally and Mr. Callahan went well," Sinclair started.

"Wait, how did you know?"

"That's why we're here, Henry," Sinclair told him. "Dex and I go way back. He and I both joined the company together."

"Yeah, I stayed in, and you went on to bigger and better things," Dex chimed in.

"Company, he worked for The Sinclair Group with you?" Henry innocently asked.

"Well, let's just say Sinclair is a wholly owned subsidiary of Dex's company."

"Wait, I don't get it."

"C'mon Henry, put it together. Dex is in the company."

"What company?

"The company, Henry."

"Wait, CIA?"

"I'm deputy director of operations for Europe and Russia," Dex told him.

"What does the deputy director of the CIA have to do with my father-in-law, and me?"

"Well, I'll let your father-in-law explain the first question."

"Henry, the Sinclair family was involved with the founding of the republic. We trace our family routes back to the Scottish Rite Masons. My great-great-great-great grandfather was the Grand Master. There were Sinclairs fighting alongside Washington in the Revolutionary War. We helped hold the Carolinas for the General. You won't read that in any of the official history books, because our people operated in the dark. We were spies, just like Dex's family. My father was in the OSS, serving alongside Wild Bill Donovan and Dex's dad. Dex and I both followed different paths. I went to Duke, he went to Yale. We both ended up in the Company. We had some successes—Panama and Berlin—and some disasters—Tehran and Bagdad."

"Yeah, Damascus, too," Dex regretted, "We got Kiev right though."

"Jesus," was all Henry could say.

"Yeah, he wasn't part of what we did. Everything we did was to preserve the republic. There are some really bad people out there that want to take us down. 9/11, as bad as it was, was actually a decapitation strike, and some of our enemies were ready to capitalize," Sinclair told him.

"I thought you were this great capitalist and entrepreneur, not a master spook."

"He is both," Dex interjected.

"The Sinclair Group is one hundred percent legitimate. We're a multi-national corporation, which sometimes allows us to operate outside US jurisdiction and laws. Sometimes the Company needs an organization to run an op that they can't have their fingerprints on."

"Which is why we're here, Henry."

"As my father-in-law will tell you, I'm not a businessman like him. I'm a political operative," Henry reminded everyone.

"You're a businessman, Henry," Sinclair insisted.

"It's for your other talents that we've had our eye on you for quite some time," Dex admitted. "You came to our attention because of that incident in D.C., when you fought off three much bigger assailants who would have murdered you and Lyndsay. We've kept our eye on you, watched your career, waiting for the time when we may want to approach you for your help."

"What could the CIA possibly want with someone like me?" Henry asked.

"We want you to help us give a bloody nose to the same people who interfered in our elections."

"The Russians?" a bewildered Henry asked.

"Yup."

"How?"

"I'll walk you through the operation, but not here. Come to my house in Scituate tomorrow morning and I'll go through the op."

"I take it I don't have a choice."

"You always have a choice," Sinclair responded.

31

Henry did not sleep much that night. His father-in-law had been a spook all this time, and the woman lying next to him had no idea. Henry wondered if his mother-in-law even knew. Probably not. He wanted to be fresh for his meeting, but he could not stop his racing mind from spinning all types of scenarios. What had they meant by Baghdad and Tehran? How involved was Sinclair in all of it? How deep did it go? When 4:30 a.m. arrived, he jumped out of bed like he had done so many times before. His habit of rising before dawn and assaulting the day had worked well for him. He longed for the time when he may sleep in like a regular person. Henry also knew he really didn't want to be like everyone else.

He was surprised as he peered out his kitchen window and saw Sinclair's Range Rover that he was planning to pack up with his daughter's things. Lyndsay was lobbying Bridgit to stay in Rhode Island and take advantage of their underused guest room, so Henry knew Sinclair may be heading back to North Carolina solo. He walked out to greet him, handing him a cup of coffee.

"Didn't know we were meeting here."

"Figured Dex's house is on the way, and you and I could chat before. Plus, I get to see my daughter off. Haven't done that since she was a kid."

"She'll be happy. She has rounds at 8 a.m. Her alarm goes off at 6 a.m. She doesn't leave here until a little after 7 a.m."

"Great, that gives us time to chat. So, take me down to this stream I've heard about in your backyard."

"Lyndsay told you about that?"

"Yeah, she says you're a bit obsessed with it, that you take everyone who comes over to the house to see it."

"I just never had anything like this in my life before."

"Well, show me."

They walked down the path Henry had carved. His wife found it ironic that he did not have time to take care of their lawn, but he did to clear and place wood chips down a path to a stream and build bridges for crossings.

"If you cross that bridge and walk down a half-mile, you'll come to the old Cranston Foundry. Dates back to 1812."

"Our family was spying on the British encampments in Baltimore back then. We're Scots, so we always had a thing for the English," Sinclair joked.

"Yeah, about that, when were you going to tell me about this?"

"Honestly, Henry, I wasn't sure I'd ever tell you. Mary doesn't even know. Certainly not Lyndsay or her sisters, and it needs to stay that way. The Sinclair family goes back hundreds of years to the founding of the Republic. We came over with other Freemasons in 1702, and we helped launch this truly amazing experiment. Republics are born, but they need to be nurtured and protected. What our forefathers created, built, and preserved is truly amazing."

"This is all just a bit unbelievable for me. I knew you were rich and part of the American aristocracy. This spy shit you're involved in, it's just crazy to me."

"I know it's a lot to handle. You're one of the few who can."

"I mean, have you ever offed someone?"

"First, don't ask me that. This is not the mafia, Henry. And no, my involvement has always been helping to finance operations. When the company needs to go outside the government for plausible deniability, we've helped set up the financing. We haven't been operational in years. Your op would be the first in about 20 years."

"Why do you do it? I mean, aren't there other people?" Henry asked.

"I suppose there are," Sinclair said as he looked up at the sunlight coming through the trees and glistening over the stream. "The reality is, Henry, we're the ones that step up when our country needs us. It's our way of giving back to the country that has given us so much. And it's always been beneficial for the Sinclair family."

"What do you mean by beneficial?"

"You'll see. Let's go see Dex, and he'll fill you in."

The drive to Scituate from Henry's house was a pleasant trek. He drove by apple orchards, a horse farm, lush green hills rolling into the pristine crystal-clear water—a quintessential New England experience. The Dexter compound was just that, more than a house or even a mansion. It was a thirty-acre estate with multiple colonial style homes dating back to the 18th century that had been historically restored.

Dex walked out the front door with his thirteen-year-old daughter in tow to catch the bus, which was picking her up at the end of the winding driveway.

"Ava, this is dad's friend, Mr. Mercucio. His name will be one to remember."

"Nice to meet you, Mr. Mercucio," she said, and then turned to her father. "Dad, I can walk the rest of the way."

"Sorry, honey, old habits. You go the rest of the way, and know I'll always be with you."

"Sure, dad," she said, and walked to the bus stop.

"Henry, come grab a coffee with Reggie and me," Dex graciously offered his guest.

The three men enjoyed espressos from Dex's Italian commercial grade cappuccino maker that was the same model used by his favorite restaurant on Providence's Federal Hill.

"Henry, Dex's espresso is the best you'll get outside Italy. It's what I look forward to most when I come here."

"So, this isn't your first visit then?" Henry asked.

"Like I said, Henry, Dex and I go way back."

"Yeah, starting to see that."

"We don't let just anyone in," Sinclair told him.

"Hey, let's go down to my SCIF," Dex invited his guests after seeing they were properly caffeinated.

"Of course, you have a secure room," Henry could not hold back.

"This day and age, Henry, I can do much of my work here, and only go to Langley when needed."

"Yeah, I can't wait to hear what Langley wants with me," Henry admitted.

"Henry, this is not going to be a Langley op. In fact the CIA will have nothing to do with this. That's why you and Reggie are here."

"I don't understand. I thought you and my father-in-law were CIA."

"We work with Reggie and your company from time to time, when we need to do things off the books, and this is one of those operations. As Reggie will assure you, let's just say we always make it worthwhile."

"Henry, as I explained, The Sinclair Group finances some of the operations. We need to protect our friends on Capitol Hill sometimes. It's almost always for the greater good," Sinclair assured Henry.

"You mean circumventing Congressional oversight. You know how many U.S. laws you're breaking? The Foreign Surveillance Act for one," Henry told them, wanting to show them that he was no shrinking violet.

"Henry, we don't invite just anyone into our world. In fact, you're the only one for this operation. And seeing what the Russians were willing to do in Rhode Island, and across the country, we figured you'd be on board, or we would not have approached you. Plus, the fact that you're part of Reggie's family."

"Yeah, that seems to open many doors for me," Henry told them.

"Sure, Henry, I've cracked the doors, but you've blown them wide open. We wouldn't be here if we didn't think you were the right one for this," Sinclair assured him.

"Alright, what are you guys looking to do?" Henry asked, his curiosity overtaking his skepticism.

"We want you to help install our candidate for mayor of St. Petersburg, Russia," Dex told him.

"What?"

"Yes, I'm serious. We want you to help us usher in a new era in Russian politics, unofficially and behind the scenes, of course."

"There are plenty of international political consultants who do that. I can give you some names."

"Yeah, we know them too. They do it for the cash, but we want someone who's going to do it for greater interests. The current regime can't last forever, and we need to groom an alternative. Our guy is Yuri Turgenev. He's one of the most outspoken critics of the regime and could use some practical political experience. He needs to serve in a major office if he's ever going to take over the Russian Federation presidency one day."

"So, you want me to run his campaign for mayor of St. Petersburg?"

"A little more than that," Dex told him.

"Like you said, Henry, we could get anyone for that," Sinclair added.

"We need to clear the path for Turgenev. We're playing the long game. The current mayor is part of the old apparatchik. And like so many of these guys he has a weakness for the ladies. He's also at the center of a major corruption ring. He and his boys have been selling off government assets, siphoning off supplies and reselling them in Eastern Europe," Dex explained. Referencing Providence's former corrupt mayor, he added, "These guys make our corrupt politicians look like amateurs, and we want to expose them."

"What does that have to do with me?" Henry asked.

"We need multiple scandals, and nothing resonates better than sex and corruption—everyone gets that stuff. We need to put together a team to work on exposing the St. Petersburg mayor, setting him up with the right girl. Then we need to make sure our guy runs a really successful race. So, that's where you come in. We want you to set up a team outside of Russia in Prague. It's close enough for you to move people in and out of Russia yet enough of an arm's distance. We need to convince Turgenev to work with you. You get Braverman on your team, and he may just go for it—all the true believers together. No offense, Henry."

"None taken, it's not like I'm calling you a bunch of old white guys trying to hold on to power," Henry said, not able to hold back anymore.

"Touché."

"So, what do you think, Henry?" Sinclair asked.

"I think this is unbelievable. From what I've already seen out there, it's really not all that different from what I've already experienced."

"Just a larger scale, with international implications," Sinclair reminded everyone. "That's why we're going to finance it. I've already deposited $10 million into a Swiss account with your name on it."

Henry would grasp the fact later that there was a Swiss bank account with his name on it. He needed to focus.

"We want you to start putting together your team for this, and I can help you with anything you need. Remember, I'm just a New England Swamp Yankee managing my family's money. Plus, you've got Reggie here who will show you how it's done. It's just a younger man's game now, and we need to pass the torch at some point."

"So you in, Henry?" Sinclair asked.

"You knew I was before you even asked."

"Yeah, I told Dex you would put up a nominal front, and that you're one of us."

***

Now it was time for Henry to start thinking about assembling his team. He didn't need to look too far for his first ask, and he knew exactly where to find him. He boarded a plane to Miami and went directly to the Ritz beach bar on Key Biscayne.

"Hello, Beako."

"How did you know I'd be here?"

"You're a creature of habit."

"Did you come down to accuse me of another murder?" he asked, referring to Henry's last visit when he had been accused of selling the drugs to Campagna's niece that led to her overdose.

"I deserve that, I do. And no, that's not why I'm here. Are you ready to get back in?"

"I mean, sipping margaritas by the beach is good and all. And

I'll miss banging my girl. Yeah, I'm ready to get back in the game. How are you going to convince Campagna to put me on the campaign after all I did?"

"Oh, no, Campagna is too pure for you, Beako. I've got something else."

"Didn't realize you were going back into political consulting. I thought you were this big business executive now?"

"An interesting dichotomy, politics and business, so often intersecting," Henry pondered aloud.

"So, what is it, Henry?"

"You have your passport?"

"Yeah, I've got my passport. We head over to the Bahamas all the time."

"Ever been to Prague?"

"Czech Republic, yeah, I've been."

"Believe they like to call it Czechia now. Better learn the lingo, Beako."

"And what am I going to do in Prague?"

"It's a whole new world," Henry said, smiled, and patted him on the back.

"Are you going to explain what you mean by that?"

"In due time, Beako. You in or not?"

"You want me to just pull out of here, just like that, based on my belief in you, Henry?"

"I do."

"What the fuck, sometimes you just have to have balls," Beako said, slamming down his glass of Jack Daniels. "Can my girl come with me? She's never been to Europe."

"Sure, why not? You can bring your teenager with you."

"Funny, Henry. We don't all get to have the perfect marriage like you. My wife divorced me and took me to the cleaners."

"With what you'll make on this, you'll do just fine."

"And how much would that be?"

"You're going to have to trust me. You will be well compensated."

"You're making me place a lot of faith in you, Henry."

"We're going to change everything."

32

Henry threw himself into his new mission. Running a gubernatorial election and the Northeast operations of The Sinclair Group was not enough for someone like Henry. An international operation to ultimately change the course of history—now that was something that truly inspired him. He also liked playing the long game. Unlike others who were quick to trade their core beliefs to earn a few bucks, Henry had learned that patience and persistence were the key ingredients to a lifetime of success, which is what he really craved.

With assistance from Dex, Henry engrossed himself in the files about the current political situation and rampant corruption in St. Petersburg. He had a full dossier on both the old political stalwart currently in the mayor's office and the new up-and-coming candidate they hoped to install. As thoroughly in-depth as the files were on the level of criminal activity, what was lacking was the 'how.' The corruption ring included selling medicine earmarked for the indigent as well as diverting armor from front-line police to the illegal arms trade and on to the black market. How did they do it? How did they get away with it? How far did the corruption go, all the way to the top of the political establishment?

Henry understood that he needed someone who understood how to run an organized corruption ring of this magnitude. As savvy as he was, he had too much of that inherent goodness to really understand how someone could sell their core beliefs for fast dollars. By no means was he a white knight. He, himself, when given the choice between preserving his future or selling his soul, had chosen the latter. And he would every time. That's why he needed someone who not only operated in the dark but relished in it. Anyone in Providence politics knew that former Mayor Donovan could never have operated an extortion and racketeering scheme without a true mastermind behind it. Terry Silberman, his shrewd and savvy chief of staff, was the true orchestrator of a 20-year-old scheme to defraud the people of Providence. It was time to put his expertise to good use.

"You told me if I needed anything to give you a call," Henry said on the secure phone Dex had given him.

"And I meant it," Dex told Henry, drinking another espresso on his deck overlooking the Scituate Reservoir.

"Just how far is your reach?"

"Depends, what are you looking to do?"

"We need to expose the mayor of St. Petersburg's corruption, right? I need someone who knows the ins and outs of how to run a corruption ring. I need Silberman, Donovan's bag man. He gets out in a few years from Danbury. I need you to get him out now."

"That's not an easy one, Henry. There's no one else?"

"He's the best we've got in terms of extortion and corruption. You want me to run this op, I need the best team to do this. I need Silberman."

"Not going to be easy. Let me see what I can do."

Not easy was an understatement. Dex had to tap into his highest contacts at the Justice Department, and he knew it would cost him in terms of future horse-trading. As much as he was in line with a group of other American elites who were in equal positions of power to help one another, they were no different than other men trading political favors like currency.

The fact that the FBI and Justice Department had bagged the bigger fish also helped. The front man for political corruption was serving a 15-year sentence, and Mayor Jack Donovan would always serve as the poster child to any political leader that no matter how powerful he was in his local fiefdom, the full weight of the American legal institution would come crashing down if he stepped out of line. Silberman had already served half of his sentence and was eligible for parole and release for good behavior in two years. It was not entirely outlandish for a high-level official in the Justice Department to lobby his associate in the Bureau of Prisons to spring Silberman from jail for special circumstances. He had earned a chip he could cash in later when he needed a special favor down the line.

None of this maneuvering surprised Henry. He didn't care about how Dex was able to break Silberman from jail, just that he got it done. It was not out of the realm of justice for Silberman's sentence to be commuted after serving half of his term. For Silberman any time out of the endless days of monotony was worth any trade. Henry suspected this, which is why he personally made the trek down from Providence to Danbury Federal Penitentiary.

"Who are you?" Silberman asked Henry, who was waiting for him in a private 10 x 10 metal room at Danbury. Silberman was unaware of his fate.

"I'm your freedom," Henry told him.

"You're that kid who ran Campagna's campaign. Yeah, I know you. So what, Campagna needs me, is that what this is about?"

"No, we don't want you anywhere near Campagna. We have

something more in line with your special expertise."

"Well, I can't be of much help to you while I'm here."

"That's why I had you released to my custody, and I'm your new attorney. You just need to sign here," Henry told him as he slid the legal document that would provide Silberman his freedom.

"And what does this cost me?" Silberman asked, as he quickly signed the document. Freedom was worth more to him than whatever Faustian bargain he was making.

"Something you're especially good at. I need someone of your unique skill set. We're going to Europe. I'll explain in full later. Let's get you out of here first."

"I'm going to need a passport for Europe. How you gonna get that for a convict?"

"The people I work for are taking care of that," Henry assured him.

"CIA?"

"Something like that."

After filling out the remaining paperwork, Henry escorted his prisoner out of Danbury. Even though Silberman was a hardened criminal, he was a man, and Henry suspected he knew what he needed after nearly three years of confinement. On the drive home on Interstate 95 they met up with Danny Conroy, who was better suited for the type of delicate meeting Henry felt Silberman craved after his lonely confinement. Danny brought a roll of hundreds with him and deposited Silberman in a gentleman's club in New Haven, Connecticut, while Henry took a ride over to Yale University where Dex had arranged some private workspace to plan their operation. Henry wanted to assure Silberman's compliance, and providing him what most men wanted after confinement helped establish further trust between the men, or so Henry surmised.

Henry knew the two men he had left had a history together and that Danny had worked for Silberman in a previous life. However, he was unaware that Danny had betrayed his boss, and that their reunion was less than cordial.

"So, I see you got yourself a new patron," Silberman said, breaking the ice.

"Yeah, meet the new boss, same as the old boss. It's not quite like that with Henry. He's the real deal. And honest, not like..."

"Not like us. Right Danny?"

"Yeah, not like us."

"Does he know how you fucked me over?"

"I didn't. That's what you don't understand. I was going to give you back the money. She took it all. She fucked us all, Terry. You, me, she beat us at our own game. Don't blame me," Danny fired back, remembering how the great flame of his life had stolen the two million they had swindled from Silberman.

"So, you're either a traitor or an idiot. I don't know what's worse."

"Hey, we can either continue here, or we can take the fresh start we've been given. Up to you, Terry."

"So, you're telling me she fucked you over too, that you weren't in on it with her?"

"That's what I'm trying to tell you. Even worse is I fell for her," Danny admitted.

"For as tough as you are, you have a soft heart. Never trust a whore."

"Yeah, I learned that the hard way. I swear, Terry, I never betrayed you."

"Alright, let's leave the past in the past. Let's get some broads."

Danny texted Henry after two hours of debauchery with a plan to satiate Silberman's other cravings. Henry was planning to take them to the best local steakhouse, though Danny told him that

Silberman really wanted to go to the Frank Pepe Pizzeria in the Wooster Square neighborhood of New Haven. Henry would not have gone to these lengths to placate a criminal if he hadn't thought Silberman's specialized expertise was absolutely necessary for his operation.

Henry had never had a white clam pizza pie. He had also never run an operation for the CIA.

"You'd never think clams on pizza. You have to admit, it's pretty friggin' good," Silberman announced to his guests. "I've been craving this stuff for three years."

"Yeah, I guess we're not the only off combination that actually works," Henry countered.

"So, you got me out of jail early, got me strippers, and now you're filling my belly. You want to tell me now what this is all about?" Silberman asked. Even though he was grateful, he understood that generosity came at a cost.

"We need someone of your talents to help us unravel a corruption ring in Eastern Europe. We need you to analyze the information we have and explain to us how it works, so we can help expose it," Henry explained.

"I'm not a rat. Why would I help you and the government?"

"Well, first, the government isn't involved. This is a private venture. The Sinclair Group is betting that Russia will open up again, and St. Petersburg is the most Western city. It presents the best opportunity for our international portfolio growth," Henry lied to him. He filled him in on the parameters of the operation, explaining who the target was and what they already knew. Henry figured that if Silberman flaked on him, he hadn't provided him enough tangible intelligence to expose the operation. He equally understood that no one would believe a disgraced criminal and his tall tales of corporate espionage.

"And what do I get for my special skills and insights?"

"To start, your freedom," Henry reminded him. "One call and I can send you back. I want you properly motivated. Upon completion of your work, $1 million will be deposited into a Swiss account. Sure, I know it's not as much as you and Donovan stole from the city. Let's just say this is a bit more honorable work."

"Please, companies like yours are the real crooks, ripping off people like me for generations. I have no regrets, and I paid the price. Don't lecture me about morality, kid."

"Here's your chance to put your special skill set to work and earn real money. It's better than doing laundry at Danbury, or a minimum wage job when you get out. You've got no pension and few other options. I'm your best one," Henry told him.

"I just don't trust him," Silberman said, pointing to Danny, not satisfied that his protege had not betrayed him.

"You boys are going to need to learn to play nice in the sandbox. Danny is going to be watching out for you while you're in Europe," Henry told him.

"Lucky me, I get to be reminded each day how I got fucked over."

"Look, Terry, I got fucked over too. And c'mon, like you wouldn't have done the same thing to me. Let's not pretend there really is honor among thieves. With Henry, we get a fresh start."

"That true, Henry, you're my new savior? Going to help redeem me from all my sins? Remember, I'm Jewish."

"I'm more of a Buddhist," Henry quickly shot back.

"Alright kid, you're sharp, I'll give you that. And you seem to have the Midas touch right now. As you say, I really don't have any better options."

"So, what do you think you need to get going?" Henry asked.

"Not what, but who, and your boy's not going to like it," Silberman told Henry.

"There's nothing more important than this operation. We can put aside our personal feelings for the greater good here," Henry lectured.

"My bet, and I have experience in this like you said, is that the guy you're looking to take down has more than one weakness. If he's as corrupt as you think, then he's going to have more than one vice. My guess is he has a thing for the ladies," Silberman figured.

"You would be correct. We think he has several mistresses, and we would need a very public scandal. Something that would even outrage Russians."

"You're going to need a pro for this, and I know the one. She's so good she even swindled me."

"Wait, you want Jana? How are you going to find her?" Danny chimed in.

"I'm not; his people will," Silberman said, looking at Henry.

"Hold on, I'm not finding you this woman so you can try to get your money back. I'm not that naïve," Henry insisted.

"No Henry, you're giving me this fresh start. I'd rather have a million free and clear than having to look over my shoulder for the rest of my life. If we're going to set up this Russian, we need a Russian speaker who understands our game. You said the mission comes first. Then we need her."

"I don't like this. We can't trust her," Danny said again.

"Danny, I think you can make this work. You're also getting $1 million and so will she. The difference is that it will be for work you both earned, because of the complexity of this operation and your unique skill sets. You won't have to run. This is legit work," Henry told Danny, which he could see was changing Danny's perspective and taking the sting away from his pride. "So, we in?"

"Yeah, I'm in. What choice do I have?" Silberman admitted.

"You telling me I can make a million free and clear? Yeah, then I'm in," Danny said.

"Today we start a new chapter."

33

Finding Jana Strakova was not easy, but if anyone could it, it was Dex. Both Danny and Terry were able to come together to provide as much information as they both knew on their common enemy. While both of them clearly seemed interested in a vendetta against her, they could put aside their feelings of betrayal to achieve their ultimate goal of considerable riches without the stain of illegality or fear of retribution.

Henry was summoned back to Dex's house for a complete dossier on his target. It was information that could not be communicated over the phone and better suited for a personal exchange.

"We found your girl. It wasn't easy, and she's quite a character," Dex admitted, which was something considering it was coming from a CIA operative.

"Where is she?" Henry asked.

"Cervinia, Italy. I'm going to get her," Dex announced.

"From what they tell me, she's perfect for this operation. I just don't know how these boys are going to handle her return," Henry pondered.

"They're professionals, plus they care more about the million dollars you're dangling in front of them. They'll figure out a way to heal their bruised egos," Dex told him, having worked with hundreds of assets and understanding what truly motivated them, mostly involving money.

"So, I'll meet you in Prague then?"

"It all starts in Prague."

***

Jana Strakova was applying her skiing lessons to a more practical matter. She did not want to raise recognition of herself by taking the tram to the top of Cervinia and then a second tram down to Zermatt, Switzerland. So, she took lessons with an Italian ski instructor, who put in the extra time with her in the hopes for a chance with her off the slopes. She was strong enough on skis to make it down the mountain, yet amateur enough to attract many a young suitor who wanted to help her up and down whenever she found herself in difficult territory.

Her trip down to Zermatt was uneventful, having hitched on to a group of college students to blend in with the other skiers. She grabbed a coffee in town and then headed to the bank where she withdrew five thousand Euros to get her through the rest of the month. Her exotic beauty had earned her complimentary drinks and dinners in Cervinia, and she had managed to live rent free by staying with her Irish boyfriend who owned the local pub in town. Jana embarked on a tram back up Zermatt to another land and put on her skis to make the short trek over the Italian border.

Crossing the Swiss-Italian border at the top of the world was usually uneventful. There were no fences or walls, and rarely any guards. This time, as soon as her skis hit Italian powder, she was surrounded by border guards. Her holiday was over. They transported her in a CATV snow personnel carrier down the mountain. Instead of locking her in the local Carabinieri station, she was deposited into a CIA safe house. Her new surroundings were less familial than the chalet she shared with her Irish paramour, and the only personal effects were a roll of bath tissue and a towel to freshen up.

"Buongiorno, Jana," a voice uttered from the makeshift living room.

"You can skip the Italian, I know you're American," Jana told her captor.

"There's no fooling a great con."

"To survive in this world a girl needs all her skills," she told her guest.

"And that's why I'm here, to put your unique skills to work."

"Why would I ever help the CIA?" she asked, showing her captor she knew his identity.

"This is not for the CIA. This is your chance to punch back at your true enemy. You're Lithuanian, right? What if you could accomplish what so many of your countrymen seek, to level a serious blow at the Russians?" he asked her, appealing to what he hoped was her sense of patriotism for her homeland.

"It's not my fight anymore. Why would I help the Americans?"

"Well, first, we've confiscated your funds and we'll be returning them to the people of Rhode Island. The money you stole from Silberman had been part of a 20-year scheme to defraud American taxpayers, and we're giving it back. So, you have nothing," Dex told her.

"I came from nothing, so what makes you think I care?" she fired back.

"I can just turn you over to the Italian police for smuggling illegal funds into their country. Or I can give you a chance to make half your money back and fuck over the Russians."

"What do I have to do?" she asked, understanding little choice was left.

"You're going to help us bring down a Russian kleptocrat."

"There's a hundred girls that can do that. Why me?"

"They tell me you're the best," Dex told her.

"Who's they?"

"Your old friends, Terry Silberman and Danny Conroy. You get the privilege to work with them again."

"Are you shitting me? There's no way they'll work with me after what I've done."

"A million dollars has an interesting way of allowing people to move past their resentments. I'm assuming you can do the same?"

"Freedom is the ultimate reward."

"That's the business I'm in."

"What business is that?"

"Preserving freedom."

"So, then what does that make me?" she asked.

"I guess that makes you a freedom fighter."

"Never thought that's what they would call what I do," she admitted.

"To protect our interests, we go to places you would never expect. That's the cost of freedom. Sometimes we need to go further than our own enemy to beat him at his own game."

"So where are we going?"

"We're setting up in Prague. The operation is in St. Petersburg."

"When do we leave?"

"We're flying out in an hour."

***

The reunion of Terry Silberman, Danny Conroy, and Jana Strakova was as cold as could be expected. The only warmth came from the bottle of bourbon Dex brought to lessen the tension. Not even a bottle of Pappy Van Winkle could soften these working professionals who had been hardened by a life of scratching and clawing to get ahead. Each knew that the first to speak often lost, so Henry took it upon himself to thaw their frost by introducing a new player to the team.

"Terry, I believe you know Gordie Beako. I think the two of you worked together in a prior life."

"Yes, made his company a lot of money and I rotted in jail. Thanks again, Gordie."

"We all knew the stakes, Terry. I lost too when Henry's white knight strode in on his high horse."

"Sorry, Terry, the fucking Ritz is not the same as a 10x10 cell at Danbury."

"Ok, so you boys all good now? Remember there's a lady in the room," Henry reminded everyone.

"I've witnessed a lot worse," Jana said in her accented English.

"Look, I don't expect you guys to all get along. I do expect you to be professional. You've all been hand-picked for this special project," Henry told the group assembled. They were in a safe house in Prague that Dex had arranged. Unlike the places Dex would set up scientists, academics, and politicos from Russia, this place was more reflective of the level of the operation. The four-bedroom, three-bath apartment was in the center of Prague and had been the home of a Russian gas executive who went into hiding in the West after the CEO of his company had been a victim of the Russian leadership's latest purge of top industrialists who posed a threat to the regime.

"Maybe if you tell us exactly what this is all about we can focus on the work, instead of on who screwed who," Jana interjected.

"No one's screwed more than you," Silberman said, not able to help himself with the easy jab at Jana.

"Let's talk about something important," Henry quickly interjected to grab their attention. "We're going to take down the mayor of St. Petersburg and help plant the seeds of change in Russia."

"And just how are we going to do that?" Silberman asked.

"Just like your guy Donovan, the mayor of St. Petersburg has his hand up the city's skirt. We need you, Terry, because you can tell us how a guy like him ticks. We need you to figure out how he hides his money. We figure you know a thing or two about that. Jana is here to distract him. It's not just your classic honey pot. She will be Beako's assistant as he's looking to do a major development in St. Petersburg. Beako's position at CampCo Development has been reestablished, and since they have been shut out of New England, they're looking to expand their holdings in Russia. The Lombardo family, with some assistance from our friend Dex, will make inroads for us into the Russian mafia in St. Petersburg."

"So then why is this kid here? He our muscle or something?" Beako asked about Danny.

"Danny is my eyes and ears on the ground, while I'm back in the states. I'll be here as much as I need to be. Danny has my full confidence, and as you know, Terry, he can handle things for you guys if anyone gets jammed up."

"How long is this going to take?" Beako asked.

"At least six months, maybe a year," Henry told them.

"And how do we get paid?" Silberman asked what was on everyone's mind.

"You each get $20,000 per month, and a million each when it's done. Everyone gets the same. You're all equal; you're a team."

"I'm in, that goes without saying," Danny was the first to go, not seeing it as a weakness.

"Well, I really don't have a choice. It's better than jail," Terry admitted.

"I don't have much of a choice either, and it's better than what I used to do for that kind of money," Jana said, realizing that everyone around her was in a similar situation. She was starting to put it together that this scheme was orchestrated by a maestro who seemed to not only have the wits but also the financial backing to pull something of this magnitude off.

"I'm just happy to be back in the game," Beako announced.

And the team was operational.

34

There was another part of the mission. For the delicate phase of this operation Henry needed someone who was on his level and in the same sphere who also sought a vendetta against the Russians. Henry knew that Charlie Braverman was perfect. Henry also understood that Charlie was not the type of person to just fall in line. He needed to also see that his involvement could have far reaching consequences for meaningful change.

Henry flew back from Prague through Frankfurt to Boston and was delivered back to Providence. His driver, Richard, wanted to take him home. Henry insisted on going straight to the Center for Politics and Policy at Brown University.

"No rest for the weary," Henry quipped to Richard. Having driven Henry around for two years, the retired technology executive turned private black car service operator had more than just a cordial relationship with his client. Henry often sought his thoughts, recognizing that Richard's street sense was an important asset.

"What's at Brown?" Richard asked.

"The future."

Charlie Braverman was settling in as the director of Brown University's outward facing international policy center. He was not so naïve as to believe that his job had not been orchestrated by powerful allies, and he was determined to show that he was not just some political appointee sidelined to academia. He planned to make a difference.

He was not surprised that Henry had called him from Prague and wanted to meet with him about an exciting opportunity for the Center. While the two bespoke men were groomed for the moment, Charlie understood that as enlightened as Henry was, he was not above calling in a favor.

In Henry's typical fashion, he did not waste time with pleasantries about his trip abroad or about how Charlie was settling into his new life. Henry was on a mission and was tunnel-focused on enlisting Charlie onto his team.

"Nice digs you got here," Henry opened with, acknowledging the 17th century setting the Center occupied on Providence's historic Benefit Street, which could rival Colonial Williamsburg for its historic architecture.

"Yeah, I owe you for the soft landing."

"You don't owe me anything. You earned this."

"Hardly," Charlie admitted to Henry.

"That's not why I'm here. I need both your heart and your mind for this one."

"This ought to be a good one, then."

"That Russian agent, have you ever heard anything from him?" Henry asked.

"No, nothing, not a peep, and I would have told you if I had. I just assume he went back to whatever hell hole he crawled out of."

"What if you could get back at them?"

"You mean the bastards that cost me the governorship, my

fiancée, everything? I mean I ended up OK here. Well, not with Christine. She's gone."

"I don't know if I can help you get her back. I can help you get back at the people who turned your world upside down. And in doing so, you might just help us start a revolution."

"Wow, Henry, you not only come to me with a chance for retribution, now we're talking about full-blown revolution. We've certainly graduated to new levels. No longer slinging politics anymore. We're now into international intrigue?" Charlie could not hold back.

"I'm into making a difference in the places where I can make a difference, just like you, Charlie. Things have opened up for guys like us. It's up to us to take the opportunity we've been given. We're not going to squander it on false riches. No we're going to do big things."

"What big things are these, Henry?"

"Let me explain."

And Henry did just that after boarding Sinclair's Cessna Citation that his father-in-law had lent him for this leg of the operation. He needed to secure Charlie's full cooperation, and nothing showed seriousness like a private jet to Europe. Even though Henry had enjoyed first class on his trip back from Europe, he needed the secure confines and privacy that Sinclair afforded him.

"I appreciate you trusting me and coming with me without a full explanation," Henry started.

"I told President Monan that her new director was flying to Europe with a major benefactor who wants to contribute to the Center and help us expand our influence overseas. This one is going to cost you, Henry. Your family is going to become one of the largest contributors to Brown University."

"I know my father-in-law is an investor in the new hospital, and our interests and the Center's are aligned. We want to see liberal

democracy thrive throughout the world. It's simply good for business. And we're willing to put our resources behind it."

"So, this is all about business?" Braverman questioned Henry.

"Isn't it always?" Henry said, giving him a wink as he leaned
back in the leather chair in the jet.

"So, really, what's going on?"

"This is going to take a drink. My father-in-law's got some good
scotch here, and you're going to need a drink," Henry said as he
pulled out a bottle of Johnny Walker Blue. "It's not a single malt, but
it will have to do. There are some rare blends in here."

"Last time I had Johnny Blue was when I won the lieutenant
governor's office. So, hope you can top that," Charlie kidded Henry.

"We do this, it's going to make you. Look," Henry started, leaning in. "How would you like to fuck the Russians up a little bit?"

"Is that what we're toasting to?"

"Yeah, to guys like us, grabbing the world by the balls, and making something," Henry said, raising a glass. They raised their Water-
ford glasses, engraved with an "S" for Sinclair, and clinked them
together.

"So just how are a couple of guys from New England going to
fuck over the largest land empire in the world?"

"We're going to help sow insurrection, just like they've been
doing to us for the past eighty years," Henry told him.

"Yeah, he whose name should not be uttered aloud for fear of
summoning the devil, ever since his days at the KGB, he's been
determined to take us down."

"As you know, the issue is he has no real opposition. We have
to help the opposition get its footing, get into power, and help set up
the next generation of leadership."

"Who exactly is 'we'?"

"Do I need to say?"

"How did you get hooked up with them?"

Henry did not speak. He looked up and around and then at the empty glass. It was clear to Charlie. Some things needed to be left unsaid. It was a long enough pause, and the silence needed to be broken. Charlie then said, "Like I've said, we're not in Providence anymore."

"A brave new world." Henry raised his empty glass which prompted Charlie to lean over and pour another two fingers of scotch.

"Yeah, this is going to take a double. I'll be out in fifteen minutes, and I suggest you get some rest. When we land in Prague in eight hours, I'm going to introduce you to Yuri Turgenev, and you're going to help convince him to run for mayor of St. Petersburg. We're going to take out the current mayor by exposing his corruption in a scandal that will even make the Russians blush. And after we pull off this coup, we're going to deposit $1.6 million into your account to replace the money the Russians screwed you with."

"OK, that's quite a pitch," Charlie admitted.

"You think I get my father-in-law to give me his Citation for anyone?"

"It's a bit unbelievable, Henry. How are we going to execute this."

"The devil's in the details," Henry told him. He reclined the seat back, folded his arms, and closed his eyes. He ended up getting the sleep his body relished.

***

On the other side of the Atlantic, Dex had been working Turgenev. An academic and true believer like him would never work for the CIA, which to him and so many Russians was no different than the KGB or FSB. Dex needed to set him up with two other Young Turks like Henry and Charlie. Time for the next generation to step up in the ongoing battle for preservation of liberal democracy throughout the world. Too often the older generation was sending the younger one to war, and that needed to end.

Old Cold Warriors like Dex needed to step back from the fight and start to let new freedom fighters take the reins. He and the other patron, Reggie Sinclair, had done their part, financing and orchestrating the operation. Now was the time that their boy stepped up to the plate. Henry was the captain, the bridge between generations. As the offensive coordinator, Dex knew the time had arrived when his quarterback should call his own plays. Henry was ready, in his estimation and that of Sinclair's, and the game plan was fully turned over to him. It was time for him to execute.

This generational meeting took place in another safe house in Prague. Upon his defection from St. Petersburg, the CIA station in Prague kept a careful eye on Yuri Turgenev. He and his fellow academic wife were on a Russian Visa. With the assistance of Czech Intelligence, they had maneuvered for a fellowship for his wife, Alana, at St. Charles University for her research in molecular biology, a coup in and of itself for the Czechs to land a leading scientist like her within their borders. This went under the radar, and the Russians were more than happy to rid themselves of another rabble rouser academic like Yuri Turgenev.

"Thank you for meeting with me, Mr. Turgenev," Henry opened with, sensing Turgenev's unease from the start.

"My wife's friend at St. Charles told me I should speak to you and your friend. That you're looking to help with my work while I'm in Prague," Turgenev revealed what he thought.

"Yes, my colleague here, Charlie Braverman, is the Director of the Center for International Policy and Politics at Brown University."

"Thanks, Henry. Mr. Mercucio is the head of the Sinclair Group, and they're one of Brown's largest benefactors. Brown has a relationship with St. Charles, and we want to open our first international center outside of Brown here in Prague," Charlie said, going along with the plan for persuasion, which wasn't in fact a lie, since as part of the cover operation The Sinclair Group was there to open an office with The Center in Prague. It was simply the groundwork for a plan to go beyond an academic exercise. Henry was about to take it operational.

"And what do you want of me?" Turgenev asked, showing his Russian brashness.

"We want you to be our director here in Prague," Charlie told him.

"So, you want me to work for the CIA," Turgenev challenged, testing his guests.

"You got this all wrong, Professor Turgenev, we're not the CIA. I'm a businessman, actually a former political consultant and lawyer turned executive."

"Yeah, like I said, CIA," Turgenev replied, continuing not to hold back.

"That's not it, professor. Mr. Mercucio's family is one of our country's greatest proponents of spreading liberal democracy around the world."

"That's my wife's family, and not me," Henry chimed in. "I'm just a kid from Boston who married way above my standing."

"You and me both," Turgenev told them. "My wife's family goes back to Russian nobility."

"And mine took off when she saw I was no longer the rising star I had promised. I guess at least she wasn't my wife yet," Charlie added in, not wanting to be left out of the conversation.

"Yeah, Charlie here was one step away from being elected governor of Rhode Island, our smallest state, but still an influential one."

"Yes, I know Rhode Island, one of the 13 original colonies. I did take American Colonial History. Your little state was the tip of the triangle trade, rum for slaves, I believe."

"Yes, my adopted state has a colorful history, just like yours, professor," Henry fired back.

"We've been oppressed for generations. This regime, they're no different than our last czars," Turgenev argued.

"Meet the new boss, same as the old boss," Henry said, reciting the verse from The Who's "We Won't Get Fooled Again."

"I saw The Who in Berlin, back when I could still travel freely," Turgenev told them. "This may not be 1917, and our day needs to come. The Russian people are victims too. Cannon fodder for NATO weapons fired by our brother Ukrainians. We all talk about the Ukrainians dying at the hands of the Russians. There's Russians dying at their hands too. Boys like you and me. Thousands of them, led to their slaughter by a regime that cares only about holding power."

"The thing about victimization, though, is it can be used as an excuse. It's why we're held back. It's why we don't rise up. We need a spark, and you, Yuri, are that spark," Henry pitched.

35

It was not what Henry expected. He had not planned for it. And it came back to his life like a bomb. He read the story on his laptop in Sinclair's Citation during the flight back to Providence.

"Former Campagna Consultant Tied to Niece's Death" was the headline on Rhode Island's most visited news website. Henry already had a message from Katrina Paul, the *Providence Journal* reporter who had doggedly questioned him when the story first emerged two and a half years ago. While his father-in-law had quashed the story once before, the emergence online provided Paul the cover with her editor to further investigate. It also helped that the *ProJo*, as it was affectionately known, had been sold once again in the constant reshuffling of print news media.

This time Reggie Sinclair could not make a phone call and shut down the story with the conservative conglomerate that was set on taking over local news in print and broadcast. Their agenda necessitated a consistent local presence and promotion of traditional values, as they saw it. Henry was now on his own with his own red notice.

He had been burned, but by whom, he didn't know. It would have to wait. He had to shut down this shit storm first. And that started first with seeing Mayor Campagna. Certain things needed to be done face to face, and this was certainly one of those occasions. Having a Citation-700 at your disposal certainly helped, and he was able to make it back to Providence only hours after the story broke.

Thankfully Henry had Campagna's secretary's cell phone number and he could call it before she left for work. He had that type of relationship with her since he had personally put her in the position to look after Campagna.

"Kristen, can you get me in first thing this morning?"

"Jesus, Henry, it's 6 a.m. I had to get up in 15 minutes anyway. It's going to be a busy morning, thanks to you," Kristen told him, her voice gaining strength as she continued to awaken.

"Yeah, that's why I need to see him first."

"Not sure he's going to want to see you. He's pretty upset."

"Look, Kristen, I need you. You gotta let me in to see him before anyone else. Please," Henry pleaded, something Kristen had never heard from him.

"OK, Henry, I'll squeeze you in at 8:00 a.m. when he does his coffee walk. Be here at 7:30 so I can put you in his office. He goes and talks to the security guys at that time, and I can get you in."

"Great, I land in an hour. I'll be there," Henry told her, thankful he had connected with the right person.

***

Kristen deposited Henry in Mayor Campagna's office before he arrived. Henry could hear her explain to him that Henry was waiting for her behind the closed doors. "I couldn't just turn him away, he told me he had to see you," he heard her say.

"Hello, Henry," Campagna said to him as he walked into his own office.

"Mr. Mayor."

"You want to tell me why I'm hearing now that you were with my niece the night she died?" he came right out and asked the question he needed to know.

"I was with her, but it's not what you think."

"Why don't you tell me then, because I don't know what to think anymore. The guy I trusted all these years…"

"You can still trust me; I'm still that same guy. You can't believe what they're saying in that so-called news source."

"Then tell me, Henry. I want to hear your story."

"I saw her that night. I had a couple of drinks with her. Well, more than a couple, I guess. I don't really drink that much, maybe one scotch, not that much. And, well, we kissed, and then I realized what I was doing, and I stopped her. She tried to, ya' know. Again, I stopped her. I didn't do anything with her, I swear."

"Then why didn't you just tell me?" Campagna simply asked.

"And say what? 'I know we're in the heat of the race, we managed to get our opponents out. Oh, and by the way last night, I almost slept with your niece, and I'm sorry she overdosed,'" Henry told him, speaking to him more like a pragmatic politician than like a grieving uncle. Campagna turned away from Henry. He did not speak, which prompted Henry to fill the void. Henry could see he needed to tone it down and fall on his sword. "Mr. Mayor, I am sorry, very sorry. I didn't know what to do. I was scared. I thought it could derail your chances, so I kept it quiet and tried to handle it my own way. The last person I wanted to hurt was you."

"Or Lyndsay, right Henry? You didn't want to hurt her either, I hope," Campagna said, breaking his silence.

"Of course not, I didn't want to hurt anyone. I made a mess of this, and I wanted to fix it. I am so sorry for your loss, deeply sorry for your niece. I never meant to hurt her. I never should have gone home with her, and unfortunately that's what happens when I drink. I lose my inhibitions, and I do stupid things," Henry admitted.

"You wouldn't be the first man, Henry."

"Thank you, Mr. Mayor."

"Come here," Campagna offered, embracing Henry and giving him a fatherly hug.

"Can we talk about your campaign now?" Henry asked, thinking they could now get down to business.

"I'm sorry, Henry. You're out."

"What?"

"It should be a relief. Now you can concentrate on whatever it is you're doing with your father-in-law and McNally," Campagna told him.

"Wait, you're firing me?"

"No, I'm releasing you from your commitment. You no longer have to be my campaign consultant."

"Who are you going to use?"

"We're in pretty good shape. Polling is holding steady with a ten-point lead. Looks like I'll be the first Providence mayor to become governor in over 70 years. My brother has good instincts; he can advise me. He's not you, but I don't need someone like you anymore."

"Someone like me, what do you mean by that?"

"Henry, don't get me wrong. I like you, and I wouldn't be in this office if it weren't for you and definitely wouldn't be having a conversation about being governor. You got me this far, now it's time for me to go in a different direction."

"Mr. Mayor, you can't spin a spin-doctor."

"That's exactly what I mean, Henry. I don't need, I don't want, a spin-doctor."

"I get it, I do."

"Do you really?"

"Not sure what you mean by that."

"Is this who you really want to be, Henry? I think you can be so much more, so much better. You seem to have stepped away from the truth. Time to come back home, Henry."

"Not sure what you mean."

"You're not the only one. Too often we trade what we know as right for the easier path. We don't want to confront the hard truth. And I'm not immune. You think I wanted to have to talk about my own depression, a private matter? I'm glad I did and wish I had done it sooner. Maybe I could've helped more people if I came out earlier."

"It was me who told you to come out with it," Henry reminded him.

"Yes, I know, and I'm thankful for that. I just don't know if you really did it to help me, the campaign, or yourself," Campagna questioned aloud, as he walked closer to Henry and extended his hand. Henry sensed that Campagna was serious about their conclusion and decided to retreat with the hope he could fight another day.

"If that's how you want it, Mr. Mayor, I understand."

"I hope you do, Henry."

Henry solemnly walked out of the office and grabbed the phone from his suit breast pocket. He had three missed calls from Kat Paul, and knew he needed to face the music.

"How did it go?" Campagna's administrative assistant asked as he emerged from the door.

"It's over." And Henry continued walking. His training kicked in even though he was again at another low point. How low, when compared to other past traumatic events, was debatable, but at this moment he felt his worst. The Journal reporter was not going away, sensing blood in the water, wanting to be first to the feeding frenzy. Henry understood this. He called her back and told her he would meet her at his office in 30 minutes if she wanted the truth. He needed to be at his office, where he could better maneuver on his own turf. His own outcome depended on it.

Paul was waiting for him in his reception area as Henry came into the office. He went in another entrance and headed straight to his office. He gathered his thoughts and his composure before greeting her.

"Kat, good to see you."

"Is it Henry? Thought you had been ducking me."

"No, just busy. The sun no longer rises and sets with *Providence Journal* anymore," he quipped, not being able to resist, and hoping to throw her off her game a bit. "Would have thought you would have taken their buyout by now."

"New ownership, as you know. Our pension's not what I thought anymore, so I have to keep working. Lucky me, and you."

"Yes, how do you like working as the mouthpiece for the right-wing agenda?"

"Cute. How do you like working for both sides, Henry?"

"Not sure what you mean," Henry replied, as he motioned her to have a seat in his office. He kept the door open, a practice he held with all visitors, even staff.

"I'm doing a story that you were working both sides in the mayoral campaign. You were extorted to throw the race by the Prescott campaign."

"Didn't know you were writing fiction these days, Kat."

"So, you're denying it?"

"No, I'm not just denying it, I'm telling you I did everything I could to win the race for Mayor Campagna. That's the absolute truth. I don't know who your source is. I think you've been played."

"You know I'd never reveal my sources. I'm also having a hard time getting a hold of Gordon Beako. I know your father-in-law's company bought out Campco, and I've called his new office in Miami. They told me he's in Europe on a project. Isn't that convenient to get him out of town when this story breaks?"

"Yeah, I heard Beako's down in Miami, good for him. Wish him well," Henry told her, not giving her anything to go with.

"So, you don't know where he is?"

"Kat, you're on a fishing expedition; there's no story here. Go let your overlords know that there's nothing nefarious going on here. Don't you have something better to cover, like the South County School Board banning books or something?"

"Always cute, Henry, and well played. Look forward to sparring with you again."

"Can't wait. Are we done here?"

"Yes, Henry, we're done for now."

"Great, let me walk you out."

"That's OK, I know the way."

As soon as she walked out, he looked at his screen and watched as she exited the office suite. He grabbed his cell and called Beako.

"You know it's the middle of the night here," Beako groggily said.

"I figured you'd be out enjoying the Prague nightlife."

"I have a major scheme and operation to run. I need my beauty sleep."

"Great, I need you to cover my back."

"I didn't know we were buddies."

"We're not, more like frenemies. You need to do something for me that is also in your best interest. That suits you, right, Beako?"

"Yeah, Henry, you and me will never be sipping Mojitos at the beach as pals."

"I will forever need to fill that void in my life…no bro time with Beako, how will I manage?"

"Look, I get it. Ours is a relationship of mutual benefit, nothing more."

"Good, money is more important than morals. So do something for me that will help preserve your current gravy train. I need you to call Kat Paul at the *Journal*. She's trying to get a hold of you at your office. Assure her that you had nothing to do with trying to get me to throw the race."

"Wait, how does she know anything about our deal?"

"Nick Dean must have sung," Henry figured.

"No, he wouldn't. He knows where his bread is buttered. Don't think it was him."

"OK, we need to contain this. Will you help me with it?"

"It's in my interest, so I'll do what I need to do."

36

Henry had more to do at home. He was meeting Lyndsay at the hospital, though not for lunch like he had done in the past. He wasn't even meeting her at Rhode Island Hospital or the Hasbro Children's Hospital, where she split her shifts as chief resident in the Med-Peds residency program. He met her at the other end of Rhode Island's sprawling medical campus at Women & Infants Hospital for her sonogram. He was determined that he would not be late, needing this aspect of his life to help return some semblance of joy back to him. Happiness was restored for a moment when he saw Lyndsay's smile upon walking into the waiting room.

"You made it," she said, as she squirmed in her chair, uncomfortable with the weight of the new life growing in her.

"Don't get up; I'm here."

"How was your trip?"

"Good."

"Just good. Tell me about it. I hope you took some time to see the city. I hear Prague is beautiful."

"I was mostly in meetings, went to dinner, had a traditional Czech dinner in the basement of a castle. That was pretty cool."

"Lyndsay Mercucio," the nurse called, interrupting Henry's feeble attempt to create an entry in his travel blog.

"That's me," Lyndsay said, uncomfortably standing, walking toward the door with Henry in tow. "This is my husband, Henry," she announced.

The sonogram was routine for both the nurse and Lyndsay. For Henry it kindled a whole new set of emotions. Seeing the outline of his child on the screen, and then hearing the doctor say that their emerging baby was healthy brought another smile to his face. He couldn't remember the last time he smiled before seeing Lyndsay or meeting his child for the first time.

"When are you heading back to Prague?" Lyndsay asked as they walked out of the doctor's office.

"I'm not."

"I thought you had to fly back, and that's why my dad's plane was waiting for you?"

"I can do what I need to from here. I already texted the pilot to head back to North Carolina."

"I hope you're not doing this for me. The baby is fine. I'm fine. I'm still going back to the hospital to work. You know, Henry, I'm not the first resident to give birth."

"I know that, Lynds. I can do everything I need from here, and if I need to go back I will. I think I need to stay home for a while. There's so much going on, and my attention is needed here."

"It will be nice, Henry. I'll make dinner tonight. It will be good for Bridgit too and will keep her busy. I showed her how to make pasta. Why don't you invite Danny over? We can have a normal dinner like regular people."

"I'm sure he'd like that. He flew back with me, and I'm sure he'd like a home cooked meal too."

"Make it happen," Lyndsay spoke in Henry's voice.

Henry had a message from Dex to swing by his house as soon as he could. He took the 20-minute drive out to Scituate, which seemed like a world away from Providence. It was late afternoon, and Henry waited as he saw Dex's daughter skip off the bus and head toward their sprawling estate.

"Henry," Dex called. He could hear him tell his daughter to head into the house. "Glad you came, needed to talk to you in person. Let's go to my SCIF." It still struck Henry that this serene setting housed a government secure room to safeguard his conversations from electronic surveillance and to protect sensitive information.

"We intercepted some communications from our Russian friend," Dex told Henry.

"Which friend is that?" Henry asked.

"Alexi Antipov, GRU."

"Oh, yeah, that fucker."

"Yeah, he resurfaced, and my buddy at NSA tipped me off. He leaked the story about you and Campagna's niece. The Russians got a hold of the photos. They must have hacked your buddy Beako's computer."

"Why would they care about a political consultant in Rhode Island?"

"Exactly my question, Henry. So, I had my buddy go back and go through their data on our Russian friend."

"Wait, what do you mean, go back and pull the data?"

"The NSA is tracking everyone. It's like a needle in a haystack. We plug in words into the algorithms the NSA has, and it spits out the data. We just need to know what to look for."

"And?"

"Well, the Russians have been here longer than we realized.

They had their eye on you, too. They like to fuck up things where they can. They wanted to help pave the way for Braverman to become governor, and they saw your guy, Campagna, as a potential rival down the road. So, they thought they could maybe take him out, and you in one swoop. They've always suspected your father-in-law is part of the Company, and going after you, his golden boy, was a bonus. Of course, you gave them plenty of ammunition. What were you thinking, going home with your candidate's niece?"

"Never thought it would end up in the *Providence Journal*, or that some Russian fucker would leak it, that's for sure."

"I'm sure you got this handled. There's something else you should know."

"There's more?"

"Antipov, he was the one who got your girl the drugs she over-dosed on."

"What?"

"Well, maybe not him exactly, but one of his people. They work with the Chinese to spike our drug supplies."

"Jesus."

"Yup, fun world out there. That's why we want to move your plan up. Need to go operational." Dex was hoping the revelation would motivate Henry.

"We're not ready. We're still setting the whole thing up."

"I've gotten the green light on this from the higher ups. This has gone beyond The Sinclair Group. We're fully backed. Your team will have the full cooperation from both the Prague and St. Petersburg CIA sections. This is the big time now."

"I'm not sure I can do this."

"You were made for this, just like Sinclair and me. In fact, he's on his way back on the plane you sent back to NC. He and his wife are going to stay with his daughters while you head back to Prague."

"You've got my life planned out," Henry said.

"You're one of us now, Henry. Welcome to the club."

***

Before Henry could put their plan in motion, he needed to confront Beako again. It was one of those conversations best had over scotch and cigars, and Prague had plenty of places for men like them to escape. Dex and Sinclair had done their part to help set up Beako's company in Miami. He had a full staff, and one of the Key Biscayne projects Henry was working with Sinclair had been taken over by Beako's Bluestar Enterprises, the hottest new development company to invade South Florida from the Northeast.

Henry saw Beako in the corner of the cigar bar Constantinople, which was off a side street in Prague's old town square. Beako was already lit up with a Davidoff Churchill cigar and sipping an 18-year-old scotch.

"You fit in well, here, Beako," Henry started.

"Don't worry, Henry, I know who resurrected my life," Beako acknowledged.

"Speaking of which, did Kat Paul from the *Providence Journal* get a hold of you?"

"Oh yeah, I called her back from the center of old town."

"And?"

"She asked me if you were working with us on the Prescott race. I told her she was reading too many Dan Brown novels, and there was no conspiracy here. She then asked me about the buyout, and of course I told her I had a confidentiality agreement that prevented me from discussing."

"Is that all?" Henry pressed.

"She's got nothing, Henry. She was fishing and I closed her

down. You don't need to worry about this anymore; it's over."

"Well, I paid a steep price for it," Henry admitted.

"Campagna cut you loose?" Beako asked. He already knew. It had circulated Providence's political circle and had already gotten to him.

"Yeah, that might actually be a good thing, because what we have to do is going to take 100 percent of my attention," Henry confided.

"Why? What's up?"

"How quickly can you be up and running?"

"I mean the company's set up. Your guys have built our legacy, we look pretty legit as far as how we look online and in person. I mean the office back in Miami is sweet. Hope I can actually work there someday. We've got a great portfolio of projects. Plus, my contacts in the Lombardo family came through for us. They've set me up with their Russian guys they've worked with before in St. Petersburg. And they'll vouch for me. Of course, the Russian mob has to have their beak wet too, so they'll be part of the development we're proposing."

"You did alright, Beako."

"Not my first rodeo, Henry. These guys are all the same and sure, they speak Russian, but we all speak the same language."

"Money."

"Yeah."

"And Jana, you good working with her?" Henry pressed, like a head coach making sure his offensive coordinator still had the game plan for their star running back to run the routes.

"She's a pro, can't wait to see her in action."

"When can you be in St. Petersburg?"

"When do you need us there?"

"Yesterday," Henry told him.

"Not much time, boss. Could really use a few more weeks here," Beako admitted.

"This operation has been prioritized at the highest levels, and we got the green light. We gotta move fast. And, of course, there's more on the other side if you pull this off."

"How much more?"

"We don't know exactly how much they have. If our girl is as good as we suspect she is, there's a huge windfall we're going to fall into. And it's ours, all of ours," Henry told him, knowing what really motivated Beako.

"You sure she's that good? I mean, what do we really know about her, anyways?"

"Danny says she's the best he's ever seen, and he worked for Silberman, remember. So, he knows talent. Plus, we got the guy who orchestrated everything in Providence on our team. He's key to help-ing us unravel everything."

"You trust her?"

"I don't trust any of you," Henry fired back.

"Oh Henry we've come so far from Providence, and now we're back in the same place," Beako reminded him.

"Yeah, we're playing for the good guys."

"Are you sure about that?"

"Never been more sure of it, Beako."

"I mean, Henry, we're not messing around in local politics any-more, this is the big time."

"Trust me, Beako, I don't have this virginal belief anymore about right and wrong. Let's say my old righteousness has been challenged. Remember what Churchill said?"

"I believe he said something to the effect that democracy is the worst form of government."

"Except for all others that have been tried," Henry finished the quote.

"So, are we Churchillian actors then, Henry?"

"He was half American, remember, his mother's side," Henry recalled, remembering his World War II political class at Boston College.

"Time to dismantle the iron curtain that the Russians want to put back."

"And help our Russian friends break free from under the curtain that's held them back for the past twenty years."

"Only twenty?"

"More like two hundred."

"Time to give them a little more of our best export—democracy," Henry proudly ended the conversation.

37

Beako and Jana flew first class from Prague to St. Petersburg on an Aeroflot jet. While Beako had never traveled before to Peter the Great's "Window on the West," Jana was returning to St. Petersburg for the first time since she was a little girl. It was grander than she had remembered. Her hometown of Vilnius, Lithuania, was considered more "Western" than even Peter's great compensation. The St. Petersburg of today was experiencing its own Renaissance, and Beako and his assistant, Jana, were just two more carpetbaggers from the West looking to capitalize.

They met their contact Sasha Dawiskiba at St. Petersburg's new Capital Grille, which was a source of pride to the Russian mobster who had worked with contacts in the States to bring the high-end steak house to his city. Prior to his journey to Russia via Czechia Beako had met with members of the Dawiskiba crime family in Miami, where they had several penthouses atop Miami's expanding cityscape. He had passed their sniff test, thanks in part to the extensive backstory Dex's people had written for him. It was made even more believable by Beako's development experience.

Upon their arrival the maître d' escorted them to the private room in the back of the restaurant. Their host stood as they walked in, and the former Russian special forces types who flanked his side scanned the guests for possible threats.

"Mr. Beako, welcome," Dawiskiba said in English. "And who is this lovely lady?"

"It's great to meet you in person, Mr. Dawiskiba. This is my administrative assistant, Jana Strakova."

"Удовольствие," Jana said in Russian, offering her hand, which the Russian gladly took and kissed.

"The pleasure is mine," he said to her in English. "Your Russian, is that a Lithuanian accent?" he asked.

"Yes, my family is from Vilnius. I live in Prague now. I help Mr. Beako with his Czech and Russian business ventures."

"He is indeed a lucky man," the Russian graciously said and offered Beako and Jana glasses of wine. "It's a 2010 Opus One. I wanted you to have a taste of home."

"That's very considerate of you, Mr. Dawiskiba. We appreciate your hospitality, and I hope you can join me in Miami when you're in town next."

"Unfortunately, I won't be in Miami anytime soon. Your county has denied me a visa even though we own half of Miami Beach."

"Well, hopefully this is the beginning of a thawing of relations," Beako said, offering a toast.

"Yes, it takes businessmen like us, Mr. Beako, to remind our governments what is truly important."

"Yes, business," Beako quickly retorted. They were now speaking his language. After three bottles of Opus and then glasses of Cognac, Beako knew the second phase of this operation was ready for execution. The Russian ordered another round of drinks. Beako saw this as his chance. He asked the Russian if he could take a rain check for their night cap, clearly seeing the Russian had his eyes on Jana.

"You Americans don't have the Russian gene to handle your liquor," Dawiskiba said with a slur to his words.

"I'm not Russian," Jana reminded him, demonstrating to the Russian that she was a strong woman, something she sensed he desired.

"Yes, you're Lithuanian. Same thing," he told her.

"Not the same, we're our own people," she did not hold back.

"No politics tonight, Miss Jana. Let's just have fun."

"I'll toast to that. More Cognac?"

"Anything you want, I own the place," he boasted.

"How about some Absinthe?" she asked.

"I like where this is heading."

Beako took his cue from Jana and made a pleasant goodbye, which Dawiskiba was more than happy to oblige. He had grander thoughts on his mind beyond a new hotel with the American. And if Jana did her job like he fully expected she would, he had more preparation to make, in research and in rest. Both Beako and Jana were living their roles which made selling the scheme even more believable. They were not going up against unsuspecting capitalistic neophytes but highly skilled kleptocrats who were indistinguishable from common thugs and opportunistic bureaucrats.

As Beako departed in his black car back to his hotel he had no doubt that Jana would fully execute her part. Success would be a meeting with the mayor of St. Petersburg, and the plan would be that both Beako and Jana would be bumped up the food chain. Corrupt business opportunities and equally easy women were shared among the ruling class no differently than they had been experienced in St. Petersburg by the czars hundreds of years ago. Some things never changed in Russia unless someone forced them. That was the goal.

To fully unravel the local web of corruption in St. Petersburg, the special operations group had the best on their team. Terry Silberman may have been fresh off his stint from Danbury Federal Penitentiary, but he was only a few years away from running the biggest corruption scheme in the United States. Silberman had thrown himself into his new task, which gave him a new purpose he had not had since he was in the Providence mayor's office where he was helping fill decrepit factory buildings with new housing or building new science labs in the city's old jewelry district. He found his Russian comrades to be no different than his Providence brethren. They were both motivated by the same thing. Greed transformed men from patriots to scoundrels. Now Silberman was playing for the good guys, or so he told himself.

Silberman pored over the documents that Dex's people had provided. The St. Petersburg corruption shared similar spider legs to Providence, and this inside player understood how it operated and could be unraveled. Just like in his hometown there were some powerful interests that controlled crime and commerce in the city. The mayor may have acted like he was the tip of the spear, but he was propped up by powerful interests who reported directly to the top in Moscow. As the traditional seat of power in imperialist Russia, St. Petersburg held a special place in the heart of the current Russian autocrat. This made the message sent from Washington via Langley that much more satiable. While Silberman fully suspected he was a pawn to the kings in their power games, he gave himself willingly to the game, no differently than his other teammates on the ground in St. Petersburg. Though each had their own reasons, Beako, Jana, and Silberman all sought the same redemption.

***

Although the mayor's office in St. Petersburg was clearly a window dressing for democracy, it certainly had all the trappings of power. The Russians historically knew how to project power and influence. The office itself was decorated more like the State Hermitage Museum fifteen minutes away. A man like Beako had always remained close to the seats of power, but even he was impressed, which was exactly the intention. Jana, however, had been around enough powerful men to understand that this charade was a show put on by men for men. She was there to serve as the primary distraction and honey pot. Even though the Russians perfected this tactic, even the most Orthodox could not resist her temptation. And the mayor of St. Petersburg was no high priest.

"Welcome to St. Petersburg, Mr. Beako," the middle-aged interpreter echoed the words of his boss, who graciously rose from his local throne as Beako and Jana were ushered into his chamber.

"We thank you for seeing us," Jana repeated Beako's words in Russian, her accented Lithuanian evident to the Russian speakers in the room. They took their seats on the couch offered to them, and Beako knew it was no coincidence that the setting had a striking resemblance to the Oval Office portrayed in so many movies.

"What can we do for you, Mr. Beako?" the mayor asked, switching to English and dismissing his interpreter.

"I wanted you to have a taste of America. It's our finest bourbon, Pappy Van Winkle," he told him, both men knowing that there was more than just a $2,000 bottle of bourbon in the package. The $100,000 of Sinclair's cash was just an entry fee for the lucrative opportunity they all sought.

"You've met my good friend, Sasha. He's coming over for a party at my house tonight. You can speak directly to him about our business. He is St. Petersburg's top developer, and you and he will be great partners."

"Yes, thank you, Mr. Mayor. I've worked with his associates in Miami, and we've done beautiful work together. We're looking forward to developing world class buildings that will add to the great landscape of your beautiful city."

"I hope you will join us too," the Mayor said to Jana, returning to his native tongue.

"I would like that," Jana replied in Russian.

"My home housed the czars. It hasn't seen such beauty since the Mystic Marriage of St. Catherine was lent to my home from l'Hermitage."

"Your wife has excellent taste," Jana said, returning to English.

"Exquisite taste," he replied in English, then returned to Russian. "Unfortunately, she is in Moscow seeing her mother, and won't be able to join us," he added.

Their mission completed, Jana and Beako were escorted out of the office. As they walked out of the ornate structure, Beako turned to Jana and asked, "So he bought it?"

"Yes, he did. Don't care if you're a Bratva or politician, you're all the same."

"Not all of us," Beako countered.

"Sure."

"Are you OK going to the mayor's house this evening?"

"Me? Not sure *you* can handle it," she shot back.

"I've partied with these guys in Providence and Miami. It won't be anything I haven't seen."

"You're in Russia, and you haven't seen debauchery like this."

***

And Jana was right again. It was like nothing Beako had experienced. While there were beautiful women from all across Eastern

Europe and the Russian Republic to entertain the St. Petersburg elite, Jana's sharp intellect helped her stand higher. The beluga caviar was scooped out like salsa at a Super Bowl party, and bottles of Dom Perignon were tossed back like Bud Lights. For Beako, it was nothing like he had even seen, and he was no stranger to the party scene from Providence to Miami. The strip clubs in Providence and the Miami bars where anything went did not hold a flame to St. Petersburg.

Jana, on the other hand, was right at home, though home was what she had fled. Her hometown of Vilnius had none of the trappings of America or Russia, which meant little excitement for an extrovert like her. It was what had driven her to Prague, a pleasureparadise in the Bohemian heartland. Even for Jana, who had taken in what German industrialists and Italian capitalists offered, this event went beyond the pale. At twenty-five, Jana was an old babushka compared to the other women, many barely eighteen. The men represented the St. Petersburg establishment, a cohort of mobsters, businessmen, politicians, and military men, all mixed together for the mayhem. The fifty-year-old Beako blended right in, and to keep his cover he indulged in the forbidden fruit. At least that's how he justified it.

Jana was on a mission. While that included giving herself to both Dawiskiba and the mayor, at least at different times during the mission, this night was dedicated to help dismantle Peter the Great's imperialist legacy. Exquisitely dressed in a tight backless dress that was fitted like a body suit, she was the belle of the ball. The one carat sapphire that adorned her neck made her even more alluring to the mayor. She had already selected her accomplice, whom she swore to herself she would send back to her hometown of Yaroslav with enough cash to help lift her family out of poverty. Just like Jana, she would have to sacrifice her sensibilities for a greater good.

As cocaine dusted the room, the men were jolted into action, and the higher members of the pecking order found their way to one of the seven bedrooms in the sprawling dacha in the St. Petersburg countryside. The underclass of the elites resorted to any space, and a wild orgy erupted with the men thinking they were Romans again. Jana and her willing accomplice followed the mayor to his chambers. The room was well appointed by a woman's touch. He at least had the decency to move the pictures of his children from the nightstand before his guests arrived. He wasn't an animal. Jana gave him what he wanted for an evening, a respite from the stress of running Russia's second largest enterprise and the equal challenges of domestic life.

The mayor's fantasy was not the only thing Jana captured. She had their threesome all on tape, thanks to the 4k camera and microphone in her sapphire necklace, courtesy of new American technology delivered to her in Prague. Jana and her young accomplice indulged the mayor in all his fantasies, with the youngest of the three taking a dominant position over the mayor. While the Russian people may have turned a blind eye to another Russian politician with young women, his wife would not stand idly by as he polluted their home. An heiress herself, her family traced its lineage to the Imperial Russian Court, and she did not look fondly on her family home's desecration.

***

Pictures of his night of debauchery were emailed to the mayor's wife directly from an anonymous source, and hell hath no fury as this woman scorned. Without her backing, and more importantly her money, he was just another loudmouth politician with little substance. He came home to their dacha to see his clothes and personal possessions burning as part of his own funeral pyre. She was nowhere to be found, her clothes and personal affects gone with her, and a picture from the night hammered into his study door. Just like in the picture, he was truly fucked now.

His problems only magnified in the following days. Jana had rummaged through his computer, stolen his passwords, and had imported a virus into the system. While the mayor had been passed out from the special cocktail she had mixed for him, she had been able to install a special software application from the Americans that scanned his computer for bank accounts. Her stunning looks masked her sharp intellect, and she was able to dupe another unsuspecting criminal who had fallen victim to her seduction. He and his patrons had just been cut off, their bank accounts discovered and frozen.

As much as his wife could break his will, the other injured parties could rip out his heart. He had managed to freeze out the St. Petersburg syndicate of the Russian Mafia from their racketeering business. From requisitioning military supplies for the local police to selling medicine meant for Russian seniors on the black market, all the proceeds from their laundering and extortion enterprise were as frozen as a Siberian winter. Only his blood would assuage the ravenous criminal consortium.

He had literally minutes to decide his future. The moment they discovered their accounts were inaccessible, they would come for him at his office and then to his dacha. And any explanation would be sought after the fact. They would kill him first, and then look to find out what may have happened, who was involved, and if they were further compromised.

After the choices he made, the only option left for this mayor was the Americans.

38

Braverman and Turgenev connected instantly, sharing a common brotherly bond, while Henry served as their pragmatic counselor. They met daily at the 3,000 square foot apartment that The Sinclair Group had rented in the center of Prague. The United States had successfully broken things, like Afghanistan and Iraq. Putting states back together into functioning governments and societies took a different skill set than simply the blunt instrument that was all too often used. And this was Russia with the world's largest cache of nuclear weapons. Even if the majority of their weapons probably did not work, they still had enough to destroy the world many times over. This reality had not gone unnoticed by Henry and his team. They were not playing local politics anymore, though their mission would involve winning another local race.

Nuclear deterrence was one of the many topics Charlie and Yuri discussed over shots of vodka. They shared a Slavic heritage as well as a strong desire to change their current predicament.

"If the Ukrainians hadn't given up our nukes in '91 we wouldn't be here," Charlie reminded Yuri.

"If they hadn't dismantled their nukes, the reactionaries in Moscow may have succeeded and who knows what they would have done. Yeltsin could have been arrested instead of becoming president. We may not be here today," Yuri adamantly argued.

"True, we could have taken a different course in history. Lesson learned, and then taught again by Ukraine and Libya. Nukes prevent invasion."

"Yeah, I guess the North Koreans and Iranians took heed."

"North Koreans and Iranians, what are you boys talking about?" Henry asked upon walking into the room. "With you too, honestly, I'd rather hear you talking about football and women," Henry joked, knowing his new pals were a different breed.

"I think we're ready," Braverman announced.

"I think I need more time," Turgenev confided in his fellow compatriots.

"We unfortunately don't have the luxury of time anymore," Henry explained. "This has been carefully choreographed. They're burning cars and buses in the streets of St. Petersburg. They need something, and someone, to look toward. They need hope, and you're their man, Yuri."

"I don't know, Henry. I'm just Yuri from the Urals."

"I'm a boy from Beantown, and Charlie here is a kid from Kiev. None of us were born into these roles. You're their white knight, the Siberian candidate."

"I'm not sure what that means," Yuri admitted.

As a fellow academic, Charlie answered first. "You're the outsider they need. Throughout history the change agent has come from outside. You're from the Russian heartland. Not an elite, not part of the corrupt power structure of St. Petersburg. You could be the spark of something bigger. Change takes time, and we need to be patient."

"Charlie's right. It's no different than in the US. It's why our own former imposter president was able to get elected. People were fed up with the liberal elites on each coast, and even though he was from New York, he spoke the language of regular people. Yuri, you can compete in any arena, at any venue. You can speak to the intellectual class in Russia and at the same time serve as the beacon to people on the streets. You're the kid they want their own children to become, someone who works hard, rises up, someone who deserves to be in charge, who has earned their trust."

"What do you Americans say, 'you can sell ice to an Eskimo,'? Why should I trust you, Mr. Mercucio? You're CIA," Yuri tested him.

Charlie stepped back into the conversation. "Henry's one of us, Yuri. He's self-made, 100%. He's come up, just like you and me. Do we have some powerful people behind us? Yeah, we do. Henry and I, we're in this with you, for the long haul."

"You're somewhat right. Do I have ties to the Company? I do. I'm my own man, just like you, just like Charlie. We've been handed this opportunity, it's now what we do with it that really matters. Consider us a triumvirate; we're all in this together."

***

All the records Yuri Turgenev had, from documents signed by Russian judges to bank transfers totaling $10 billion, were released online, and the Russians could not shut down the Internet. St. Petersburg had not seen such a barrage since the Germans shelled the city 80 years before. The Russian people witnessed the true nature of their government officials and the oligarchs and elites who backed them. This brought out thousands to the streets, not witnessed by the city since the first days of the Ukrainian War. While the police had suppressed the outrage over killing thousands of their fellow Slavs before, they were having difficulty containing the college students, factory workers, and Russian mothers who all came out together to protest Russian injustice and corruption. And then the next salvo hit the city.

The video first circulated through social media feeds, and an elite unit of the CIA made sure cell and WIFI service went unfettered. St. Petersburg was free to witness their mayor with a clearly underage girl defiling him. The mayor was nowhere to be found, having abandoned his post for a sanctuary from a wrath greater than his wife's. Both the mayor's and Sasha Dawiskiba's accounts had been hacked and looted, leveling a devastating blow to the Russian Mafia in the city.

Dex's special operation brought St. Petersburg to its knees. Silberman, Beako, and Jana had executed flawlessly, and their service to the state would be well compensated. The $20 million Jana helped steal earned her and Beako a five percent commission. Another million dollars each on top of what Sinclair was paying was a good pay day, and they would not have to look over their shoulders. The Mayor looked like the fall guy, and the Russians didn't even know about Beako or Jana, who made out quite alright. Not the mayor of St. Petersburg though, he was pegged as the poster boy for depravity.

For Silberman's first part of the operation, he earned a cool million dollars. His work was not complete, and he had an additional chance to earn even more than he had originally swindled from the Providence taxpayers. The second phase of the operation was now underway. The Foreign Intelligence Service of the Republic of Estonia, once a vassal state of the Russian empire, was more than happy to aid their fellow NATO intelligence service to smuggle Beako, Jana, and the mayor of St. Petersburg out of Russia. That was followed by Yuri Turgenev and his wife being ushered back into St. Petersburg.

Another artillery wave hit the city in the form of a two and a half

minute video that higher authorities assured saw the light of day. Yuri
was with his wife, Alana, together with their newborn son. It was perfectly choreographed from a studio in Prague, and amateur shots of
the protests appeared in the background of the video. With the use of
the green screen, the video was powerful enough with footage of
Molotov cocktails being tossed and mothers, students, and workers
united. However, it still had an amateur feel, which ensured it looked
home-grown, not foreign produced.

Yuri delivered the message he had always wanted to tell his
countrymen:

"My family and I have returned to Russia at our own peril to
fight for something larger than ourselves. Our mayor has fled, not
only with personal disgrace but with your money. Funds that were
supposed to pay for roads, bridges, schools, and our seniors went to
line the pockets of the oligarchs and elites, not for you, the hardworking people of Russia. We have stood too long idly by while our country's great resources are pillaged by a few at the expense of the many.
Look at how they have used your money," he said, as the video cut
to shots taken from Jana's necklace that featured many identifiable
members of the St. Petersburg hierarchy in compromising positions.

He was not finished, continuing his impassioned plea: "When
will we stand up, open our blind eyes to the light, and take back our
city? We need to break free from the shackles of victimhood and
reclaim our lives."

"My son, Peter, will grow up in a country where there is opportunity for all, not for only the strongest and most corrupt. That's why
I am announcing my candidacy for mayor of St. Petersburg," he
stated, making a direct shot at the leadership in Moscow.

His populist tones had been added by Charlie Braverman, and
his delivery was coached by Henry. They all understood that for this
war to be won, Turgenev needed to insulate himself. He had to create

such outrage that not even the new czar in Moscow dared take him out because of the insurrection that would follow. The storming of the Winter Palace in 1917 was part of the Russian people's collective anger.

While Yuri was consumed by the unfolding events and his new role in Russian history, his wife, Alana, was focused on matters at home. She was not convinced that coming to St. Petersburg with their infant son was the best move for their family. She was concerned less with what happened on the streets of St. Petersburg and Moscow, than what happened in her own kitchen and living room. She cared first about nourishing her son's future. Prague was better suited for her family, and she too was a Russian patriot. There were other Russian sons and daughters who did not have the same advantages she was raised with, and she above all else believed her husband could in fact help deliver substantive change. At the same time, she was not going to let Yuri know that, considering the upheaval he had caused in their lives.

"I hope you know what you're doing," Alana said to her husband.

"I'm going with my instincts," Yuri told her.

"And that's what concerns me," she admitted, not the first wife to question her husband's fanciful dreams.

"And don't tell me you're doing this for our son, for our family. You're doing this for you."

"Alana, I am doing this for us. You and Peter are my world. And I would give my life for you to have a better country to live in."

"And that's what concerns me, my mayor-to-be."

"I have to do this, Alana."

"I know you do, but we need you first. Peter needs a father, and I need a husband. Not a martyr. Your son needs a dad to show him how to play football and hockey, to read Pushkin and Dostoevsky, to understand Karl Marx and Adam Smith. He'd rather have a father than a martyr."

"I want to be both, not a hero but a leader and a father. Why can't I?"

"You can, I believe in you. I'm afraid for our family," she said what she felt.

"What do you want me to do, Alana?"

She waited before she answered. She looked straight into her husband's watery eyes. "I want you to be you."

"Then why didn't you just tell me that from the beginning?" Yuri asked her.

"Because I'm scared for us, for our son. You're not just a local annoyance anymore. I'm worried how they're going to come at us now. It's not just your writing anymore, or your articles that expose their corruption. You're now a full-blown revolutionary."

"Do you trust me?" Yuri asked his wife.

"Trust you?"

"Yes, do you trust me? Do you believe in me?" he persisted.

"What is this? Of course I trust you, and yes, I believe in you."

"Then why are you saying this to me?"

"It's them I don't trust."

"Who's that?" Yuri asked.

"Your CIA overlords."

"I'm my own man; they're not pulling my strings, if that's what you mean," Yuri insisted. "Charlie and I are friends. Haven't had one like him since I was a boy."

"That's exactly how they get you, act like they're your friend. They're spies."

"Charlie's not a spy, he's a kid like me. He grew up in New York. His family is from Kiev. His parents were born there. His father fought for us. I mean not us, the Soviets," Yuri corrected himself.

"I don't trust them, especially that Henry guy," Alana added, changing her tact.

"He's a businessman."

"Is that what they call it?" She continued to question.

"Honestly, I'd like to bring more men like Henry and Charlie to St. Petersburg. Look, I'm not naïve. I know who they are. And I know I'm being played. We all want similar things. They want a free Russia just like us. A free Russia is less antagonistic toward them and the rest of Europe."

"They're in it for the money," Alana continued to argue.

"And so what if they are? Maybe they are out to make some bucks. I don't think so. I think it's about more than that."

"OK, my love," she conceded the fight. She had had enough and now seen enough from her husband. He was still in it for the right reasons, and she was completely behind him. She just needed to remind him that while he was his own man, she still provided oversight.

39

It was time for Henry to go home. Danny accompanied him back to Providence in Sinclair's Citation jet. Eight hours in flight gave Danny enough time to catch up with Henry before he departed for a two-week stint. Dex had arranged for him to visit the Farm, the CIA's clandestine training facility. Henry was quickly rising up the ranks, and they needed someone he trusted around him to ensure his protection.

"So, you're coming over for dinner?" Henry asked him, looking up from his tablet.

"Yeah, I'm coming. This is not a setup, right?" he asked as he handed Henry a scotch and then also poured himself one.

"No, not a setup, just dinner. My wife loves making her home-made pasta. She's gotten really good at it. Her sister is still with us, and I need a wingman while they reminisce about their privileged childhood."

"Hey, did you see this?" Danny asked him, handing over his phone. Like so many, he had been scrolling through his phone while talking to his friend.

"What is it?"

"Looks like Campagna's facing a shit storm."

Henry looked at the headline, scanned the story and then went to another local news website. It was the lead story across all Rhode Island media. The hospitality workers had walked out of Providence's restaurants and hotels, bringing the city to its knees.

"Holy shit."

"Not your problem anymore, boss," Danny reminded him.

"Wrong, it's all our problem. And how is it all of a sudden, in the middle of the campaign, they decide to walk out? No, there's something, or someone, behind this," Henry thought aloud.

"You think it's our friend?" Danny asked.

"Doesn't matter who it is right now. We'll deal with that later. Right now, we have to help Campagna or the whole state is screwed."

As soon as they landed, Henry's phone lit up with all the missed calls. Lyndsay, McNally, and Campagna all had left messages. Having evolved as a husband, he called Lyndsay back first and told her he would not be late. He assured her that he was still bringing Danny to dinner.

Then he called Campagna. "I didn't think we were talking," Henry started.

"It's not like that, Henry. Even though I'm the mayor and may be governor, if you prick me do I not bleed?"

"Quoting Shylock now?"

"Yeah, I thought I'd speak your language. So let me ask you, what would you have done if you were me?"

"I would have fired my ass."

"And if you got jammed up, who would you call?" the mayor asked.

"OK, so how can I help," Henry offered.

"There's been a mass walk out. They did it on Saturday night, half of them just walked out. Waitresses, bartenders, even the cooks leaving food on the stove. Sure, a few stayed there, not wanting to lose their jobs. They have families to feed themselves. And the front desk staff at the hotels too, just got up and left, and of course didn't tell anyone, so I had to send police officers just to make sure the hotels stayed open. Imagine walking in to check into your hotel after driving all night and a Providence police officer greets you? A great look for the city. It was total chaos. Then Sunday comes and an army of restaurant workers march down Federal Hill into the city. They're joined by the hotel workers who pour out onto the streets, and they all congregate in Kennedy Plaza demanding a $25 minimum wage, health insurance, and student loan forgiveness."

"Is it just in Providence?" Henry asked.

"For now, but we're hearing they're going to Newport next. Middle of the summer in Newport, do you know what that would do?"

"I intentionally avoid Newport in the summer for the crowds. I can't imagine the hit these local businesses would take if there's no one to work," Henry said.

"I've been good to the local union. We've been talking, and they know there's no real possibility of that minimum wage. Plus, so many of their people make way more than that. There are waiters and bartenders in this city making six figures," Campagna said.

"It doesn't make sense. There's got to be someone behind this. I know the chairman of the Hospitality Association. Let me start with him and see what he knows."

"Just so you know, he's got his own problems. I heard they're going to walk out of the casino, so you better catch him now," Campagna told him.

Henry called Carlo Russo, the general manager of Rhode Island's only casino. They had served on a local board together and had become friends over the years, sharing a love for Porsches and storytelling.

"Henry, what's going on? I heard you were in Prague trying to help the Bruins sign the next Czech star," Carlo joked. They also shared a love for hockey, especially the Boston Bruins.

"I heard with what you're up against you're going to need another set of my center ice tickets at the Garden," Henry offered.

"Never seen this. I'm doing everything I can to stop our guys from leaving. They're getting so much pressure to walk. I set up a buffet for them, and I'm about to start handing out c-notes to keep them from walking. I could really use you up here, Henry. I know it's slumming it for you with all your world travel and deals. We could really use your talents. How about one more time, for old times' sake?"

"As much as I'd love to get into a sparring match, I now report to a higher authority," Henry told him.

"Your wife."

"My very pregnant wife. I'll come up first thing in the morning and help you sort this stuff out. You can count on me."

"Always have, Henry."

"So, tell me, Carlo, who do you think is behind this? It seems way too organized, even for our friends in the Locals."

"I agree, Henry. They're using social media, and it's spreading like the Arab Spring. All kinds of fake stories out there. People just make shit up and half of it isn't even from Rhode Island. They used a photo from a restaurant in Iceland for fuck's sake."

"There's someone stirring this shit, and they want Campagna to look bad, like it's his fault, like he didn't take care of the city workers and then it spread throughout the state. And at the same time, they want to attack one of our most important economic sectors. It's way more than minimum wage anymore. This is economic sabotage."

"We're all fucked if we don't fix this," Carlo told Henry.

"Alright, give me until tomorrow and let me think this through. We'll come up with something."

"That's what I needed to hear. I'll tell my guys the great Henry is on the job and that will settle them down. I'm serious, buddy, I just say your name, and it calms people down."

"OK, let me take care of business at home first. After being out of the country for a week, if I don't see my bride you may have to put me up in your hotel."

"Go take care of your family, Henry. I'll see you tomorrow."

Fortunately for Henry, Danny had already gotten their luggage to their driver, Rick, who had met them on the tarmac.

"Where are we going, boss?" Rick asked.

"Home, please."

Henry was not in the car for more than three minutes before his phone buzzed again. This time it was McNally, and Henry figured the call would not last longer than the ride home.

"You hear about this shit?" McNally started before Henry even greeted him.

"Yeah, I go away for a week and the whole place falls apart. I'm heading home now. Need to see Lyndsay, then I'm meeting with Carlo in the morning. Do you know anything?" Henry asked.

"It's not our guys behind it. The Casino Union was caught off guard too. They got hacked and emails and social posts went out under their name. They swear they did not organize this, and I believe them. You and I both know who the only one who could do this, his parting shot at us from Siberia or wherever he's holed up," McNally figured.

"Well, the genie is out of the proverbial bottle now, and now we have to put it back in. We got to get everyone back together—the unions, Hospitality Association, Chamber Coalition. Can you organize it, let Campagna take the credit? It will make him look like a governor, bringing all sides together."

"Yeah, I can do that, and I'm gonna drop a bomb tomorrow. We need to take the attention off of this."

"Congressman, what are you going to do?" Henry asked and pleaded at the same time, sounding like a parent using a child's full name.

"Nothing you need to know about, Henry," McNally told him.

Henry got the reprieve he needed with Lyndsay, who even in her uncomfortable state was still working as a chief resident at the Hasbro Children's Hospital and as the primary consoler to her second sister, Bridgit, whose short-lived marriage had been annulled. In addition to the homemade pasta and sauce, Danny was served as the primary distraction for the evening. What had been billed as Henry's home reunion after a week abroad was also a chance for a loving older sister to signal that there were many fish for catching off the Rhode Island shores. And Danny did not disappoint. His enigmatic personality and Irish charm were just what Bridgit needed. If anything, Henry wanted him to tone it down a bit as he watched how Brigit was beginning to swoon over him. It's all Henry needed right now. His wife's glare at him told him to stay out of it. A wise man, Henry did just that.

Henry crashed at 9 p.m., a bit of jet lag and mental exhaustion. Wide awake at 3 a.m., he checked his phone first. It was another busy news day in Rhode Island, and this time the tables had turned. The online news source, *GoLocal*, had the story first, and Henry figured all the newsrooms at the *Providence Journal* and local broadcast stations were scrambling right now to cover their own angles.

Chad Stevens' mug, along with the head of the Gaspee Militia, was plastered on every screen by morning. The dark, grainy video made the scene appear even darker and the audio clip that accompanied the imagery much more sinister.

"Welcome to politics in Rhode Island, Mr. Stevens," Henry thought to himself. He would sort out the fallout from this bombshell. First, he needed to prepare for his meeting at the casino. He knew his buddy Carlo would pull out all the stops and that McNally would come through by delivering his guys.

The meeting was at 8 a.m. in the high rollers room at the casino. As expected, Carlo came through. He put out a spectacular spread, a complete buffet with eggs and issues.

McNally started, and did his best Marlon Brando, "How did we let it get this far?" It was the right line for the audience and broke the ice. He introduced Mayor Campagna and gave him the microphone. McNally by now knew when to exit off stage right.

"I've worked with many of you ladies and gentlemen before. I'm here to get our people back to work. Tell me what we need to do; I'm listening," Campagna offered.

It was a far cry from having a deal dictated to them. Recognizing that, the local union president spoke first. His name was John Bouchard, a son of a French-Canadian carpenter, who had served six terms in the State Senate and graduated up the union food chain. As the president of the Casino Union, he had already cut his deal with Carlo Russo, earning his guys five extra paid holidays and a five percent across-the-board raise. The casino could afford it, and their shutdown was averted. Part of the deal also was that he would step up in an effort to get the other unions to fall in line.

"You know me," Bouchard said, looking directly at the heads of the other two unions in the room with him. "I tell it like it is."

"You've always been a straight shooter, Johnny," one of the other union heads acknowledged in front of everyone, which now numbered a dozen in the room.

"This is fucking insanity," Johnny did not hold back. "Get your people back to work. There's mouths to feed for fuck's sake."

Campagna took his cue and spoke up. "The city will work with you. I've already talked to both the city council president and the chair of the finance committee. We're going to use some ARPA funds to get your guys and girls a thousand-dollar bonus."

"That's chump change; you've got millions," the other union steward spoke up.

"The mayor's going out on a limb using those funds for these bonuses. It's federal money, and it's supposed to be used for long term infrastructure," McNally explained. He still had considerable influence in this room.

"It's not all we're giving you," Campagna said, regaining control. "I'm going to put in legislation in the city council for paid sick time. If your people miss a shift, they make $25 per hour for an 8-hour shift. We're also using the ARPA funds for this."

"That's great and all, but what happens when the ARPA funds run out? The Feds aren't bailing us out forever," the union steward reminded everyone.

"It will give us some time to all sit down together and work out something that's fair to everyone," Campagna argued. Look, I'm with you. I worked as a dishwasher, then busboy, waiter, made it all the way to barback. I never got to be a bartender. My wife thinks I am when I make her margaritas. I've got to squeeze fresh limes for her. Won't drink it any other way, so I feel your pain, I get it."

This earned a polite laugh by the male-dominated audience and a courtesy smile from the two women in the room. Until one of them decided to make her voice heard.

"As the group that owns half the property that the restaurants sit on, and several of the restaurants themselves, I have a few things we'd like to add," said Jenna Lombardo. Standing under five feet tall, her stunning auburn hair prevented her from being overlooked.

And she did not hold back. "What's next, paid paternity leave? What da' ya' wanna be, Italy or Greece? Their economies aren't exactly role models."

"Thank you, Ms. Lombardo, for that interesting take," Carlo jumped in to show solidarity with the Hospitality Association's biggest member after the casino.

"You know how this works, don't you? We give into them now, and what's next? We can't reward this type of extortion."

"Sorry Ms. Lombardo, we don't break legs anymore," Bouchard fired back, a subtle reference to her family's ties to organized crime from a bygone era. While Jenna's father had been the head of the Lombardo crime family, he had insisted that his exceptional student attend Dartmouth and pursue an MBA at Harvard. She one-upped her father and added a JD in with her MBA. Her wit was only matched by her superior intellect.

"She's real subtle," McNally said under his breath to Henry. "That's why they call her the *red fury*."

"You guys," she said, starting to walk out of the room. She turned back and fired a salvo at those standing in her way. "You do this, and you set a dangerous precedent. They will want more. The only reason I'm here is because of Campagna." She turned toward McNally, "And you, my father backed you all those years. You can't call your union boys back?"

"I wish I could, Jenna. It's out of my hands. It's not like the old days when we could control them. It's new leadership, and they don't respect the old ways your dad and I did things." He left out the part that their strings were being pulled by a dangerous foe. "And you're right, Jenna, we can all trust the mayor," Campagna reminded everyone, reducing the tension in the room.

"Yeah, he's not going to be mayor for much longer," the union steward reminded everyone.

"Yeah, he'll be our governor," Johnny quickly fired back.

McNally looked over at Henry and shot him a wink. They had fixed it. There was that other matter of McNally leaking the Stevens goods on his meeting with the militia. Henry filed that off into his memory for another day. Today he savored the win.

40

Henry was back in every respect. His home life was secure and his political world on course, but he had one last piece to fix. The assist came from Dex. They met again at Dex's house, this time for a scotch and full file folder as they enjoyed a sunset over the Scituate Reservoir.

"What's this?"

"It's a single malt, 30-years old."

"No, not the scotch, the folder," Henry asked.

"Read it."

"It's new orders for RITECH, switchblade drones, plus HIMARS and howitzers."

We need to resupply all the stuff we're blowing up in Ukraine," Dex told him.

"These orders are from the Czech Republic, Poland, Slovakia, Austria…"

"Finland, Sweden, Norway, Netherlands too," Dex added.

"What's it worth?" Henry asked."

"Company made over $800 million last year. These deals will put them over a billion in profits. Only if you're chairman of the board, that's the deal."

"What?"

"That's right, Henry. You knew we would take care of you."

"How am I going to do this?"

"Really, you're asking me? Aren't you the mastermind?"

"Yeah, this is different. This is big business."

"Different, really? How's it any different? It's all politics, you know that, in everything we do. So go in there and take what you've earned."

"And exactly how do I do that?"

"What, I gotta tell you?"

"So, I call Campagna and ask him to get me my seat back on the board. He owes me, so he'll do it. Plus, they know he's going to be governor, and there's talk of new submarine contracts coming to our state. RITECH will want a piece of the torpedo business."

"Now we're talking, and..."

"Then I go to Tim Teller and tell him I want chairman, and I dangle the deals we've secured."

"Yup, Timmy will see the value in those contracts. The new contracts will earn them over $100 million in profit per year. That's a $5 million bonus for him, on top of his salary. He'll do it," Dex assured Henry.

"And that's how it works, even at this level?"

"Yup, that's how it's always worked."

"My father in-law, is that how he did it?" Henry asked him. Dex was a master spy and not about to reveal all company secrets.

"Henry, it's always been done this way. Contacts become currency, and just like when you were trading political favors with state senators, we're doing the same thing at a different level. Your father-in-law saw this in you, and we don't just let anyone into our world.

Once you came on our radar, we carefully followed you. Honestly, it's been quite impressive."

"So then, what's next for me?" Henry asked.

"Dubai."

"What's in the UAE?"

"We're going to fuck with the Iranians, a little payback for the Taliban as a little test."

"Like we haven't fucked up that country enough?" Henry questioned.

"Not enough," Dex told him, his tone changing and facial expression betraying the cool outward image he often portrayed as he thought of his true intended target, Iran. "I lost my dad in Baghdad in '91. He was a Marine intelligence officer. It was the Iranians who took out his barracks. Now, the son has the chance to avenge the father."

"You think that's a good idea, Dex?"

"Really Henry, you mean like how you raided the company you blamed for your father's failures? That little fire you had your boy set took out the whole complex. I could see the smoke plumes from my summer house in Newport. Honestly, I loved it, and it's what made us want you even more. If you had the balls to do that, I figured you were one of us."

"So now that I'm one of you guys, what exactly am I going to be doing?"

"The Iranian protests over that poor girl, you know she was my oldest daughter's age," Dex reflected. "They've been going on for a year now, and we need to continue to stoke the fire."

"And how are we going to do that?"

"You think you can get the band back together again?"

"My team, yeah, they'll play. They love the money."

"At least we know what motivates them," Dex acknowledged.

"We all have our reasons. For some it's money, for you it's honor. For me, this one, it's revenge. I want to take away from the people who killed my father what they cherish most."

"Power?"

"Staying in power."

"We need an alternative, a leader, and no one has emerged yet."

"And that's where you come in with your buddy, Charlie. We got to bring one up, like we're doing in St. Petersburg. And our girl, Jana, her special skill will work over there too. And she can help track down some of their funds. They're in the same Swiss banks she's using, so that will help. Definitely we'll need Silberman again. You think he was corrupt? The Persians take it to a whole new level. He can help you understand it, and then unravel it."

"When are we doing this?"

"After Campagna's inauguration in the New Year."

"We don't need to wait. He's got this thing all buttoned up. After McNally dropped the goods on Stevens there's no way he recovers. I bet Campagna wins by 20. That's a landslide today. He'll have a mandate and can actually bring some substantive change."

"I've seen crazier shit happen, Henry. It's not over until election day."

"And even that's changed."

"Yeah, we can't take anything for granted anymore."

***

Jana flew from Prague to Milan, took a train to Turin, and then the bus to Cervinia. It was her own homecoming, and though Italy was not her native land, Billy was her new home. She bought a slope side apartment in Cervinia and settled in to hibernate for the fall. For a girl from Lithuania who had cut her teeth in Prague, skiing on a glacier in October and nestling with her Irish boyfriend was a true respite from her other life. She could get the hang of it. After paying cash for her apartment, her first stop back in town was to Billy's Irish bar.

"I thought I saw an angel and now she appears," Billy said as she made her grand entrance into his Irish bar at the base of the Italian side of the Matterhorn.

"I told you I would reappear," she said with a coy smile.

"You always do make your grand entrances and exits, love."

"I'm here to stay for a while. How about a drink?"

"Bourbon?" Billy the bartender asked her.

"Sure."

"Angel's Envy?"

"Of course."

"And how long are you going to stay?" Billy asked. He knew birds like her could not be caged and would fly away again.

"For a while, like I said. I bought a place here," Jana told him.

"Why? You could always stay with me. I told you that before you left."

"A girl needs her space and privacy. Plus, I thought you could always move in with me. No offense, but I have no desire to live above a bar. We could turn that apartment into a night club. That's a better use of the space. We make that balcony into a terrace, put a few tables out there, and then expand your seating capacity. Now your space will yield profit," she told him.

"Where am I going to get the money to do that, love?"

"How about a partner?"

"What kind of partner?"

"A silent one."

"Love, I don't think you could ever stay silent." If we're going to do this, I'm going to need some type of commitment," Billy told her.

"I'm here, aren't I? I came back just like I told you."

"For how long?"

"I have roots here now; I'll always come back home."

***

Gordon Beako was on his own island. Roatan off of Honduras afforded him a resort home with an infinity pool overlooking the Caribbean Sea and access to a port visited three days per week by cruise ships, his connection back to the real world whenever he wanted it. He even brought in his Miami girlfriend, who after his pleading and even begging, was convinced to join him. The diamond necklace that Jana had helped him pick out in Prague with their new earnings helped seal the deal.

For Beako it felt like halftime during the game. He was happy to be called back in, having come off the bench and thrown the Hail Mary pass into the endzone. Guys like Beako needed the game to keep them alive. Their greatest punishment was being sidelined, but his recent work in St. Petersburg had earned him a new long-term contract. For right now his job was to lay low. That was made all the easier by his posh, tax-free living with his twenty-eight-year-old girlfriend who kept her fifty-year-old boyfriend young and active.

The only article on Beako's girlfriend was her diamond necklace as she laid by the pool soaking up the sun. It wasn't easy to leave her for a trip into town. Remembering what he was coming home to every night provided him that added relief. He took his Porsche Boxster for the short drive to the port and parked next to the taxis and tour drivers ready to whisk excursion enthusiasts around the island.

His cell service was unreliable on the island, and he and the rest of the team had been advised to lay low off the Internet to avoid

Russian bots searching for a possible American team behind the men-
acing in St. Petersburg. To communicate with the outside world,
Beako relied on more traditional methods. The cruise ship he used
stopped in Miami every seven days, and Beako had befriended one
of the ship's security guards. He supplemented his meager pay, which
he sent back to the Philippines, but the money Beako used to grease
him paid for fun on Roatan. The security guard saw Beako in his
usual spot, and they exchanged envelopes. The guard's envelope had
a hundred in small bills for the local gentlemen's club, while Beako's
had a simple note. It read, "Abu Dhabi, 1.4."

It was his call back to the game. In January, he would book a
cruise back to Miami and fly to Abu Dhabi to meet Henry.

***

Terry Silberman was a new man. He had 2 million bucks and a
new sense of freedom. It was not nearly enough, but he had plans.
He realized his talents were in demand. After all these years toiling
away under a boss who was half his intellect, he was finally his own
man. If he was going to hang out a shingle, he figured he should land
in a place that historically had cultivated strong men. From emperors,
to popes, to el duce, Rome was a perfect place to set up his new consulting practice. And he figured the CIA would come calling again.
They had not fooled him. There was no way that Henry Mercucio
alone could pull all the strings. There were strings behind even the
master puppeteer.

Silberman became accustomed to his new life. He walked to
Piazza Navona every morning for cappuccino and biscotti. He always
threw a coin in the Trevi Fountain and made sure to climb the Spanish Stairs each time. This was truly Dolce Vita for Terry, a far cry
from Danbury Federal Penitentiary. He wondered how the mayor

was doing since he had left him behind. It was only courteous to send him a postcard from Rome. He had millions in a Swiss bank, and he guarded those bank account numbers like it was his only lifeline. He would not be fooled again.

The night for Silberman was a different scene. He was alone, in a foreign land, no commitments and no limitations. Rome had every distraction he could enjoy, and he was going to take full advantage of being a Roman for some time. He could even find authentic food from his childhood in the Jewish quarter of the city. Now in his mid-sixties and only recently having satisfied his pleasures in a brothel in Prague, he had sworn off the illicit sex scene in Rome and went out to a bar like a regular person. He had been out of the dating scene for nearly a decade. Back in his days in Providence he could just have women served to him at his beck and call. It would be nice to meet a woman in his golden years. This was a new start for Silberman.

41

"We did it again," Campagna told Henry on the phone.

"Congratulations, Governor."

"Looks like it's going to be an 18-point win once all the ballots are counted. Pretty sure that's a mandate. What do you think? You're the pro."

"I think it's a fucking mandate, Governor."

"Henry, you know I'm not a boy scout either. I got to tell you, the swearing, it's not you. We're not gangsters. You're better than that."

"You're fucking right. We're not gangsters, we're politicians," Henry jokingly replied. "No, you're right, Governor, I need to up my game."

"It's how you want to present yourself in the world, how you want people to see you. Do you want people to look at you as some cocky kid, or a respectable businessman?" Campagna asked.

"The only problem, Governor, is I've seen both. And let me tell you the higher I go the more treacherous it becomes."

"Yeah, I see that too. What if we handled it differently, actually became the people we were meant to be?" Campagna pondered.

"And who would that be, exactly?"

"Henry, you have a baby coming…"

"Yeah, any day now."

"What do you want your child to see?" Campagna did not hold back.

"Man, I thought this was going to be a congratulatory call, not a moral evaluation. I hear you, I do."

"Do you, Henry? Do you understand what I'm telling you?"

"No, honestly, I really don't."

"It's something I've always wanted to tell you, ever since we first started working together. You're better than all of this. It's time to get out of this business before it fully swallows you whole."

"What are you saying?"

"I know what you're doing with Jerimiah Dexter. I know what he is. I get intelligence briefings now, and I know what the Russians were up to. I also know what you did for Charlie Braverman. You saved a good kid."

"Yeah, he's one of us."

"I want to tell you, Henry, I'm doing this for one term, and then I'm out, for good this time. And I know you're going to tell me not to. I'm going to announce in my inaugural address that I'm only going to serve one term."

"Great, you'll be a lame duck before you even start. Are you sure you want to do that?"

"Politics and government, it's not supposed to be a career, it's supposed to be about service. It's not about the accumulation of power, but about what you can do for other people. Sure, call me naïve. That's what I believe at my core. Plus, my kids are young. They'll be in high school when I'm done with my 4-year sentence, and I want to be there for their formative years."

"Well Governor, maybe you can show us all how it's supposed to be done. I think you're crazy, but I can't say I don't respect it."

"So, what's next for you, Henry?" Campagna asked his consultant.

"I'm going to make things happen, hopefully improve some people's lives along the way, and not just the elite. This is for everyone. For all the guys and gals who came up from different neighborhoods, we're going to show them how it's done."

"And what is going to be done?"

"Well, first you need to come out early with a win," Henry said, shifting away from his own plans and back toward the Governor. "You need to get wind behind your sails, and then you'll be difficult to stop. Everyone will want to get on your bandwagon. We've got some time to think this through. You can't do anything until you're seated in January. That's why it's going to be important to surround yourself with the right team. And please, please, don't announce you're a one-termer."

"I'll think about it."

"Please do. In order to do the things you want, you'll have to demonstrate your power. The governor's office in this state is just a big bully pulpit. The General Assembly will run right over you if you show weakness. And announcing you're already not seeking a second term will take you out right from the beginning."

"OK, I won't say anything until the time is right. I'm serious, I'm only doing one term."

"Sure you are, Governor."

"Do you have anything practical for me, like who I should bring in for chief-of-staff?" Campagna asked his chief confidant even though he was no longer on the payroll and was his own man, which is why he sought his counsel.

"Yeah, I've got someone in mind. The female me."

"Oh, can't wait to meet her."

"Christine Smith. She was Braverman's aide. They were actually engaged, and then when the shit, I mean stuff, hit the fan, she bolted back to the West Coast. Can't really blame her. A lot to handle. I think she'd come back. It would be good optics to have a Gen Z woman as your chief-of-staff."

"Optics is one thing. Isn't she a little young? What, twenty-five? Can she do the job?"

"Yeah, she can do the job. I was running McNally's campaigns when I was her age. She's sharp, and you're going to need someone like her to help keep the wolves away."

"I thought I had the biggest wolf now?" Campagna asked.

"I'll always be here for you, just a call away. I'll be traveling a lot, and then we'll have my new kid. When I'm not away I need to be home with Lyndsay and my baby."

"I know you want to see the world. Everything you need is right here in Rhode Island, don't forget that."

"Yeah, I wanted to get back up to Boston, but Rhode Island is my home."

"Remember, there was a reason Roger Williams left Massachusetts. We're much cooler down here, you know, with the whole religious freedom thing and all."

"So, we good, Mayor, I mean Governor? I gotta go, actually need to see my shrink. Yup, you heard that right, I'm in counseling, even on meds too."

"I'm really glad to hear that, buddy. I've seen what you're capable of. I can't imagine what you can do after you've slain your demons."

Henry ended the call and walked into Dr. Lou Kelleher's office. The whole conversation occurred from the back of his black Suburban within earshot of his driver, Rick, and his most trusted advisor, Danny. Danny was also packing a Glock and little did Henry know that Rick had also been trained by the Rhode Island State Police, as a courtesy to the Feds, on defensive driving. The vehicle itself had been replaced with a retrofitted Rhode Island State Police Suburban and included some enhanced features like bulletproof glass and reinforced steel doors. They had important cargo to protect, and Henry was unaware of the precautions already being implemented around him.

Henry contemplated how much had changed since he had last visited. A new governor had been elected, another mayor had fallen, and a brighter future was emerging. Not a bad year for Henry. A new baby was coming, his dream opportunity was emerging, and the life he had envisioned was within his grasp. He just needed to wrap his hands around it and secure it. That's why he was back in Boston. It was time to extinguish those demons for good.

"How are you, Henry?" Dr. Kelleher asked.

"That's a loaded question."

"Is it loaded?"

"OK, here we go. I didn't mean anything by it. Really."

"I'm messing with you, Henry. Come on in."

"You got me. Good for you, doc. So, you're probably wondering why I'm here."

"I didn't know if you'd ever come back. You seemed to have figured things out on your own and weren't sure you were serious about therapy. I'm glad to see you."

"I think I'm good without the meds. I want to get rid of them, and I want to talk to you about weaning me off."

"You're on the lowest dose of Sertraline. Twenty-five milligrams is not going to slow your ambition, or take away your drive, if that's what you're worried about. It just takes the edge off a little bit."

"I can't afford to have any of my senses dulled. You did your job and got me through the depression. You helped me understand what I've been through and how it's affected me. With the meds, I was going to just stop cold turkey. My wife asked me to talk to you first, so that's why I'm here."

"Did you stop to think that maybe the Sertraline is working? You sure you want to risk falling back into a depression? If I told you that you had high blood pressure, would you take medication? If you had diabetes, would you take insulin? So, why is this any different?"

"And in both those cases I would take those medications. The difference is, with what I'm up against, I need my full faculties. I need to be the sharpest I can be right now."

"OK then, Henry, break your pills in half and take the halves for two weeks. After that, you can stop altogether. You feel sick, headaches, anything you call me. Also, if you want to go back on it in a month, six months, a year, you don't hesitate. You call me. Is that a deal?"

"It's a deal." Henry knew that everything in life was a negotiation.

***

"Charlie?"

"Christine, you're back?"

She walked into his office at Brown unannounced. Charlie waved off his secretary and closed his door for privacy.

"I was asked to be Campagna's chief-of-staff. How do you feel about that? If you don't want me to, I'll leave."

"You don't have any problem picking up and leaving. Does the governor know that?"

"I deserve that, I do. I want you to understand. I freaked out. I know I'm no angel, hardly, but Russian spies and dark money? I freaked out, I did. What did you expect?"

"You left me at the altar like a fool."

"Is that what this is, your fragile male ego? And don't be so dramatic, I didn't leave you at the altar. They hadn't even cashed the check for the deposit on the wedding."

"I was no longer your golden boy. That's it, wasn't it, why you left?"

"No, it wasn't like that," Christine pleaded. "I love you, I always have. I freaked out, that's all. I mean, really Charlie, can you blame me? One night we're with a girl in Prague, next thing we're getting engaged and you're running for governor, and then our whole world blows up."

Charlie didn't immediately respond. He really didn't know what to say. How he responded could determine whether she stayed or was gone for good, and he was not sure what he really wanted. He had found his new calling now. He loved his position at Brown University helping to spread democracy through intellectual studies, and he was able to put academics into action through his work with Henry. He was excited to be opening a new Democracy Institute in the Middle East and was scheduled to travel with Henry to Dubai later in the new year.

Even though he was not the one who had left, he started with an apology. "I'm sorry," Charlie told her. "I'm sorry for what I put you through. I'm sorry for what we did in Prague. I'm sorry for being so stupid to be duped by that Russian, who preyed on me and exploited my weaknesses. I'm sorry for it all."

"And I'm sorry for leaving you without an explanation. Do you think we can be friends?" she asked.

"Friends?"

"Yeah, friends."

"You once told me that men and women could not be friends. There would always be that sexual tension."

"I said that?"

"Yeah, you did."

"Well, I talk a lot of shit, you know that," she reminded him.

"And how do I know you're not still talking shit?"

"Because I didn't need to come back here on my knees groveling to you. Here I am, all of me."

"OK, Christine, we can be friends then."

"Good, because the governor is going to need allies going forward. You would have been a great governor, Charlie, I have no doubt. Maybe it just wasn't your time yet, but some day. We both know there are always second acts in politics."

"Yeah, it's not like I got caught with a dead woman, or a live boy. Do they still say it's the only way you get ruined in politics?"

"Something like that, and you seemed to end up pretty good."

"Thanks to some powerful friends," Charlie admitted.

"Those friends would not have gravitated to the Charlie orbit if you hadn't earned their trust and respect because of your talents. Don't forget that, Charlie," she told him.

"Good to see you back, Christine."

42

Lyndsay was ready. She woke Henry and told him it was time. Henry jumped out of bed with the drill instructor in his head ordering him to attention. Their baby was coming. Henry had his go-bag ready and helped Lyndsay down the stairs. Rick, his driver, had insisted that Henry call him when that time arrived, but Henry insisted on taking in his wife on his own. He revved up the Porsche Cayenne and off they went to Women & Infants Hospital in Providence. They were there in less than 15 minutes.

Lyndsay was no martyr and happily took the epidural that was offered to her. She had vivid memories from her OB/GYN rotation of those women who insisted on delivering the natural way. Not Lyndsay, she planned to take advantage of what modern medicine offered. After several hours in labor the epidural was wearing off and Henry witnessed a level of pain he could not comprehend. They had explained that she may need a c-section, which prompted him to react.

"If that's where we're heading, let's get it done. There's no reason my wife needs to be in pain a minute longer," Henry pushed them. It did not matter that he was an internationally sought-after political consultant or business tycoon. In the hospital he was just another father. Henry was escorted out of the delivery room as they prepped Lyndsay for surgery. He waited alone wearing the scrubs they had given him, because damn right he was standing by her side in the delivery room. It was the longest half hour of his life. Could this c-section go wrong? Would he have to choose between saving his wife or his baby? Lyndsay had told Henry in no uncertain terms that if he had to make that choice, he was instructed to choose the baby. They called him in, and he saw his wife. She grabbed his hand. They were indeed in this together. What they waited for was revealed moments later with the announcement, "You have a girl."

Henry was asked if he wanted to see his daughter, and he realized at that moment he would be the first in his family to see her. He turned to the doctor and said, "Only after you show her to my wife." Henry's request brought a smile to the obstetrician and a comment she actually did not utter to all the parents, "You two need to make more babies. She's beautiful."

Henry was ushered out of the delivery room so that the medical team could stitch Lyndsay up. Henry was alone with his daughter in a separate room, and what happened next caught him off guard. Henry broke down in tears. It had finally all caught up to him. All the pressure, all the stress, and now the overwhelming joy—his baby girl was here, and he swore to himself that he would change. No more running around like a lunatic from one conquest to the other. It was time to settle down. Lyndsay and his daughter were his home, and he would do anything to preserve it.

First though, he had a job to do. He picked up his phone and FaceTimed his mother, brother, and in-laws, in that order.

"Meet Kate Mercucio," he told each of them when he called.

3JOHN HOULE

Henry looked at the innocence before him. She represented everything he had fought for, and the future was going to be different. It didn't take a failed blackmail attempt. It wasn't about self-serving politicians, unscrupulous businessmen, or vengeful Russians. What caused Henry to change was his seven-pound, blue eyed daughter.

One of the delivery nurses checked in on Henry and the newborn.

"Do you need anything, Mr. Mercucio?"

"Yeah, I want to hold her, but I'm afraid to pick her up."

"Let me show you."

And as Henry held his daughter, he felt in that moment that everything was going to be alright.

***

Mary Sinclair was annoyed with her husband. He knew they needed to catch their 6 a.m. flight to Providence to meet their first grandchild. What was the purpose of owning their own jet if they had to take an early morning flight, she thought to herself. Both she and her husband wanted to be up in Providence when their daughter woke up. Lyndsay's sisters were even packed and ready, so excited at the prospect of being an auntie that they barely slept.

Her husband insisted on taking their dog for a walk before they left. She swore he liked that dog sometimes more than her. And now the beagle was howling her head off like bloody murder. Another rabbit in the yard or squirrel invading their property, she figured, and gave it little thought. The howling persisted, and Molly the beagle was relentless.

"What now with this annoying animal?" Mary muttered. "Good thing we don't have neighbors nearby."

What she saw from the window shocked her. Reggie was on the ground, and the dog was wailing. He was not moving. She ran down the stairs, grabbed the defibrillator from the mud room, and sprinted across the lawn. Molly refused to leave his side, and Mary jumped into action. She pressed the defibrillator to Reggie's chest and prayed.

The ambulance was there in minutes, and the paramedics took over. Mary went with her husband in the back of the ambulance, and she called her sister from the road to come and watch her girls. She was not leaving her husband and would do everything to prevent him from leaving her.

This was not going to be Reggie Sinclair's day to leave anyone behind.

He was flown by helicopter to Duke University Hospital and rushed into surgery. Mary had to navigate this one on her own with her eldest daughter still in recovery from a c-section and her second daughter also away in Rhode Island. Mary's own sister was now watching her two younger girls, and the most important decisions of her family's future rested with her alone. Sinclair was only sixty-six and in considerably good shape. She had told him to stop with the weekly cigar and scotch with the boys, but it hardly seemed like a lethal vice. It just did not seem like he should just drop from a heart attack. There had been no warning signs, and while his EKG indicated a minor abnormality, he had a strong heart.

The heart surgeon on call came out to greet Mrs. Sinclair. She was expecting that it was a false alarm and that he had fainted from dehydration or some other explanation. She was alarmed by what she was told. "Your husband had a heart attack. It's a blockage of the left anterior descending artery, the largest artery in the heart. It supplies about half of the heart muscle's blood," the doctor explained. "We've found a ruptured plaque with a blood clot, and we need to operate now. As his wife, I need your consent."

"Yes, of course, do what you need to do," she said, signing the consent form.

"Mrs. Sinclair, you've already done your most important job for your husband. I have no doubt if you hadn't used the defibrillator on him, he would not have made it. Now, you have another important role, to serve as his advocate and make the tough calls when needed."

"Thank you, doctor. We're just not supposed to be here. Our daughter just gave birth, and we were heading out to see her."

"Right now, your job is to be here for your husband."

"Can I see him?"

"He's being prepped for surgery. There was significant damage to his heart muscle. I want to do a coronary artery bypass graft surgery, or CAPG. We're going to use your husband's leg vein to bypass the narrowed area around his heart to restore blood flow."

"Is he going to make it?"

"We're certainly going to do everything we can."

"So, what do I do?"

"We have a family room you can wait in. I think your family donated it. I'll have someone bring you some coffee. Do you want something to eat?"

"No, thank you."

Mary soon realized that she was not alone. Very serious looking gentlemen appeared around her with earpieces and long coats concealing automatic weapons. A young woman, who could not have been much older than her daughter Lyndsay, approached her and offered her condolences.

"Mrs. Sinclair, I'm Special Agent Adams with the FBI. We're here to secure the floor with a security detail for your husband. I have a friend who would like to speak to you," she said, offering her phone.

"Mary, it's Dex. I heard about what happened to Reggie. Don't worry, he's one tough son of a bitch, and he's going to make it through this. The FBI agents, this is just precautionary, nothing to worry about," Dex assured her.

Dex was taking every precaution himself. While he wanted to personally investigate what had happened to Sinclair, he also needed to protect his family. He had planned for such an occasion. He knew Sinclair would do the same for him.

"Dex, I don't understand. Why would the FBI need to protect Reggie?"

"Reggie has been identified as one of the key industrialists and when something happens the FBI just wants to make certain there's not an additional threat," he lied.

She really had no reason to doubt her husband's friend of forty years, and little energy at the moment to focus on anything else. Dex told her that he was calling on his way to the airport and he should be in North Carolina in a couple of hours. Quite frankly, she was happy to have someone to talk to and people around her.

Dex wanted to oversee this personally. Of course, men at Sinclair's age had heart attacks, however Dex also didn't believe in chance. He knew all too well that the Russians had toxins they used to make it appear like their targets had suffered heart attacks. There were specific tests that Dex could insist on to screen for certain agents that an academic hospital would not ordinarily know to use.

Dex was on a mission now, and this one was personal. It very well may have been a regular heart attack brought on by bad genes and not from an outside actor. Dex was not willing to take any chances. His wife and kids were taken to his parents' place in Connecticut, which was less than half an hour away. Rhode Island State Police watched his wife's vehicle and then handed off protection to their Connecticut colleagues. Dex also had select members of the CIA's private army of contractors patrol the grounds of the family farm. He just did not know yet how deep this plan went.

43

Henry was urged by the nurses to go home and get one good night's sleep. Though he stood vigil by his wife and baby daughter, the chief nurse on the floor explained to him he would be better help if he in fact received real rest than what a chair could provide him. As soon as he was home, he crashed on his bed.

Henry's property had acres of woods behind his house with a stream he proudly showed off to visitors. The property was his little sanctuary. The turkeys, deer, foxes, and the occasional coy wolf were the only living creatures who ever emerged from the woods into his backyard. A far more sinister predator came out this evening.

They were a three-man hit squad. They had trekked through the woods from the main road and followed the stream toward the coordinates they had been given to Henry's property. Dropped off at the main road in the cover of darkness, they walked in past a small stone bench marking the area's former heritage as the Cranston Foundry from 1812. A stone path ended about one hundred feet in, but they made their own way through the brush, past an old stone wall dating back 150 years. Henry had made their job even easier with the bridges he had made across Furnace Brook. He liked to take their dog for walks in the morning close to home in a place that felt worlds away.

Henry had been tracked home from the hospital, and they had figured he would be alone. They weren't animals. They would not harm a newborn and mother. They were patriots, or so they told themselves. As members of the Gaspee Militia, they had sworn an oath to eliminate all enemies of the State of Rhode Island and Providence Plantations. Their pledge was to a different state, not the liberal bastion that had removed "Providence Plantations" from their name to appease the cancel culture radicals, so they believed.

They had been instructed to kidnap Henry Mercucio, and if they faced resistance, lethal force was permitted. Harley, the mixed breed beagle and chihuahua pup, affectionately referred to as a cheagle, was happy his master Henry was home. Some people thought they were masochists, to raise a puppy and baby at the same time, but Henry was practical. If they had to dramatically adjust their lives, why not go all in? Harley's snout was against Henry's leg in bed, and he had crashed pretty hard after the events of the last few days and the whole year. Something awakened Harley, who leaped from the bed and howled bloody murder as his paws and claws tapped on the hard wood floors.

The hit team knew Henry had a puppy and came prepared. They gave the dog a bone, complete with the meat still on it, to feed the dog's primary instincts and immediately eliminate the sound of their entry. The dog was neutralized, and they continued on with their mission. That was the thing about racists; they loved animals, hated people. Henry's security system had not been activated. He had been so tired that he could not be bothered to hit the four-digit code. The team had been prepared to deactivate the system, but Henry made it easier for them. It was like he was almost inviting them in to do their job.

While Harley's barking had not awakened Henry, it had startled Henry's sister-in-law who had been staying with them in the guest room. It also had roused her guest.

Danny did not believe in innocent noises in the middle of the night that went bump. He only knew threats from those who wanted to rob him of who he had become. His senses now alert, he heard glass breaking, which triggered his training, making him operational. He searched under the bed for the gun locker, pressed four quick buttons and grabbed his Glock. He placed his finger over his mouth, motioning to Bridgit to stay quiet, and he slowly opened the guest room door. Bridgit did her best to stay calm. She had been rattled enough over the past six months with the unraveling of her marriage and its ultimate annulment. She was no longer sure what she had gotten herself into now.

Danny brought his decade of street smarts and his recent CIA training to calmly meet his prey. The hunted was now the hunter, and these wolves had no idea they were coming upon a leopard. He could hear their footsteps, and they were beginning to ascend the stairs. Danny slowly emerged from the upstairs hallway. As the stairs came into view, his training kicked in, guiding him to make a split decision between a threat or a friendly. Hooded men in black Kevlar were only there for mayhem, and within seconds Danny tapped three shots, one to each of their heads. The tap, tap, tap that he heard in his head sounded more like a thundering explosion in Henry's foyer.

Shocked and disoriented, Henry rushed out of his bedroom, wondering why his associate was standing in his hallway with a smoking gun. "Holy shit, Danny, what the fuck?"

"Henry, please go back into your room and get under your bed. We don't know if there are more coming."

The more that came was local SWAT. Upon seeing her new lover exit the room with a gun, Bridgit Sinclair called 911 explaining there were intruders. She was on the phone with dispatch when the gunfire erupted. Cranston Police were at Henry's house in five minutes. On the scene was Lieutenant Michael Palazzo, night patrol commander of the Cranston Police Department. When the 911 call had been rerouted to Cranston PD, he quickly dispatched SWAT and accompanied them to Hines Farm Rd. He knew Henry Mercucio personally, played golf with him at The Alpine Country Club just eight minutes from the scene, and was not going to let a bunch of thugs come into his city and take out his friend. The FBI had shared the considerable chatter with Rhode Island State Police that local militia were planning big hits, and the information was disseminated to all 48 law enforcement agencies in the state. Lt. Palazzo was not taking any chances. He grabbed his M4 carbine assault rifle out of the trunk of his patrol car and accompanied SWAT into Henry's house. He and the SWAT team stormed in through the front and back doors and cruisers blocked the street in and out of the neighborhood.

Danny could tell the difference between the thugs he had just dispatched and the professional operators arriving on the scene, so he immediately dropped to the floor, pushed his weapon away, and spread his arms. Bridgit came out of the room and yelled, "That's my boyfriend, don't shoot."

"Miss, I need you to get down on the ground," the SWAT officer yelled. Another SWAT operator checked the vitals of the fallen militia men. All the lights were turned on in the 3,500 square foot house with SWAT starting to take defensive measures. They did not know if there was a second wave coming.

Another attack did not come to Henry's house that evening. The only perpetrators were some sorely misled Rhode Island rednecks who had been duped into taking action and were put down by a professional. The SWAT team searched the deceased for identification and photographed each of the attackers. It was determined through facial recognition software that these men were members of the Gaspee Militia and had been on both Federal and State watch lists.

Attacks like this did not happen in Providence's leafy suburbs. These were different times. America was changing, and danger was now at her doorstep. Fortunately for Henry, the only casualties today were the perpetrators themselves. He was relieved to hear a familiar voice pierce through the chaos and alleviate his shock.

"You alright buddy?" Lt. Palazzo called for Henry.

"Is that you Mikey?"

"Yeah, it's me. Who are you with?"

"My sister-in-law and a guy from my office. He took out the shooters."

"Didn't realize you had a bodyguard."

"I didn't either. Also didn't realize he's with my sister-in-law," Henry said, looking at Danny.

"You're lucky he was tonight. I don't think we would have gotten here in time. This would have been a much different scene," Lieutenant Palazzo told him.

"Mikey, what's going on?"

"Not sure, Henry, we don't know if this is one isolated event or if there's more to come. We need to sit tight."

"Bodyguard, you have a weapon?" the lieutenant asked Danny.

"Name's Danny Conroy, and I'm in the Federal Law Enforcement database. You can look me up. And yeah, I've got weapons."

"You agency or something?"

"Yeah, something like that. Special detail."

"Really, Danny? You didn't think to tell me you're sleeping with my sister-in-law and that you're working for the Agency too?"

"Which one do you want me to address first, boss?"

"Doesn't matter, Danny, I owe you my life," he told him, putting out his hand to Danny, who countered with the biggest bear hug.

"Thank you, brother."

"I finally got to repay you for everything."

"Repay me, you kidding, for what?"

"For my life, Henry."

"Don't mean to break up this bro fest, but what the fuck?" Bridgit intervened. The question was addressed more to Danny than Henry.

"Yeah, Bridg, I've been assigned to protect Henry, Lyndsay, and you. And I know it sounds cliché that I fell for one of my protectees."

"I didn't know you liked blondes, thought it was brunettes," Henry joked. Bridgit shot him a stare much like Lyndsay gave to express she was less than amused. Henry was rescued by his puppy, Harley.

"My baby, where have you been?" he spoke to the dog like a child. The dog jumped into his arms and licked his face.

"That friggin mutt may have saved us all," Bridgit realized.

"It's what woke me up," Danny admitted.

OK, guys, sorry to break up this lovefest, but we need to move you," the lieutenant demanded. "Henry, you got a safe room here?"

"Yeah, my father-in-law insisted on one. I thought it was overkill, but I guess he was right. It's in the basement."

"Danny, my boys checked you out. We're all good. We could use the extra firepower. There's a lot of chatter, and we're not sure what exactly is going down."

"What about my wife and baby? They're at Women & Infants," Henry reminded everyone.

"My sister, the baby, you got to go get them, Danny," Bridgit insisted.

"I'll go with you, Danny," Lieutenant Palazzo announced. "I'll call Providence PD right now and have the hospital locked down and your wife secured. Danny and I will go get her and the baby and get you all into safety."

Bridgit's cell lit up. It was her mother. She always seemed to call at the worst moments.

"What is it ma? It's not even 6 a.m., and all shit has broken out here."

"It's your father, Bridg, he's had a heart attack, and they're taking him into surgery. They're taking a vein from his left leg and doing a triple bypass."

"My father had a heart attack, and they're taking him into surgery," Bridgit announced, her face revealing how frightened she was from the whole state of affairs.

"Jesus, could this day get any worse?" Henry said his thoughts aloud.

"Yeah, it could if we don't lock you down and get you and your family to safety. Henry, we gotta go," Mike told him. "Danny and I will get Lyndsay and the baby, come back here, get you and Bridgit, and then get you all to safety. My SWAT guys will guard your house, but we need you and Bridgit to get into the safe room. And no matter what happens you don't open it."

"Got it. I'm calling the pilot and getting the jet back up here. We're going to my father-in-law," Henry told him.

"OK, buddy, that's a good plan. We'll be back in less than 30," Mike told him.

"And Henry, don't open that door for anyone. I'll open it when I get back," Danny insisted.

"You got it."

Danny followed Mike to his cruiser, and soon they were heading up 95 with lights flashing. Providence and Warwick police had blocked off Routes 37 and 95 letting their colleague pass unfettered by any traffic, friendly or hostile, they just didn't know who yet. Women's & Infants looked like a federal building locked down during

9/11. Providence Police had been lent one of the fire trucks by Providence Fire to block the entrance, and the police were able to bring out one of their reconditioned Humvees for this special assignment.

Mike and Danny were escorted in by Providence Police SWAT and taken to Lyndsay's floor. Mother and baby were sleeping soundly. Danny was smart enough to take off his black Kevlar helmet and mask that had been given to him by Cranston SWAT.

"Lyndsay, it's Danny. I'm here to bring you to Henry and Bridgit."

"Danny, what's going on? Is Henry OK?"

"Yes, he's fine. There's been an incident, and we need to move you and the baby."

"An incident, what do you mean? Is everyone OK?"

"Yes, everyone here is fine. Your father had a heart attack, and we need to go see him," he explained, only telling her half the story.

"What, my father had a heart attack? When?"

"Earlier this morning on the way to see you. He's being taken into surgery. We want to bring you, the baby, Bridgit, and Henry to see him when he recovers, and be there for your mom," Danny explained.

"Danny, we gotta move," Mike interrupted.

"Wait, who's that with you?"

"Lyndsay, it's Mike from Alpine. Henry asked me to come get you."

"Mike, why are you here? What's going on?"

"Lyndsay, we'll explain on the way. We gotta go."

Lyndsay slowly rose from her bed, her abdomen clearly strained from the life that emerged from her. She went to the crib next to her bed and retrieved her baby. Kate was swaddled in a white blanket and escorted out of the room with her armed guards.

***

Fifteen minutes later the Mercucio family was reunited at their home in Cranston. Sinclair's Citation jet was set to land at TF Green in an hour. They wanted to get Sinclair's family out of Rhode Island. There was something brewing, and they needed to get Henry and the clan to safety.

"Conroy, that you?" the voice asked over the phone. Danny ducked into Henry's home office while Henry, Lyndsay, and Bridgit were making coffee. The only relief Lyndsay had was the coffee she was finally able to enjoy after pregnancy. She was going to need to be fully caffeinated for whatever lay ahead.

"Sir?" Danny asked.

"It's me, Dex. You got them all secured?"

"Yeah, Lyndsay, the baby, Henry, Bridgit, and me. We'll be in Raleigh by Noon," Danny told his new boss.

"Good, you did good, Danny, real good. This could have been a disaster. We could have lost Henry."

"Yeah, I know, not sure I would've been able to do it if I hadn't gotten that training you sent me to."

"Yeah, you would have. The Farm may have shown you how to react, but what you did was instinctive. You did real good, kid. You're going to get a nice bonus for this."

"Don't care about money, sir."

"I know you don't, but you're getting one anyway, a nice pile of cash."

"I don't do it for that, sir."

"I know you didn't, Danny, but it'll be nice to have."

"Sir, what's really going down here?"

"We really aren't sure how big this is. Right now, we need to secure our people and regroup. This may be the start of something much bigger."

"Sinclair going to pull through?"

"Sure as God hope so. It's too early. His wife saved his life, and his dog, believe it or not. If he had been on the ground maybe a minute longer it would've been a different story.

"You think it's a coincidence that Sinclair goes down and then there's a hit on Henry?"

"No, I don't believe in coincidences, do you?"

"No, of course not, but who?"

"My guess, it was pay back."

"Our Russian friend came back from the dead."

44

Alexi Antipov came out from the cold and was enjoying the stifling air in Dubai. He was indulging in a cocktail in a Russian safehouse with his Iranian colleague, who drank vodka like water even though he portrayed himself as a tea-totaling cleric. Waleed Al Hassan headed up the Intelligence Organization of the Islamic Revolutionary Guard Corps. He had helped secure the Russians the Shahed-131 and Shahed-136 drones dropped on Ukrainian civilians. They had been battle tested on the Syrian rebels, and the Iranians now had a new market to sell their technology since the West had cut off the Russians. Both Antipov and Al Hassan subscribed to the ancient proverb: "The enemy of my enemy is my friend."

"You drink like a Russian Orthodox Bishop," Antipov told him.

"And you scheme like a Persian Assassin," Al Hassan retorted.

"Touché."

"Have you heard about the shipment?"

"They should be heading up Narragansett Bay. They're being smuggled in through the port and could be operational by tomorrow night."

"You think these people are going to know how to use them?" the Iranian asked, proud of his countrymen's technology.

"We have criminals from Tyva firing them in Ukraine. How hard could they be?"

"Point taken. We need to make sure the Americans don't think it was us. I don't need American and Israeli bombs hitting Tehran," Al Hassan expressed his fear of reprisals.

"Don't worry, my people stripped the serial numbers and registered them with the FAA under the names you gave me," Antipov assured him.

"Why Rhode Island, why not New York or even Boston?"

"Too hard to hit New York now. And Boston, we've tried, and it's equally difficult. But Rhode Island, they won't know what hit them."

"So, it's just an easier target?" the Iranian asked his Russian counterpart, intrigued by his tactical sense.

"Not just that, it's also psychological. We want to remove a state from the map. What would the effect be for the pompous Americans? Imagine, we overthrow one of their states."

"Also, a good test run for a bigger operation down the road," the Iranian thought about what his country could learn for their own future strikes.

"Exactly. Those arrogant Americans think they can meddle in all our internal affairs. Time to teach them a lesson they won't soon forget."

"Agreed, they need to feel what we have felt."

"And you know the best part?"

"What's that?"

"It's going to look like they did it to themselves," Antipov told his unsuspecting guest. Al Hassan knew he was supplying some drones to be smuggled into the United States. He did not understand the magnitude of the operation.

"How so?"

"I can't tell you all my secrets."

"I thought we were allies," the Iranian pressed.

***

George Francisco had no idea what he was doing. His job for the Gaspee Militia was to steal lead paint from an old factory in Warren, Rhode Island. The factory was being turned into new apartments and a brewery, and large drums of lead paint had been found in the basement. One of Francisco's drinking buddies from his corn hole league was talking about what they had found, and he mentioned it to the colonel. He wanted to impress the colonel and demonstrate his usefulness to the cause, and as a result he found himself dragging barrels of paint from the 1970's onto a U-Haul truck. Not what he expected to be doing on a Saturday night while other men his age were chasing women and throwing back beers. He thought he had a higher calling.

The new Patriot movement, or so they thought they were, was highly compartmentalized. Different cells were not always aware of what other so-called freedom fighters were doing. The lead paint drum was heading to a farm in Scituate, where fellow countrymen would use it for a special operation. Another cell was focused on the state capitol. The Independent Man, who triumphantly stood atop the largest state house in the country, was shedding a tear for what was brewing again in rogue's island.

A new man had emerged. And he was not for religious liberty and separation of church and state. He certainly was no fan of liberal democracy or even representative government. He preferred the top-down approach, and not trickle-down economics that catered to the rich and elite. The new man was an anathema of the liberal cancel culture that pervaded the fabric of colonial Rhode Island. And this man had new allies. While there were plenty who shared his views in the United States, he found kinship in Russia, Iran, and even parts of Germany, Spain, Japan, and China. A new order was being tested, and Rhode Island was fertile ground to gauge if it could flourish in the Americas.

It was an epic battle between democracy and fascism again. The war never really ended after World War II, and the struggle continued. There were strong fighters on both sides, each attempting to claim their piece of the power prize. And there were plenty of pawns to sacrifice.

Thomas Wilson was not afraid to lose a few good men. It was the price to be paid, and what true patriots needed to endure. He did not care where all the funding or the weapons were coming from either. The mission was all that mattered. Freeing Rhode Island from the corrupt politicians who pulled the liberal reigns was his true calling.

"There's been a complication," his top lieutenant Andy reported.

"What is it?" Wilson asked.

"We lost a few guys in Cranston. That Mercucio guy had an armed guard who took out our guys."

"Then we hit the hospital," the local militia commander coldly replied.

"Providence police have it surrounded. No way we can get in there and kidnap the woman."

"And what about the congressman?"

"We got him, but there was collateral," the lieutenant told his captain.

"How bad?"

"There's a congressman tied up and a young girl, maybe 25, in a dominatrix suit. Their brains and blood are splattered all over a suite at the Omni."

"Tell me you have pictures."

"Oh yeah."

"And can you see his face?"

"Yup."

"Great, I want them all over Insta, Facebook, Twitter, everywhere."

"You got it, Captain."

"Your team's ready for what's next?"

"Born ready, Captain. We're finally taking back our state from the corrupt elites."

"Don't be overconfident. Nothing ever works out exactly as planned. I learned that from the Colonel. He was there before us. We gave the land we took back to those animals. And then we're surprised that they don't honor our agreed-upon pull out. You can't negotiate with these people. The only language they understand is power," the Captain lectured.

"We talking about the towel heads or our people, Captain?"

"Both. What's worse is our own people have become too soft, too weak. If we don't start taking a stand now, our children will be speaking Chinese."

"As long as it's not Spanish," the lieutenant joked.

"The tree of liberty must be refreshed from time to time with the blood of patriots and tyrants. It is its natural manure."

"Who said that, Captain?"

"Thomas Jefferson."

"Didn't he have slaves too?"

"Yes, he did. Fathered black babies too, according to liberal revisionist history."

"Jesus."

"Jesus would not recognize this world of ours," the captain

lamented.

"No wonder he couldn't wait to get back to his father," the lieutenant joked.

"At the right hand of God are the seven seals. The Lion of Judah opens the first four of the seven seals. This summons four beings that ride out on white, red, black, and pale horses."

"Where's this from?"

"Revelation 6:8," the captain explained. "I looked, and there before me was a pale horse! Its rider was named Death, and Hades was following close behind him. They were given power over a fourth of the earth to kill by sword, famine and plague…"

"What does it mean?" the lieutenant asked.

"The prophet John saw the four horsemen of the Apocalypse. They describe conquest, war, hunger, and death. The fourth rider was death. Death is followed by Hell, claiming a quarter of the world."

"That's about two billion people."

"Consider it a fresh start."

"You really believe this, Captain?"

"Nah, I just play it up for the crazy religious zealots and racists who hoped COVID would kill a billion Chinese."

"What do you really believe?"

"We've let those faggot liberals run things for too long. If we continue down this path, we'll be taken over by the Chinese or Russians. Maybe even the North Koreans. Wouldn't be surprised if they started lobbing some missiles over at us."

"Those fucking North Koreans."

"At least their leader's got some balls. Not like our guys. It's time we hit the reset button on the United States of America, and it all starts in little Rhody."

***

The truck was loaded with 55-gallon drums of lead paint and was headed to the Scituate Reservoir Causeway. It was 1 a.m., and the plan to take back America was underway. It was a carefully orchestrated plot with many players out front and behind the scenes. But Rhode Island was not ready to become another footnote in history, not today. Michael Denning was driving his Suburban for the Providence Water Supply Board Private Security Unit tasked with patrolling the shores of the Scituate Reservoir, which supplied sixty percent of the state's drinking water. A Marine in his youth, and always faithful, the only action he saw in his retirement job was chasing away kids who wanted to fish and swim in the pristine water.

Today was a different day. A U-Haul was parked on the side of the road right past the Causeway. In total there were six overweight, out of shape wannabe commandos on the scene. They were hooded, cloaked in black from head to toe, and clearly up to no good. Denning and his team had been briefed before their shift to be on the lookout for anything out of the ordinary. There were some real concerns that Rhode Island's primary water supply could be a target.

Denning did not come to this party alone. In the back of his Suburban he had a 12-gauge riot gun, M-4, and 45 caliber pistol. His buddies on the State Police had told him about an Arab looking man who had fled after they pulled him over. He had enough explosives in his box truck to take out the major dam and kill potentially thousands of Rhode Islanders. With this in mind, he wasted no time waiting for back up. His Corps training kicked in. He grabbed his M-4, holstered his pistol, and put his 12-guage in his backpack. He saw one of the terrorists open the drum and start to empty the liquid contents into the Reservoir. He fired a shot at his midsection, baptizing the Reservoir with his blood. One of the man's comrades raised his weapon, and the Marine took him down. Then the driver started up the truck and attempted to pull away. He then saw what looked like a second U-Haul coming across the Causeway looking to join the party. He grabbed his 12-guage and blasted away. The U-Haul's window was shattered, and the truck crashed into the Reservoir. Denning decided it was now time to call for backup.

***

Steven Malone was another man of privilege who had lost his golden ticket. Replaced by technology, he lost his job as a camera operator at Rhode Island's leading television network to a remote-controlled operator out of Texas who ran the cameras for a dozen stations from one central hub. His buddy had hooked him up with a landscaping job over the Summer but had to let him go when some liberal Rhode Island lawmakers passed a ban on gasoline mowers and blowers. He was another victim of advancement.

He wasn't going to just lay down. He hoped to better himself and taught himself how to fly drones. He even managed to pass the FAA test and received his drone pilot's license. Feeling banished to his parent's basement, he spent an equal amount of time online visiting hate websites and fell fully for their White Supremacist rhetoric. He was a perfect soldier for the new revolution.

Malone looked at his Special Forces watch that the captain had given him for passing his FAA test. It was 1 a.m., go time. He fired up the drone from the base of the Roger Williams statue at Prospect Terrace Park and directed it toward the State House dome. The fourth largest self-supporting dome in the world, it was an attractive target. Today, however, was not his day. Malone was used to flying his Mavic Air 2, not the drone the colonel told him to fly. He had only tested it once before this night. Tonight, they were going to make history. His adrenaline was pumping. He couldn't wait to take down the symbol of those fuckers who robbed and pillaged his great state.

Someone needed to take a stand, and he felt so fortunate to have met the colonel. This great moment had chosen him.

All he had to do was fly the drone into the big white dome. And then he panicked. The combination of the adrenaline firing on all cylinders with the two Red Bulls and pack of cigarettes he smoked made him lose his nerve, and the kamikaze drone crashed into the apartment building adjacent to the Rhode Island State House, sending a fireball into the air. The dome didn't come down. No legislators were sacrificed. However, eight unsuspecting college students met their untimely fate, never afforded the opportunity to understand why they had suffered such a shortened existence.

They were the first innocent blood to be spilled. The war for Rhode Island's future had begun.